TRUTH AND OTHER LIES

THE NINE WORLDS RISING BOOK 1

LYRA WOLF

RAVENWELL PRESS

Cover design by Dominic Forbes

Ravenwell Press

eBook ISBN: 978-1-944912-26-0
Paperback ISBN: 978-1-944912-36-9
Hardback ISBN: 978-1-944912-40-6

First Edition

To Cait, who gave me the courage to write the stories in my heart...You lost me my last chance at being a normal, well-adjusted adult. Thanks.

Hell is empty, and all the devils are here.

— William Shakespeare, *The Tempest*

1

GODS AND MONSTERS

Present Day

Basel, Switzerland

He stood naked on the altar, staring up at the crucifix.

He claimed he came to destroy the world.

This wasn't the first deranged man I encountered inside the Münster Cathedral, but he was the most tenacious in his ravings.

When I called the police, the woman on the phone sighed. A naked man inside a church did not constitute an emergency.

I strongly disagreed.

She sighed again, then said an officer would be here in twenty minutes, if one was available.

I cleared my throat, wanting to alert the man of my return.

He turned and met my gaze. Sharp eyes of green cut into

my core, almost into my very being. I didn't know if they wanted to love me, or end me.

I forced myself to speak.

"I found this suit in the rectory. It might be a little short for someone of your height, but it should do the job."

He tilted his head, his eyes trailing to the pressed suit in my hands. A wave of energy from him struck me, kicking me in the chest like a mule.

Fierce, raw, alluring...

He descended the red, sandstone steps, each stride determined and powerful. Feline. I knew I should run, but I also, inexplicably, wanted to stay.

Flicking back his head, he ran his elegant fingers through shoulder length copper hair. His every muscle and movement tensed with careless danger, though his air remained at ease. He possessed a sublime and menacing beauty I'd only ever seen captured in the *Lucifer of Liège*.

Taking the suit from me, he caressed the fabric beneath his thumbs. He smiled, a wry, devastating smile. For a heartbeat a torrential thrill lit my blood.

"You people never were fond of public nudity," he said.

His voice. Soft, yet lethal. His every word resonated within the buttresses.

Who was this man?

He pushed his arms into the shirt and flicked each button into the little slits as if savoring each step, though he grumbled at the lack of gold embroidery.

I checked my watch.

Ten minutes more to wait. Damn. He would leave before the police arrived. For his own safety I couldn't let that happen.

"I...I would be remiss if I didn't ask why you intend to destroy the world?" I pushed out.

A frown tugged his lips, as if I had caused him great insult.

"No, not the world," he said, shaking his head. "All worlds. All universes. I will shatter everything. Is this suit silk?" He shoved his legs into the pants and zipped the fly. "I've missed the sensation of fine clothes against my skin."

I didn't like the deadly flash in his eyes. The irreverent laughter behind his pupils.

I rubbed the back of my neck, my fingers gliding over cold sweat.

"Isn't wanting such destruction extreme?"

"I only know extreme."

He smiled that smile again.

Where the hell were the police?

Smoothing out the creases of his suit, he glanced over his shoulder at the side vestibule. Anger hardened his lips, erasing any hint of their seemingly constant amusement.

He flickered. Flickered?

Two overlaying images raced between each other. They flipped back and forth, over and over until the one beneath flashed to the surface, fierce and vivid.

Pinpoint punctures surrounded his mouth. A map of scars stretched across his face. Twisting in thick red lines, the marred tissue traveled down his neck, disappearing beneath his white oxford shirt.

My breath stopped. A sickening chill gripped my stomach. This couldn't be real?

I blinked, hard.

His beauty returned, unobscured by the horror. Unobscured by anything. He was, once again, perfect.

The low lighting, alongside my nerves, played with me. That was the explanation.

It had to be.

"Where are they?" he growled.

He walked to the plain cross standing beside an open Bible. A single, white candle sat to its right. He curled his hands into fists, the skin pulling white over his knuckles.

"Where are what?"

"The beeswax candles. The trays of sand."

His rage crashed against my chest in violent waves. Why should he be this upset over a Catholic tradition?

"There haven't been prayer candles in the Münster for five hundred years. Not since the Reformation. You must be confused with another church," I said.

His shoulders dropped. His skin paled. For the first time, he appeared fragile. Fatigued.

"Five hundred years?" he whispered. Pain lanced each word.

He neared the candle, his footing no longer anchored. He stared at the wick, his gaze lost somewhere, someplace.

"I'm sure there is someone out there looking for you. Is there a phone number I can call?" I wanted to divert him. It all started to unnerve me more greatly.

"Five hundred years?" he yelled. No, screamed. "I've been imprisoned in that hell for five centuries?"

The arches shook, and the ground quaked. My heart pounded in my throat, and a fresh crack of terror split through me.

He sank to the floor. Broken. Defeated. He buried his face in his hands and flickered a second time.

Webs of deep scars laced between his fingers and over his hands.

I blinked. Again.

And again, he returned to his nearly divine form.

Twenty minutes had now passed. Still no police.

Pity overtook my fear, and I reached out to touch his

shoulder. He might as well been marble. For a second, I believed he truly was the *Lucifer of Liège* come to life.

"What's your name?"

Searing heat burned through his clothes and scorched into my palm. I yanked my hand back.

I stepped away.

The candle wick ignited on its own. He rose to his feet, lengthening and seeming much taller than I first recalled. The flame blazed hotter, brighter, throwing him in shades of gold. Even the red of his hair burned.

But his eyes...

Fire, an absolute inferno, exploded within them.

This was no man.

And the police weren't coming.

My pulse thundered in my ears and terror, cold, bitter terror, consumed me. I took another step back.

He took one towards me. And another.

I made to run, but I stumbled and fell into the timeworn, oak pew.

In a second, he was on me as if I was his prey. He leaned over my trembling body, the heat rolling off his skin broiling my cheeks.

"You have no idea who you're dealing with, mortal man," he said. "I am Loki. Loki of the Aesir. Loki of the Jotun. The god of mischief. The god of lies. The trickster. The evil-doer. The sly one. I *am* chaos."

Dread pounded in every beat of my heart. My veins iced.

"But, that's...all a myth."

He chuckled, as if I told him a hilarious joke. His eyes returned to their normal green, and his skin cooled.

"I am no myth."

"Are you going to kill me?" I asked.

His lips pulled into a charming smile. It sickened me how much it made me want to like him, despite his threats.

"Yes, but at another time. Please don't take it personally. I will kill you as I will kill every living creature. It's quite fair, I assure you."

He held out his hand, offering to help me back to my feet.

"But why?"

I pushed myself out of the pew, refusing his help. He shrugged and let his hand fall back to his side.

"For the same reason your God destroyed His own creation with a flood. Judgement."

I shook my head and swallowed down my panic despite all reason and good sense. I would not shrink. I would not waver. I couldn't. Not when everything was on the line.

"This isn't judgement. This is extermination. Whatever grievances were committed against you, you must forgive."

The laughter in the lines of his face faded, a bleak emptiness taking root instead.

"You don't know what they did." He whispered the words. "After what they've done, they deserve no forgiveness."

He stared once more at the candle beside the open Bible. At somewhere in the past.

The intensity of his gaze sent cold sweat trickling down my back.

"What have they done?"

2

A WEDDING TO DIE FOR

Five Hundred Years Earlier

Asgardian Year — Two Thousand and Eight, Sixth Age

Jotunheim

(Somewhere in the middle of nowhere)

"I will never forgive you for this, Loki Laufeyjarson," Thor told me.

A set of grinding teeth gleamed through his thick beard.

I forced his head to the left and stuck an orange blossom in his wild hair. It complimented his fiery red mane quite nicely, as well as his blue eyes that grew with hatred for me by the second.

"Do you want Mjolnir back or not?" I said, powdering his nose, struggling to lighten his ruddy complexion.

Tyr pushed back his blonde hair from his angular face, trying to stifle a snicker. He crossed his brawny arms over his firm chest and leaned against a boulder, enjoying our spectacle way too much.

I should have known better than to bring him along. The god of nobility and justice. Nice guy, but a banner killjoy. But no one wielded a broadsword so expertly as Tyr. I didn't anticipate bloodshed, but this was a prickly situation.

Thrym, the warlord of Thrymheim, stole Mjolnir, Thor's beloved hammer and the very safety of the Nine Worlds.

The brothers Brokkr and Eitri forged the hammer in the hearths of Svartalfheim. Made of Dwarven steel, it never missed its mark and always returned to the hand of its owner after being thrown. It could also crush giant skulls quite adeptly.

Odin did not find the loss of such a weapon particularly pleasing, and so, once again, it was up to me to save the day.

Now I was stuck in Jotunheim, where there were only pine forests and thicker pine forests, and a lovely biting cold that raced down from the Northern mountain ranges making the climate simultaneously freezing and humid.

Digging my fingers into the blue silk of Thor's gown, I adjusted his bodice until it hugged his massive chest smoothly. No creases, no puckers. Still, something remained off.

Perhaps it was the muscles.

And the beard.

Jotnar liked a woman with some meat on her bones, but this was a touch ridiculous. All the orange blossoms in the world couldn't mask the truth. But, Thrym demanded a bride in exchange for the hammer, and a bride I would give him.

"Are you sure you won't let me cast an illusion to give you a more, uh, *feminine* form?" I asked. "He's expecting the goddess of beauty and fertility. I don't mean to be rude, but you make an ugly Freya."

Thunder cracked overhead, and his eyes lit white with lightning. I took that to mean a no.

"You leave all my bits and pieces as they are," he spat. "I don't trust your magic, lie-smith."

I sighed. They never forgot.

"I turned you into a salamander one time." I tried not to smile at the memory. "If you had protected Mjolnir better, we wouldn't even be in this mess. This is all on you."

He cursed beneath his breath as I stuffed his fierce beard behind a thick veil. It kept springing back out of the fabric.

"I will break every bone in your body if you tug my beard again..."

"Now that is language very unbecoming a goddess."

I ducked just in time to miss his fist slamming into my nose.

Stepping back I admired my good work, though "good" was a stretch. Thor's broad shoulders forced the seams of his gown to their breaking point, while his waist reminded me of a tree trunk wrapped in a tent. But, the true travesty was how stupid the delicate silk appeared against his burly hands.

I scrounged through the pine duff for wild flowers until I collected a modest bouquet of blue monkshood and rampions. I pressed them in his grip, arranging the blossoms to better hide his chunky knuckles and the tufts of hair on his wrists.

It would have to do.

Besides, it was my turn now.

Casting an illusion over myself, my waist thinned, and my eyes widened along with my hips. My lashes lengthened, and my legs curved. I arched my back and stretched my arms as I grew an exquisite pair of breasts. At least one of us would be a true beauty, and it might as well be me.

Tyr couldn't hold it together anymore. His broad chest heaved and a crack of laughter escaped his lungs, causing the pine trees to shake around us. Pine cones dropped like hail at our feet.

"By Odin's ravens, you both look ridiculous!" he exclaimed.

He wiped tears from his small eyes. Thor's lips stiffened and stretched tight across his teeth.

"Shut up!" Thor growled.

He stomped towards Tyr, the hem of his gown almost getting trampled beneath his heavy boots. He was most definitely not graceful in a dress.

I pulled him back. Tyr only cackled harder.

"It's not worth breaking your laces, Thor," I said. "We're only an hour's trek from Thrymheim, and you want to look like the goddess he anticipates."

"Yes, don't break your laces, Thor," Tyr mocked.

Thor glared at him, and his right eye twitched.

"I've never been more humiliated in all my millennia," Thor said. "Everyone will think me a fool."

I dragged my hand down my face. Did they not already think that?

"There are worse things to be thought as," I said. "One of them being a coward because you aren't willing to do what it takes to get your property back."

His nostrils flared.

"But..."

"This should be a fairly simple deception, *if* you don't lose your head," I interrupted. "I will be by your side the entire time as your maid servant. There's nothing else worth fretting about."

Thor's shoulders relaxed and he nodded, almost imperceptibly.

Tyr shoved off his rock and circled Thor. He gave a hard sniff in approval.

"This plan of yours better work, Loki." He scratched his trimmed beard with the tip of his iron hook he used in place of his missing right hand.

If only he knew the truth. There was far more riding on this mission than just getting Mjolnir back.

"It will." I smoothed my own gown of deep purple. "A sacred object such a Mjolnir is necessary to bless Thrym's marriage to a Vanir goddess. He is a Jotun man, and she is unattainable to him in any other circumstance. Don't you think he will bring Mjolnir out of hiding to make this union valid?"

"For your sake, I hope you're right," Tyr said. "I don't like when you negotiate with Jotunheim on your own. If I catch one whiff of trickery..."

His gaze narrowed, and his knuckles pulsed as he gripped his sword hilt. The message was clear.

As I said. Killjoy.

Crossing my arms I sighed, unimpressed.

"My skin is in this game just as much as yours."

"I know, but I still don't see why you had to go by yourself," he said.

I rolled my eyes.

"Because I'm the only one that hasn't completely burnt my bridges with Jotunheim. You need to learn to trust me."

His grimace turned into a smile. A laugh belted out from deep within his gut.

"Trust you, lie-smith? Now that is a capital joke!"

Pain spread across my jaw from clenching my teeth

together. I hoped he didn't notice. I didn't want to give him
the satisfaction of having gotten beneath my skin.

I turned my attention away from Tyr and back to Thor.
He nibbled the rough edge of his thumbnail. He almost
spawned pity in me for him.

Almost.

"I'm sorry I called you an ugly Freya, Thor. Blue really is
your color, and you look positively radiant!"

He looked positively absurd. Luckily for us, Thrym had
a broad taste in women.

"Let's get this over with," Thor said. "And when we
return to Asgard, not a word to anyone."

"Cross my heart," I lied.

* * *

MUSIC SWELLED within the feast hall, rough fiddles and
pulsing tambourines pounding into my chest. This didn't
compare to the celebratory roar of increasingly intoxicated
Jotnar. They reveled as hard as they drank and laughed as
loud as they belched.

I lifted my heavy brass goblet to my lips and took a sip of
the dark claret, almost spitting it out involuntarily. I'd
forgotten the bite of Jotun wine, if what they served could
even be called wine. The rustic manners and tastes of Jotunheim reminded me why the Aesir and Vanir viewed Jotnar
as, to put it nicely, *provincial*.

A rush of peril hit me recognizing my cousin, Hymir, at
the table dead across from us.

Roasted boar flew out of his mouth as he hurled lewd
jokes to the crowd, each garnering a rumble of laughter
down the scarred oak tables. If only Hymir knew I was here
without his permission, right beneath his nose...

The risk was entirely electric.

Splatters of meat hit my cheeks as a rather ravenous "Freya" tore and pulled at a roasted ox beside me. Awe filled Thrym's gaze as he watched his new bride in admiration.

Now *this* was a problem. I forced down another gulp of acrid wine.

Thor growled pulling flesh off massive bones with his teeth, smacking his lips as he chewed like a forest animal. Dropping the leg bones at his feet, he moved on to the seafood platter. Grabbing a salmon, no, eight salmon, he wolfed and gorged on the pink meat beneath his veil.

Scales and fishbones flew everywhere, including landing in my hair. I giggled daintily as I pulled a sharp bone out of my braids.

"You know how fond the Vanir are of their fish," I said in the rough Jotun tongue.

I grabbed at any excuse.

Thrym didn't respond, his mouth hanging open in reverence. His bride downed an entire barrel of mead in ten seconds flat. A reverberating belch followed the victory. Adoration melted into bewilderment.

This was Thor's third barrel. Even Tyr couldn't keep up.

Several other Jotnar stopped their feasting to applaud. I only hoped their wonder wouldn't turn into suspicion. They might be provincial, but their torture methods for those who crossed them were anything but.

I kicked Thor beneath the table, reminding him we hadn't come all this way for the free food.

"When will it be time for the blessing of the union?" I asked Thrym, almost screaming over the clatter of dishes and drunk Jotnar. "We are most eager to see your marriage happily sanctified."

Thrym leaned in my ear, his gaze refusing to leave Thor who now picked up a string of sausages.

"I've never seen a woman eat like this," Thrym replied, not answering me. "I imagined your mistress Freya to be of a more delicate nature."

Thor pulled the entire wedding cake towards him, cramming fistfuls into his mouth.

"Yes, well...There is a perfectly reasonable explanation." I cleared my throat, hoping he didn't notice the sweat collecting on my brow. "After Loki returned from negotiations with you and told her she would be your bride, she grew heated with love for you. She was so nervous in wanting to protect her figure, she didn't eat for eight full days."

Thrym shook his head, and his lips sank into a frown.

"Poor lamb!" he said. Thor belched again. "She won't have to fast ever again as my wife."

He took Thor's hand, causing him to drop a cream puff, and kissed his freckled skin. Thor's shoulders tensed, and a split of thunder rolled overhead. I prayed he could keep it together a little longer.

"I love a woman with a healthy appetite," Thrym said to Thor, rubbing Thor's thick wrist with his thumb. "You are already exceeding my expectations, my dearest Freya. Let me peek beneath your veil. Don't be shy."

Before I could stop him, Thrym lifted the top veil only uncovering Thor's eyes.

I bit my lip, bracing myself for the fallout.

"Handmaiden, your lady...Her eyes are fiercer than any I've ever seen," he said to me. "Blazing red and ferocious."

I forced another feminine laugh.

Until Thor retrieved Mjolnir, we three were sitting

ducks. I refused to let this be the way I died. It would be an embarrassment.

"You must understand, her longing for you was so great, so consuming, that not only didn't she eat for eight days straight, but she also didn't sleep. This is why my lady's eyes are so fierce Lord Thrym, they are fierce with yearning for you."

Thrym smiled at this and placed his hand over his heart, as if overcome by my touching tales. I loved how easily he fell for my flattery and lies.

"She is pure goodness," he said.

I couldn't help my own lips from smiling now.

"That's why you shouldn't keep her waiting to sanctify your marriage. Nothing will give her peace until your union is finalized."

He nodded ardently.

"You speak the truth handmaiden. Freya, I will not make you wait a minute more. You and I will be man and wife this instant!"

Thrym clapped his hands, and four Jotun women went to a locked, carved wooden chest.

Thor squirmed in his seat. Nervousness plagued the lines of Tyr's face.

I shoved a plate of marzipan in front of Thor. If food would keep him quiet, then I would give him as much as he wanted.

Thrym took Thor's hand again. Thor didn't stop eating.

"My dearest Freya," he said. "I have a great gift for you, one that will make our unorthodox marriage binding and blessed. Are you ready to be mine?"

A muffled sound, I'm sure one of protest, pushed through Thor's stuffed mouth. Thank gods for marzipan.

The Jotun women approached carrying a red, velvet

pillow. On top, lay Mjolnir. A short, thick handle wrapped in fine leather joined to a solid block of Dwarven steel. The polished metal appeared almost gold reflecting the firelight. Dried blood of past enemies filled the etched runes on the hammer's face, making the engravings black.

They placed it on the table before Thrym and Thor.

Thunder quaked outside the fortress.

My heart raced. Tyr dropped his hand to his waist to be nearer his sword.

"Now, my dearest, loveliest Freya, grasp Mjolnir's handle. Yes, like that." Dishes chattered from another crack of thunder. Thrym laid his hand on top of Thor's. "Feel the power of this formidable weapon? I swear it is nothing compared to what you will grip your hand around tonight."

Thrym smiled, but it did not compare to the murderous glee dancing in Thor's eyes.

A vein of lightning tore through the sky outside the leaded windows, the ensuing peal of thunder rolling in my bones.

I stood up from my seat and stepped back. Tyr did likewise, unsheathing his sword.

"Thank you, Thrym. I've been dying to plunge my hammer into your skull all night to shut you up," Thor growled.

Shock filled Thrym's expression as Thor ripped his hand away. His thick beard sprung out as his veil fell from his face, and the blue silk gown split into tatters as he jumped onto the battered table.

Thor lifted Mjolnir above his head, darts of lightning sparking and sputtering around the weapon of Dwarven Steel. His eyes flickered white, revealing his true aspect of thunderous violence and danger.

Rage washed away Thrym's surprise as he stared up at

Thor. He pulled out his broadsword, pointing the deadly tip up at Thor's gut. His confidence was adorable, really.

"You dare trick me, Thunderer?" Thrym barked. "You will feel my blade for this mockery."

Thor laughed filling the room with more thunder.

Lifting Mjolnir higher, he swung the hammer down with all his strength towards Thrym's head. The face of Mjolnir plunged into his forehead, the resounding crack of his skull louder than the roaring storm outside.

His neck snapped, and his head sank between his shoulders, his bones fracturing and splintering from the force of Thor's blow.

Thrym's sword slipped from his hand and clanged against the stone floor. A thud followed, as his body fell forward. Dead.

Shrieks crashed against each other accompanied by pounding feet as rather angry Jotnar rushed us.

Well, the wedding was nice while it lasted.

Thor beamed as he struck a Jotun man square in the jaw, producing a satisfying snap. A woman hit at his feet with a mace, while another latched onto his arm and tried to claw at his face. He kicked his thick boot into the delicate nose of the first, while thrusting his hammer into the stomach of the latter.

Hot blood sprayed my face. Worse, it soiled my dress.

"Come on Thor, it's time to go!" I screamed over the din of breaking dishes and bones.

"In a minute." Thor brought down his hammer on a man armed with a morning star, splitting his seventh skull.

Tyr only grunted, swinging his sword and slicing it through the guts of three Jotun warriors.

Unlike them, I knew when a party was over.

I sprinted towards the doors. Muscular arms wrapped around my chest and yanked me back.

"Not so fast, little lady," a Jotun man breathed into my ear.

"I am but a weak woman!" I said, rolling my eyes. "Have mercy."

Steel flashed. His dirk bit into my throat. I took it mercy was off the table.

"You will pay for what you've done." His breath stunk of that sour wine I detested. That was enough to kill him.

"Oh no! Whatever will I do?"

Making a fist, I thrust it between his legs into his groin. He yelped and released me. Spinning around, I reached inside my bodice and pulled out my dagger in time to stab it deep into his right eye.

Blood ran down his cheek as he screamed and stumbled backwards into a tower of honey cakes. Springing towards him I pushed him down and straddled his hips, my knees squelching in the butter and sugar.

"You should have known better than to assume a woman incapable of saving herself," I said.

I plunged my dagger again, this time through his chest. I loved the thrill as my blade scraped past his ribcage until it sank firmly into his heart.

"Asgardian scum!" another screeched at me.

He ran at me, raising an axe over his head. I stood and thrust my arm upwards, burying my blade into his liver. His blood gushed warm over my hand, slipping between my fingers.

The rush was scintillating.

The Jotnar refused to retreat, fighting with fists, weapons, and whatever else was at hand. I ducked as a roasted peacock flew over my head.

Thor jumped off the heavy table, forcing Mjolnir down onto a group of Jotnar armed with spears. Thunder quaked the halls as he broke their collarbones and tibias. Thor laughed as he continued his assault, as if having the best day of his life.

Lightning illuminated the gore in flashes of garish white. Hemingr, another distant cousin of mine, lay dead, his brains splattered alongside crushed apples and eggs.

My stomach churned.

While I loved a good fight, the unbridled chaos of it all, I didn't like wasting blood. We got what we came for, we didn't need to make a point.

Besides, there were more pressing matters of business I needed to attend to back in Asgard.

Against all good sense, I searched for Hymir among the throng of fighting Jotnar. I smiled catching sight of him. He tried to pry a battle axe off the far wall.

Thankfully, Thor and Tyr remained too engrossed in their killing to notice me cast an illusion. Snapping my fingers, I split from myself creating a perfect duplicate me. Fun little trick of mine. Very useful in such sticky situations.

I couldn't help but admire my female form thrusting and parrying, a dagger clutched firm in its slender hands. Damn, I looked good.

Leaving the mirrored image of myself behind in the thick of the fighting, I ran to Hymir and pulled him into a dark hallway. Pinning him against a wall I pressed my dagger against his wide neck, forcing his own blade out of his hand.

"Don't kill me!" he gasped.

Dearest cousin. Always so brave.

"Does Thrym still keep his boats at the base of the fortress?" I asked.

His eyes swam with confusion, most likely from how an Asgardian hand maiden would know such private information.

"Tell me!"

"Y...yes," he whimpered.

"I suggest you surrender now and gather your compatriots and take the langskips. Make for Utgard. You'll be safe there."

His face twisted.

"It's against our code to surrender," he said.

I sighed. Damn everyone and their codes.

"Do you prefer to be dead?" I asked. "You know Thor and Tyr won't stop until they crush all your skulls. You know you stand no chance against Mjolnir. If you love your life at all, if you love Jotunheim at all, stop this now and get out."

My earnestness surprised me.

I didn't know if this benevolence was born purely of my impatience to get back to Asgard, or from a remaining sliver of sentiment for my first home of Jotunheim. That disgustingly sweet thought sickened me.

Hymir took in a deep breath, then nodded.

I released him, letting him run back into the fight. He yelled over the clash of steel and flesh to retreat. The others blinked as if he lost his mind, but when Thor and Tyr roared charging them with Mjolnir and blade, they all retreated and ran towards the passage that would bring them to Thrym's langskips.

My heart slowed.

I snapped my fingers, ending the illusion I created of the duplicate me fighting. It wavered, flickered, and then dissolved completely away, allowing me to return to the feast hall no one the wiser to what I had done. If they ever knew I tried to save any Jotun...

"Come back, you cowards!" Thor cried after them. "Don't steal my property if you can't handle the consequences."

Tyr smiled and held out his hand, well, his only hand, to Thor. Thor gripped it and yanked him into an embrace.

My lips pulled into a smile seeing my plan come to fruition. Thor got his hammer back, got to have some fun, and could see I was true to my word after all.

I had delivered Mjolnir to him literally on a velvet cushion.

"You are a master at taking a Jotun down," Tyr complimented Thor, returning to the smooth Asgardian language. "It's beautiful to watch."

Thor nearly blushed.

"Aye, but you wield that sword of yours more masterfully than any other I've witnessed. Sliced that one almost in two with a clean swing!"

I dragged my hand down my face from their gushing, self congratulations.

Stretching my shoulders, they widened along with my chest. My breasts flattened back into lean muscle as I returned to my usual male form and perfect jaw. I ran my fingers through my copper hair, taming the waves that moved like flames when I walked.

"I told you if you listened to me you'd get Mjolnir back, and just look at you!" I said, prodding them to acknowledge my part in this gambit. "I dare say no Jotun will ever steal from you again. They will tell tales of this night."

Thor's lips flattened. Tyr scratched behind his ear.

"What?" I asked.

Thor shook his head and stared at me.

"This never would have happened had you not

promised Freya to Thrym," he growled. "You negotiated all this behind our backs, now look at the resulting carnage."

He pointed at the bodies littering the floor, slumped over oak tables, or smashed beyond recognition.

"Yes, it is a shame," I said. "That limestone will never quite be the same with all those blood stains."

"Can you ever take anything seriously?" Thor asked.

"That depends if you can say anything of consequence. I will not be blamed for your ruckus."

Tyr sighed.

"So, you think yourself innocent?" Tyr asked.

"I did what I had to do," I seethed.

"No, you only did what you wanted," Tyr spat. "As you always do, without thought of repercussion."

My throat tightened, and I tried to keep the bile in my stomach from rising. They never ceased to amaze me with their hypocrisy.

"I never told Thor to bash Thrym's brains out," I said. "That was his decision. All he had to do was grab Mjolnir and make a break for it." I turned to Thor. "You never can control your bloodlust, just as you can't control your appetite. You damn near gave us away."

Thor stood not a breath apart from me and pressed his finger into my chest. I grabbed his hand, his skin rough and dry beneath my fingers, and pushed it away. I would not be reprimanded by him.

"The fact remains this entire operation was reckless, as is everything you touch. This could cause war, Loki."

I swallowed, hard. I didn't like that thought.

An impromptu war with Jotunheim was the last thing I needed to deal with.

Especially when a significant threat already sat at Asgard's door.

3

CLARET FOR TWO

Asgard

All the gods celebrated Mjolnir's return in Asgard's grandest hall.

I leaned against a marble pillar watching them from the shadows.

Bragi twanged his harp singing songs he composed in Thor and Tyr's honor, while Idunn and Freya accompanied him with rattling tambourines. Mead flowed continuously into freshly drained horns, and laughter rose with each repetition of the tale of Thrym's fall to Aesir might.

I crossed my arms tighter against my chest as my defeat grew with every toast and cheer to Thor and Tyr. The warriors. The victors. The heroes.

No one raised a glass to me. No one offered me glory. No one even had the decency to thank me, the one who alone masterminded Mjolnir's rescue.

This hurt my feelings, which I hated. It made me admit I had feelings in the first place.

What I hated more was I failed in gaining their trust, which was the entire blasted point of offering my help at all.

They kept a secret from me, you see.

Danger swelled within Asgard. A faint pulse of some ominous presence lingered in every corner of every hall, as if a grim aura had descended over us and prepared to feast.

It began as a dull ache between my temples, a vibration in my blood with all things dire and bleak.

I ignored it at first, but as this sinister force strengthened, so did the throbbing in my head.

If I drank heavily, or lost myself in passion, it would go away for a spell. But it always returned, which vexed me.

I despised discomfort, but I despised being left out of a good secret even more.

These past months I caught their tense whispers echoing in narrow corridors. I sensed chaos smoldering in their souls when they lied to me. When they told me not to worry. To leave it to them. To stay out of it.

As if that was a possibility for me when this secret, this tantalizing threat, seemed absolutely delectable. Dangerous. Thrilling. All the things I loved rolled up into one fascinating enigma.

I just had to crack the gods open like a walnut.

But for now, I needed something to lift my spirits.

I snapped my fingers.

A green snake materialized right before Balder the Beautiful's fancy boot. He yelped, his voice reaching a falsetto I didn't know quite possible, and jumped back from the snake.

His heel caught on the sheepskin rug behind him, sending him crashing to the floor. A magnificent arc of mead cascaded out from his drinking horn and splashed all over Thor and Tyr, drenching their best tunics.

I stifled my laughter as sticky, honey wine soaked their beards and dribbled down to their laps.

Someone tugged my arm, forcing my gaze away from my entertainment.

Sif, Thor's wife, faced me.

Blonde hair shimmered like gold as it spiraled down her back. Her violet gown hugged her delicate waist, and her pink lips matched the crimson inflaming her cheeks.

The woman was insatiable! She couldn't keep her hands off of me. Seven times the night before, and still she wanted more. I realized the effect I had on women, but this was getting ridiculous.

"Fancying another round? I suppose I could be persuaded," I said.

I leaned towards her, destroying the space between us.

She narrowed her hazel eyes, their usual naivety washed away by anger. But anger and lust are such close cousins...

"Don't speak so loud," she hissed through clenched teeth. "I can't have the others ever discovering—"

"What?" I interrupted. "That you experienced the greatest pleasure you've ever known? I warned you I'd ruin you for anyone else. I'm quite addictive."

Her expression dissolved into pure vinegar. She pushed me back, the little minx.

"You orchestrated this whole charade of Mjolnir's theft and rescue, didn't you?"

I gave her my most devastating smile. Catching one of her soft ringlets, I rubbed the strands gently between my fingers. Rose water and jasmine filled my nostrils.

"You seem troubled, my dear Sif. Why don't we retire to my rooms for a drink? I'm a very good listener."

I tucked her curl behind her ear, letting my fingers skate down her hot cheeks.

She slapped my hand away. The spark of pain only excited me more.

"Tell me the truth."

Oh, she was funny.

I laughed, and she shifted in her deer skin slippers, peering behind my shoulder if anyone heard me.

"Sorry, telling the truth isn't exactly what I do."

She crossed her arms, letting out an irritated sigh.

"Sleeping with you was a mistake. I've known none as loathsome as you."

I frowned at this.

"You're beginning to make me think you aren't interested."

Actually, I was glad. She was quite average when it came to lovemaking.

I made to leave. She gripped my wrist, digging her nails into my skin like needles.

"If you won't admit the truth I...I will tell Thor what you've done."

Now this accusation was getting serious.

I smiled again, checking the cuticles of my free hand.

"And what, exactly, will you tell him Sif?"

She blinked.

"That you planned all of this. That you manipulated Mjolnir's theft. That you used me."

I nodded, considering her words.

She was clever to figure it out.

Convincing Thrym to steal Mjolnir was a personal triumph of mine. Quick, clean, and most importantly, no one able to blame innocent little me when the gods realized their prized weapon was missing.

Of course they would need me to help them win it back. I was the only one able to negotiate with Jotunheim, after all.

"You mean, you will admit your infidelity to your husband?" I let my lips graze her ear as I spoke. "That you allowed me into your bed, instead of guarding Mjolnir? That you had me get Thor so drunk he spent the night in the pigsty so we could enjoy a little *lust-and-thrust*? That as you screamed my name all night, you gave Thrym the time he needed to sneak into your rooms and take Mjolnir?" Her entire body stiffened now. "Is *that* what you will tell him?"

Her eyes narrowed.

"You bastard."

"I could never have pulled it off without your help, Sif. Don't take it personally. Lies and tricks are my speciality."

She clutched hold of my tunic and forced me to look at her. Spite and hatred tightened every muscle in her face.

"Maybe it's not Thor I should tell, but Odin. You've admitted to treason to me. He will skin you alive for this."

She reminded me of an angry Chihuahua. Vicious, but harmless.

"Please," I said. "You won't betray my secret without revealing your own. That you slept with the lie-smith. That you allowed me to make your husband a cuckold."

She swallowed.

Her gaze searched me, as if hunting for some weakness, some thread she could grasp to destroy me. She let her hands fall from my tunic, defeated.

"You are disgusting, Loki. Foul to the core," she said, her voice quivering. Shaken.

As if I'd never heard that before.

"Funny, last night I remember you calling me magnificent."

Her mouth fell open, and her right eye twitched. I turned and left her to her guilt and anger.

I was done being reminded how much planning and effort I put into the whole plot, only to fail. What's the point of manipulating a theft and sleeping with another man's wife if I couldn't even enjoy the fruits of my good labor?

I massaged the spot between my eyes, trying to stop the slow throb threatening to explode.

They might have all been fools and idiots, but I was the biggest one of all to think I could get them to trust the god of lies so easily. I wouldn't concede defeat yet.

Not when these bloody headaches still plagued me.

* * *

SOFT HANDS SKATED across my chest leaving fire in their wake. Katla branded a trail of kisses along my neck. Our knees sank into the layers of feather mattresses as we embraced, tangling our fingers in each other's hair.

Her lips captured my own, and I swallowed her moans one after the next like brandied cherries. Each coiled the heat tighter between my legs.

I explored Katla's mouth with my tongue as a second set of fingers, these stronger, dug their nails into my back, pulling agonizingly slowly downwards. The little bites of pain he caused forced me towards the edge. Ivar knew what I liked.

The shapes we three made together in my private rooms were delightfully taboo in most of the Nine Worlds.

I turned from Katla to him, brushing his straight brown hair away from his eyes black with desire. Away from his pretty mouth parting and glistening as he licked his lips. I needed his mouth against mine.

He gasped as I caught him in a kiss, surging my tongue between his lips. We fell into a heap of pillows, the satin cooling my hot skin.

I savored how the ridges of his stomach flexed beneath me. A beautiful contrast to Katla's soft breasts brushing my shoulders as she attacked my ear with her teeth.

My blood ignited, desperate to sink myself into either of them.

A throat cleared beside us.

Dammit!

I threw off the silk sheets, ready to rip out the spleen of whoever interrupted us.

I gulped instead.

Odin stared down at me, his expression frosted with annoyance.

For two seconds fear washed over me. Had I underestimated Sif?

Katla and Ivar gathered the blankets around them and took off out the oak doors.

I laid back against my pillows and stretched. Unlike them, I was used to being caught in precarious positions.

Besides, I couldn't look guilty.

"You always have excellent timing," I said, brushing my hot fingers through my tousled hair.

He smirked, raising his eyebrow above his only eye. The blue of his iris contrasted the black silk eyepatch covering his right empty socket nicely.

"Maybe you should be more careful to lock your doors," he said.

He had a point.

Pressing my fists into the layers of my mattresses, I pushed myself out of bed. The marble chilled my bare feet as I walked naked towards my rumpled tunic. Picking it up off the bearskin rug I pulled it over my head.

I turned back to Odin. He traced the intricate pattern of inlaid wood of my table with his forefinger, as if remembering an old friend. The crackling fire bathed him in soft gold. The Asgardian sea rolled through the open terrace, flooding my rooms with the dull roar of crashing waves.

"Won't your wife be furious when she finds you've been back here? With me? Alone?"

Not that I cared. She hated me, which flattered me greatly. I enjoyed knowing my existence could inspire such extreme emotion in another.

A tiny echo of pain fluttered behind his lips. His eye bore into me.

"You know I don't care what Frigg thinks," he said. "Not for a long time."

Since me, he meant.

Without thought, or out of old habit, I went to a lacquered table pushed hard against the back wall. I took two green glass goblets and poured them both to the rim with claret. I handed him one.

Surprise brightened the fine lines around his eyes. He scratched his russet beard, and I couldn't help admiring the handsome angles of his jaw and cheekbones. Though thousands of years old, his face remained that of a man in his prime. Rugged, pensive, dangerous.

"Like the old days?" he asked, taking the glass. "I thought you hated me after..." he paused. "Well."

I did hate him after what he did, or at least I wanted to. That was the lie I told myself, anyway.

I forced a grin.

"We agreed to always remain friends. Brothers," I said.

He held my gaze. Sorrow settled in his face, though he smiled through it.

"If only we could have remained more."

He drank down the claret, not even bothering to savor the black currant and plum.

My stomach squirmed, and I spun my silver onyx ring around my middle finger. I didn't like this turn in conversation. I didn't like the feelings he tried to wake in me again.

Feelings sucked all the fun out of everything.

"Have you come to admire me naked, or to scold me?" I asked, done waiting to discover if Sif had betrayed me. "I don't blame you if you came for the former. I'm quite irresistible."

He chuckled beneath his breath.

"Neither. As unbelievable as it may be, I actually came to thank you."

Relief mixed with shock washed down my spine. Dear Sif. I knew I could count on her pride and discretion.

"Oh?"

"You did a great thing today, Loki. You succeeded in bringing Mjolnir back home to us. I am grateful to you."

He made to put his hand on my shoulder, but stopped himself. He knew better.

"Don't tell that to Thor and Tyr," I said. "To them I've apparently started a war."

"Don't worry what the others think. Only what I think, and I am pleased with you."

Renewed excitement rippled through me. Perhaps my endeavor to regain the gods' favor wasn't a complete failure after all.

"You always have my loyalty," I said. "I will never break my promise to you."

"I hope so," he whispered.

Something else lurked behind his words, like a somber riddle. I disregarded it. Anticipation sizzled my skin far too deeply to care.

Hoping to further loosen his tongue, I poured a second round of claret. Hoping he would finally reveal what threat I sensed in Asgard.

He always was like a strawberry trifle with his secrets, forcing me to dig through one astounding layer after the next.

I gave him the fresh glass, trying to not let our fingers graze as he took it from me.

He sat on an embroidered chair by the fireplace as he had done so many times in the past. For a heartbeat, I was back in that time when I loved him.

I still loved him, but I wouldn't admit it.

"It's been ages since we last sat here and talked," I said, egging him on. "We shared everything with each other then."

He rubbed his thumb across the smooth glass, a soft smile creeping across his lips. I knew he must be inhabiting the same memory I had just visited.

"It was your decision to stop them."

This again.

"What did you expect?" I said. "Choices made us become different men."

He turned from me and stared at the Persian rug beneath his feet in response. The fire spit and cracked beside us, filling the silence along with the thundering waves outside.

"Do you remember when I made you what you are?" he asked.

Of course I did. That was the day my life changed forever.

It's widely believed gods exist outside birth and beginning, but that's not completely accurate.

We are made.

Odin was one of the first. Ambition and wisdom pulsed untamed within him, until one greater than he took notice and breathed him into a celestial.

Alone, Odin searched for others like him who contained pure elements. Finding beauty, law, strength, love, war, and of course, chaos, he collected us like precious jewels for his new kingdom of Asgard.

Sinking his fingers into his chest, he pulled out a small piece of his own element and pushed it into our bodies, transforming our elements, making us gods.

Making us immortal beings like him.

"I can still recall the rush, the force of your power, as you plunged your ambition into my heart and I became the god of chaos."

"Then I offered you something greater."

I looked down at my wrist, where a faint scar reminded me of our link.

"Brotherhood," I breathed.

"I never offered such a vow to another, nor have I ever since. Our blood oath bound us together in fealty forever."

I went with him to Asgard after that, leaving the country of my father for the country of my mother. I took her name and became a Laufeyjarson and stepped into a world I was not prepared for as Odin's blood brother.

He leaned towards me, the groaning wood breaking me out of his spell.

"Your chaos remains as beautiful as when I first caught sight of you, Loki. You deserve all I gave you."

I smiled.

Odin always was a first rate con.

He never flattered unless he wanted something, and he loved the game as much as I did.

But right now, I rather he get to the point. He was sucking away valuable "me" time.

"I'm sure you've rehearsed a grand performance trying to swindle me with all this ooey gooey sentiment, but I prefer you cut to the chase."

Confusion knit his brow as if he had no idea what I was talking about. Oh, he was good.

"I told you, I came here to thank you."

I rolled my eyes and let out a sigh.

"I'd stop while you're ahead."

The corner of his mouth twitched, but he kept my gaze. I tapped my foot.

A guilty smile spread from ear to ear.

"You always could call me out on my shit, even when I'm acting my heart out," he said.

I enjoyed the tingle of excitement having beaten him this round. In the past we tried being honest with each other, but we were better at games.

"There's a trick to that. You're always full of shit."

A laugh burst out from deep in his gut. I couldn't help giving a chuckle myself. A warm familiarity seized me, remembering how it used to be between us.

"Fine. Truth is, I'm concerned about you."

Ok, now I really laughed. This was brilliant.

"I didn't think you capable of such concern. You are full of surprises."

His mirth calmed, and he cleared his throat, making his face more serious.

He narrowed his eye.

"There is too much free time for you in Asgard, and it's not serving your mind well," he said. "You are either sulking, drinking, or what I caught you doing when I walked in here."

"And the problem is?" I asked. "You said I wasn't to be scolded."

He pinched the space above his nose and shook his head.

"I'm not scolding you. I'm simply offering you an opportunity to escape what is becoming routine. You hate routine."

He made another point. Damn.

"And what is this grand adventure?"

"I'm attending a carnival in Switzerland. I swear it is the three finest days in Midgard. Costumes, drums, masks, and eager humans, all in a frenzy to celebrate the end of winter."

How tempting...

"Not interested."

He frowned.

"I've never known you to turn down a fun time. This would be perfect for you. The chaos alone is thick and ripe."

"Because when I think of a fun time I immediately think of the Swiss," I said. "I know your offers. More importantly, I know their price."

"Which is?"

"I'd have to go with you."

"Is that so terrible?"

"I thought that obvious."

He shook his head.

"Loki, I want us to move forward. I want to travel together again and stir up trouble like the old days."

Old days.

I didn't like how his words churned in my soul. They made me want to forget my pain and anger. To forget the promise I made to myself to never go back to him.

"Still no."

He stepped even closer, his fine linen tunic brushing against me. I tried to ignore the heat from his body sinking into my skin.

"I miss us, Loki."

I gave a sad smile, more genuine than I liked.

"I'm not the reason we lost what we were," I whispered.

The lines of his face tightened.

"I admit I've made horrific sacrifices. But I did what was necessary for the survival of the Nine Worlds. I wish you could understand."

He stretched his hand towards my cheek. Again, he stopped himself from touching me.

I knew of the sacrifices he spoke of. After all this time he still tried to justify what he did. Fury crackled within my heart from his stubborn arrogance.

"That's the problem. I *do* understand."

I was done listening to him.

I passed him and walked to the door.

He gripped my wrist, stopping me.

My body tensed.

Beneath his hand the utter vastness of his element opened to me. The edges blurred where he ended and I began. A deep ocean of ambition consumed me, crushed me, surged into my nostrils and into my mouth. It filled me to the brim, and I greedily drank it all in.

I had forgotten how he felt.

How my reckless soul hungered for his of raw ruthlessness.

"I never intended to drive you into the shadows," he said. Pleaded.

Pain splintered within my skull, hot and fierce. For once,

I was thankful for the return of my pounding headache. It broke through the maelstrom that was Odin.

I pulled out of his grasp.

"Didn't anyone ever tell you excuses are unbecoming?"

I no longer cared if Odin shared what this threat was with me or not. It wasn't worth the risk of him eating me whole again.

4

SECRETS, SECRETS

I rubbed my temples trying to lessen the throb pulsing between them. A fresh wave of menace crashed in my brain with every stab.

This pounding in my head was starting to get extremely irritating.

I needed something to take my mind off it all, without blackening my mood further. Mead seemed the best option.

Slinking through halls and corridors, I placed my hand on the brass door handle that led to the cellars.

I stopped.

Voices whispered inside. Oh, this was too perfect.

I swung the door open. Thor, Tyr, and Balder's jaws fell slack, as if my very presence spoiled everything. How marvelous.

"My, my! Are we throwing a party? You know how I love parties."

I stepped in, letting the door shut with a bang behind me. I wouldn't miss this for anything.

Balder's chiseled features sharpened, and he bared a white set of teeth.

Everyone said he was the most beautiful of the gods. That he beheld the truest of elements. Goodness. Light. I didn't see what all the fuss was about.

His short, blonde hair was nothing to write home about, same for his lean physique. And his smile? Poems were written about its charm. To me, it only screamed *I'm the biggest prick this side of the Ifingr River*.

"What are you doing here, Wolf's Father?" Balder asked.

I tutted.

"Your mother really failed you at manners," I replied.

"I'm also surprised by your being here," Tyr added. He scratched his chin with his hook, rustling the dense whiskers of his beard. "By now you are typically stumbling drunk into your rooms where you commit all manner of sins the entire night."

Odin was right. I guess I had formed a routine. Such a travesty sickened me.

"I already accomplished one of those tasks today, now I'm working on the second. I am horribly sober, so if you don't mind." I grabbed their bottle of mead off the table and took a large swig.

Balder tore it out of my grasp and threw it to the ground. Froth and foam splattered across our boots, and good mead ran through the grooves of the limestone floor like miniature rivers. He really was the worst.

"Get out before I make you." He dropped his hand to the dagger at his hip.

Excitement rippled through me at the thought of him spilling my blood. His threats were always cute.

I stepped towards him, my lips pulling into a smile as his knuckles tightened around his hilt.

"Go ahead," I said. "A brave man wouldn't be afraid to do it."

A heavy hand clapped over my shoulder and pulled me back. Pine and sweat rose from their skin. Thor.

I grumbled internally he should end my fun.

"I didn't realize you cared for mead," Thor said, releasing me. "You said it wasn't strong enough for your tastes."

He cast an apologetic glance at Tyr. I could surmise the meaning. They believed this spot a safe refuge from my prying.

"I hate to be predictable," I said.

I picked up the bottle from the ground, and drank what little mead remained. Honey and blackberry warmed my throat and stomach. Better yet, it lessened the pain still burrowing in my skull.

"Regardless, this is a private matter, and it's time you leave," Tyr said.

I smiled.

"Private matter? How could I possibly leave now, when this sounds absolutely riveting?"

I pulled out one of the battered oak chairs and sat. Leaning back, I clopped my boots on the heavy tabletop, making myself quite comfortable. I wasn't going anywhere.

"No, Loki," he said. "It's for your own good that you go."

I chuckled, despite Tyr crossing his twenty inch biceps across his fifty inch chest. He was built like a very muscular whale.

"If I did what was good for me, I'd never have any fun."

Thor shifted in his boots, gaining my attention. He seemed nervous. I could always count on him to slip.

"Dearest Thor, we've always been friends," I told him.

"Well..."

"Of course we have. We've travelled, feasted, and fought together."

"Yes, but..."

"Tell me, *friend*, whatever could be the reason for your little meeting tonight? Could it be, I don't know, the danger that threatens Asgard?"

Sometimes it's best to aim right for the throat.

Silence descended on us. Awkward silence. The best kind of silence. It meant I hit a nerve.

Thor twisted his fiery, red beard between his thick fingers. I loved the sweat collecting on his freckled brow as his brain struggled to formulate an answer.

"No...Nothing like that," he spit out, scratching his head.

Chaos flickered in his soul and rose from his skin like a woman's fine perfume.

Liar.

Being the god of chaos allowed me the ability to sense the turmoil in others, their lies. Except for Odin, that man was like a steel cage of secrets.

"So you were talking of the weather, then?" I asked. "Only something crucial would bring you three together."

"We were just discussing a...Jotun squabble," Tyr covered. "The fallout from the wedding you caused. That's all."

More lies.

I smirked.

"I'm sure it is," I said.

Irritation flared in me. They were persistent in keeping whatever this threat was from me. If I missed a good battle because of their tight lips, I would be extremely put out.

"You know how Jotnar can get," Balder said. "You and your brood always cause trouble."

I leapt up from the table, letting my chair fall and crack against the limestone.

"My brood?" I ground out. "Don't forget most here share Jotun blood."

Malice glinted in his blue eyes, the same blue as Odin's, and a sneer curled his flawless lips.

"True, but only you share blood from a Jotun father. Your Aesir mother was a whore to bear Farbauti's spawn. It's why you took her name instead of his. To hide your shame, Loki *Laufey*jarson."

Red washed my vision. I twisted my fingers in his tunic and pulled him against me. Gripping my dagger I placed it against his soft throat.

"Do you recognize what this is?" I said. "Dwarven steel, the deadliest of all metals. It was a gift from my mother, the only thing I have of her."

He squirmed beneath me. I pressed the razor edge deeper into his thrashing pulse.

"Get off!"

"You might be the favorite god of the Nine Worlds, but don't think that protects you from me," I said. "Nothing would give me greater satisfaction than cutting into your supple skin with her blade."

Fear flashed in his eyes, his fine, blonde hair sticking to the sweat beading at his temples making me flush with heat and delight.

"Show some restraint for once in your life, Loki," Tyr shouted. "You're constantly rash and short tempered."

Noble Tyr, always trying to keep the peace. Always a wet blanket.

I loosened my grip and pushed him away. He rubbed the fine red line on his neck.

"Thank you, Tyr," I said. "You've kept me from making a terrible mistake. Balder's blood would have stained my favorite tunic for sure, and that would have been truly tragic."

"What's gotten into you?" Thor asked. "You're worse than usual."

"He can't help it, brother," Balder snapped. "Don't you see what he is?"

I crushed my nails into my palms. Even his voice grated my nerves.

"And what am I, Balder?"

"Monstrous," he spat. "You spawn wolves and snakes. You sully these sacred halls with your filth and base lusts. Asgard was meant to be a beacon of wisdom, truth, and honor. You diminish what my father built with every breath you take."

I chuckled at the notion of Odin being honorable.

"You know nothing of your father, Balder. His ambitions, or his sins. A place like Asgard cannot be built by honor and beauty alone. I may be many things, but at least I'm not naïve, like you."

His shoulders loosened, and the anger in his face melted into amusement. He laughed. The little shit.

"If you say so," he replied. "One day my father will realize he never should have brought chaos to Asgard. Then we will see which of us is truly the naïve one."

The tone of his words stung like needles. Like there was a joke I wasn't let in on.

"You three really throw the worst parties," I said.

I snatched another bottle of mead from the cupboard and left. They closed the door behind me, a soft *click* of a lock echoing through the empty hall. As if that would achieve anything against me.

Casting an illusion, I let my footsteps carry away into the

distance. I remained by the door, pressing my ear against the rough wood grain.

Their voices carried through the murk of mumbles and murmurs.

My breaths increased along with my excitement.

"Is this still the best course of action?" Thor asked.

"It's the only course Odin allows," Tyr replied.

I pinched my ear harder against the door. I didn't want to miss a word.

"This never should have been agreed to," Balder said.

"We thought we stopped it," Tyr followed, fear clinging to his every word. "We thought we escaped our fates, but now, without reason, the threat returns."

Silence followed, but not the awkward silence of earlier. This was the kind of silence that sank into the roots of your heart and tugged.

"Odin's dreams are nothing but ash and death, and the Destroyer at the center of them."

Destroyer?

A shock of absolute agony exploded between my temples, hard and wicked.

Pain crushed me, twisting into my bones, mixing into my marrow. Even my blood stung, pumping towards my heart where it squeezed.

I fell to the limestone, grinding my fingers into my scalp begging it to stop.

Sounds filled my mind, an awful pounding coming from outside me and from within. Steel split bone. Fire seared timber. Cinders and charred flesh filled my nose. Horror overtook me.

My headaches had never been like this before. Before were only warnings. This was real, and it wasn't fun anymore.

It was deadly, and it was coming.

Whatever *it* was.

I usually thrived on the thrill of the obscure. The rush of danger. But now, I only felt terror. I was unused to the sensation, and I didn't like it.

The throbbing started to weaken. I wiped sweat from my brow, ignoring the tremble in my hand.

I had saved the gods countless times before. I rescued them from ruin. I helped them in war. Now, when they needed me most they preferred to shut me out? Expected me to sit back and let my fate be in their idiotic hands? We would all be dead before supper.

No thank you. I loved my life far too much to allow that. And I hated admitting it, but I was rather fond of Asgard, too.

I had been an utter fool. All this time I wanted their trust because I simply detested being kept in the dark. Now, I saw I needed their trust to let me save all our necks.

But how?

5

MEMORIES TO BURN

Midgardian Year — 1526

Midgard

Basel, Switzerland

"I'm glad you changed your mind about coming with me," Odin said.

"You made it too tempting for me to resist. I had to see what all the fuss was about."

Actually, I found Midgard quite dull, but this trip offered me an opportunity to regain Odin's trust, which I needed if I wanted to discover more about this "Destroyer."

It should be relatively straightforward. Seduce him, win his favor, try not to collapse in on myself like a dying star.

Easy.

"Can you smell that?" he asked, opening his arms wide to the Midgardian air.

"Shit?"

"Life."

I raised my right eyebrow.

"They have life in other realms too, you know," I said. "Ones far more advanced."

"But not ones filled with such hope and drive. Human bodies are weak. The slightest chill in the wind and they fall like timber, but their souls..." His lips pulled into a wide smile like a child daydreaming of summer. "There is a strength in them you don't find in beings a hundred times stronger."

Odin always could spin poetry out of muck.

The Rhine river raced beneath us as our boots snapped against the wood planks of the bridge that led directly into Basel. White buildings gripped the stone banks, almost as if the city rose out of the rushing waters. And above the tile roofs and lime plaster homes towered the two red spires of the Münster Cathedral.

Sharp notes of fifes lilted through the night in celebration of carnival, or Fasnacht, as the locals called it.

We passed beneath the Rheintor, the immense gate that separated greater Basel from its smaller sister. I chuckled. High on a corner laughed a stone face of a king, its tongue sticking out towards the opposite rival bank.

The Basler's cheekiness impressed me.

Stepping into the narrow lanes of Schifflande, we barely missed getting stampeded by one of a hundred different marching bands. The bright tones of their fifes pierced my ears, and their trilling drums battered my chest.

Revelers crowded the streets, filling every nook and cranny of the city. Their drunken songs and laughter added to the thick dissonance surrounding us.

"I told you, there's nothing like this," Odin yelled over the din of the crowd.

Someone tugged my Midgardian doublet from behind,

forcing my collar into my neck. Small hands stuffed a handful of rough barley husks down my back scratching my skin. Laughter from children grated my nerves.

"You vermin!" I screamed after them as they ran into the throng of costumed men and women.

I twisted in my doublet, trying to free myself of the barley husks slowly crackling into pieces and falling at my feet. I hated these new restrictive human fashions, but Odin insisted we "blend in."

Odin laughed, deep from his gut.

"I thought you enjoyed mischief?" he asked, rubbing a tear from his eye.

"Only when I'm the one causing it."

He smirked.

"Then why don't you?" he asked. "This is the three greatest days where chaos and mischief are worshiped. I'd think you ill if you didn't partake."

I brushed the remaining dried pieces of husk off my shoulders.

"Is this a dare?"

A spark lit his gaze, deviousness playing in the lines of his face.

"It's Fasnacht, Loki. Anything goes."

My blood lit at the chance for unbridled abandon.

"May the greatest rogue gain the victory."

Purple and red lanterns bobbed above our heads as we pressed our way through the dense throng of masks, drunks, and pranksters.

In Barfüsserplatz I guzzled at least ten carafes of hippocras spiced wine, while Odin started to slur his words after nine. Our blood thoroughly heated, we ran to Clara-platz where he slunk off with two maidens with peacock feathers in their braids, while I found a trio of glittering masked beauties.

I had a reputation to uphold, after all.

The city blurred into a cacophony of drums and alcohol, and I lost myself in the rich scent of broiling gruyere cheese and savory flour soup.

Finding a low wall that overlooked the Rhine I pressed my elbows against the rough limestone and leaned over. Moonlight flashed in flecks of white and gray on the water's surface, and I couldn't help but smile.

Sucking in the cold air, I closed my eyes letting the chill douse the fire from my cheeks. Unfortunately, I actually enjoyed myself tonight.

Odin approached and joined me. The breeze tousled his russet hair, the fine wisps caressing his angled cheeks. The wine made me want to catch a piece and tuck it behind his ear, as I had done countless times before.

I wouldn't let myself, though.

"The Rhine reminds me of where we first met along the banks of the Ifingr River," he said. "You were so spirited then."

"Am I not spirited anymore?" I jested. "Did you not see me throw that onion pie at that cardsharp in *The Goldenen Sternen*?"

He chuckled, and a prick of desire nicked my core. I forgot how much I liked making him laugh.

"All I mean is I've enjoyed seeing it again tonight." He pressed his hands together, rubbing his thumbs over one another. "I've felt like a stranger around you since we fell out."

He kept staring out over the water.

"That's never been my intent," I said. "I would never hurt you."

And I wouldn't.

A smile fluttered across his lips, as if a sweet fool spoke to him.

"I'm happy you came," he whispered. "If you knew what it meant."

He caught my gaze, and I held it.

"As am I," I lied. At least, I thought I did.

I hoped I did.

Cautiously, he reached out towards me.

His fingers trembled as he rested his hand over my thundering heart. I didn't move away. I didn't want to move away, which scared me the most.

He lowered his gaze, staring at where he touched me. He let his hand trail down my chest, as if savoring every inch of me, until it fell away. I sank into his scent of sage and clove.

Don't forget what he did. What he is.

"Your chaos, your fire, bewitches me still, Loki," he whispered, his breath cascading over the dips and arcs of my face. "Since the beginning."

My pulse rushed in my ears. I knew what he wanted.

"Odin, I..."

Odin, I can't, is what I wanted to say. But I remembered, there was more at stake now than my heart. I couldn't become a trembling virgin now.

I swallowed hard.

Stretching my hand towards his fingers that rested on the cold limestone, I grazed them and opened myself to him.

He clasped my face between his hands and leaned his forehead against mine, hungry for my inferno to sear his chambers and sinew.

I gasped. His ambition pulled through my veins in a frigid rush, crashing and mixing with my fiery chaos. My depths quaked as we bared ourselves to one another, my soul drowning in the euphoria of a savage and terrifying love.

I forgot the intoxication of him. The pleasure of what he was.

And I wanted more.

Don't forget what he did. What he is.

"I never should have fallen in love with you," he said.

"Neither of us could control our hearts."

Our breaths softened, if we breathed at all.

"Knowing everything, I still wouldn't want anyone else but you."

Everything?

Our lips brushed, destroying the question. Only he and I existed, a tempest of colliding ruthlessness and potential.

Don't forget what he did. What he is.

"If that's true, then let me in. Share with me what burdens you, and let me alleviate it," I whispered, my every word calculated.

He pulled back.

Staring into my eyes, he looked through me, as if lost peering into some terrible future. I shivered.

"Odin?"

He returned from wherever he went. Smiling, he rubbed his thumb across my cheek. I wanted to rid the sage and clove from my nostrils.

"I promised you an escape from troubles, I don't want to burden you with what is only mine to bear."

I guess he was going to play hard to get.

* * *

THE DEEP CRIMSON Rathaus dominated the city center of Marktplatz. The clock showed an hour before dawn.

Groups of costumed fifers and drummers continued to beat beneath its golden turrets, while the painted figures against the red pigment appeared living in the flickering torchlight. Winged basilisks embraced the city's coat of arms of a black bishop's staff.

The city seemed obsessed with basilisks. They watched from high on plaster homes and curled their scaled tales around fountains. Even the name of Basel paid homage to the great creature.

I couldn't help thinking of my son, Jormungand. He was rather *intense*, and that paired with his ability to shift into a serpent the size of a small planet...

Well, that little party trick of his made the gods rather nervous.

Odin decided it would be best for him to be exiled from his home in the Ironwood. Same with my other son, Fenrir, and my daughter, Hel.

My heart ached at their memory, but banishing them was the only way to protect them from a worse fate. The Aesir were not known for their understanding and mercy.

"What do you think they'd make out of Jormungand here?" I asked Odin. "He'd give these basilisks a run for their money."

Only fifes and drums replied.

I turned around only to have two teenage boys pelt me with inflated pig bladders. They cackled and took off, leaving me with wishes of murder.

Where the blazes did Odin run off too?

Grumbling, I shoved into shoulders, trying my best to dodge my toes being stomped on by heavy leather boots and general morons. This had all better be worth the aggravation.

I stopped.

Nestled within the drunks and dregs, glowed a perfect blue sphere. Peace gently rippled out from it, lapping whispers of constancy, of hope, across my prickling skin.

I quivered at such an unusually wholesome sensation, and I wanted more.

Sharp notes cut through my concentration, hurtling me back into the hectic celebrations. Where did the sphere go?

My pulse pounded as I scanned the revelers and musicians, hunting for this tantalizing energy.

There!

Blue light skittered between the men and women who all bustled and shoved against one another to get from one side of Marktplatz to the other. I forced my way through the tide of elbows and knees, keeping my gaze firmly on the shimmering blue racing up a narrow street.

Its radiating serenity beat against my chest, and my pulse thrashed in my ears with my rising excitement.

In all my millennia of life I encountered nearly all elements of the universe: love, war, thunder, wisdom… But I never beheld the rarest and most delicate of these forces. Fidelity.

I ran across the cobblestones chasing the sphere as it skipped and hopped. Just a little closer to glimpse the creature who possessed it.

My breath caught in my throat.

Honeyed ginger hair fell in long wisps out of a golden threaded snood. Her blue velvet gown cinched her waist and hugged her arms. She glimpsed behind her shoulder, revealing a face of soft curves and arcs. And in her chest, bright and strong, burned the most beautiful and sincere fidelity.

I tilted my head, laughing softly at the delightful impossibility that a simple human contained the most precious of elements within them. Their bodies were far too fragile to contain such raw energy, and yet, this Midgardian woman defied everything I knew.

Curiosity ignited my blood further.

I had to get even closer.

She walked briskly towards the Rhine, her arms straining holding onto her wicker basket.

"Where are you off too in such a hurry, pretty lady?" a coarse man asked her.

"Hurrying to rid myself of idiots like yourself," she replied.

I liked this one.

She ascended the steps of an alley, the plaster houses squeezing us as I continued to follow. She exited into a street, took a sharp right, and flew down a steep, cobbled hill. Water gushed from a small waterway beside us. A paddle wheel thumped somewhere in the distance.

We were quite alone now, the bright tones of the fifes dying in the night air.

A shadow spread over her. Thick fingers gripped into her skirts and pulled her back, causing her to fall. Her basket split open striking the ground, and small, metal pieces clattered across the cobblestones.

"Sigyn, not so sure footed now," he said, his voice gruff.

"Go to hell, Bertolf," she spat.

Pressing her palms into the stone she pushed herself upright. I didn't like the amusement glinting in his tiny eyes. She made to pick up her basket when he kicked it away from beneath her hand.

"Imbecile!" she yelled.

She dove for the scattering metallic pieces, but he clasped her arm in his beefy hand, preventing her. His fine silk clothes and lace were of a gentleman more than thief.

"I invested money in good faith in your brother's business venture. I, and several others, were promised a handsome return." The creases in his pockmarked forehead deepened. "Since he left for Portugal, I've not received one blasted franc. I demand to have what he took from me returned."

"Your foolishness in believing he knew anything about wine or trade is not my problem," she said.

His lips stretched into a sneer, and he wrenched her against him, towering over her.

"It already is," he growled. "I know you're hiding Simon from me. You can either tell me where that cheater is, or we can have a very different conversation."

Her element glowed bright at his words, the light in her chest even diffusing through the pores in her skin. The very idea of surrendering her brother disgusted her. I expected no less from such an energy.

And I would not see it destroyed.

I made to emerge from the darkness and break Bertolf's sweaty neck, but stopped.

A knife flashed in Sigyn's free hand. She pressed the edge against the length of his rounded nose, the tip threatening to pierce the corner of his eye.

I couldn't help but smile. She was absolutely charming!

"Skin and cartilage cut easily." She forced the blade deeper until his flesh almost split. "You just have to decide if you prefer having a nose, or to know a woman bested you."

Her element nearly blinded me from its strength, its devotion to her brother. Bertolf shuddered, unhooking his fingers from her gown. She stepped back, keeping her knife before her.

"Bitch," he growled, rubbing the side of his nose. "You'll regret this. Mark me."

He stepped away, withdrawing into the shadows.

"Bastard," she breathed, returning her knife to the belt of her hip.

She took in a deep breath, then knelt against the stone and scavenged for those curiously precious metal bits.

Pity swelled in me as she retrieved five out of a hundred small pieces from the cracks and grooves of the street.

I walked to her and knelt beside her. My heart stopped as her fidelity warmed my cheeks, wrapping me in an embrace I never wanted release from.

Sigyn gasped, and the light sank back into her. She dropped her hand to her knife. I put my hands up in the air, making sure she understood I meant no harm.

"I only want to know if you're hurt?" I asked in perfect Swiss German. An odd little language mixing harsh inflections with a cute lilt.

Her brown eyes met mine, and I expected her to blush. All the other Midgardian's I encountered always filled with carnal fascination when they saw me. But her eyes filled with something else.

I believed it to be annoyance.

My blood raced at this intriguing difference.

Her shoulders relaxed.

"I'm fine, thank you," she said.

She started gathering the pieces again and placed them in her broken basket. Black ink smeared her fingers, leaving dark crescent moons beneath her nails. Smudges and stains spotted her expensive bodice, and as she wiped her brow, a sheer streak of ink remained behind.

I smiled again.

I searched out the pieces to help, my own fingers now getting stained by ink. A small letter M protruded from the lead square. I found an R next. Then an E.

What odd things to fret over.

"What are these?" I asked, inspecting the letter Y. Humans always had such inventive ways to get past their inadequacies.

She clawed at another pile, dragging them in a rattling mess towards her.

"Typeface. For printing."

"How trivial!"

"Trivial?" Her cheeks flushed red, and she grasped the piece away from me. "These *trivial* letters have changed the world. Where have you been?"

I couldn't very well answer that.

"Of course, my apologies. I'm only curious what need you have with typeface at this hour?"

She sighed.

"My father owns a printing press. Johann Webber. The lettering is all set wrong. Not only that, the apprentice finally came clean that even certain characters are missing entirely. I need to get it all sorted before sunrise. I've worked too hard to get off schedule now."

She squinted shifting typeface in her hand to catch the light.

I closed my eyes savoring her energy rolling off her shoulders and legs. It took everything in me to resist reaching out and touching her wrist, to feel her pure fidelity against my skin.

It seemed silly a being of chaos should be so entranced by one of true heartedness. But here we were.

"The D is bent. It's useless now. Thank you, Bertolf."

The weariness in her voice caused distress to ruffle through me. I swallowed down this new feeling.

"Who was that man?"

"I don't discuss private family matters with strangers."

"Then let me correct this. My name is…"

She'd hardly believe me if I told her the truth. And if she did believe me, I'd have to put up with all those tiresome questions about divinity and what life all means.

Best to avoid it entirely.

"Lukas," I said. "My name is Lukas Lanter."

She raised her right eyebrow.

"Sigyn Webber."

"See, now we are no longer strangers."

She smiled, and I wished for her to smile at me always.

"I suppose that's true."

We placed the final pieces into her basket, and she rose to her feet. I didn't want her to leave.

"There's a carnival going on, if you haven't noticed," I said, my words wanting to stick in my throat. "Let me buy you a cider, or an onion pie to get your day started."

She bit her lip, as if considering. Turning her gaze over her shoulder, she looked out towards the lightening sky, the first streams of pink stretching beneath the stars.

"Sorry, I must go. I've been detained too long as it is."

"Let me escort you at least?"

"Thank you for your help, Lukas, but I've walked these streets myself my entire life. I'm perfectly capable on my own."

Before I could say another word, she turned on her heel and walked off. The first woman in the Nine Worlds to ever deny me.

I combed my hot fingers through my hair.

A hand clapped over my shoulder. Dark ambition iced my veins, shriveling the warmth and hope of Sigyn.

"Where have you been?" Odin asked.

"Looking for you, as it so happens." It was half true.

I turned, surprised that Tyr stood beside him.

"I don't remember inviting you," I said.

"Loki, we have to go, and I want you by my side." Odin said.

Wanted me by his side? This was brilliant. I hungrily craved this moment, but I couldn't look too eager, not yet.

I nodded and crossed my arms.

"I see," I said, contemplatively.

"Yes, against my behest, and all good judgement, Odin feels you will be an...asset. I told him you would only be an ass."

I'd let him have that one.

"You've yet to tell me what's so urgent?"

"They are marching towards Asgard."

"Who?"

"The Jotnar are furious about the death of Thrym and want revenge."

"Somehow Hymir escaped the night of the wedding with several compatriots and has since raised an army."

"Loki, are you even paying attention? You really are hopeless," Tyr said.

I shook back to their worried faces, unaware my glance had fallen to the horizon where Sigyn had disappeared. My thoughts along with her.

I scratched my head.

"Sorry, I'm just trying to take it all in."

"What's there to take in?" Odin asked. "We're at war."

6

A BUTTERFLY IN WINTER

Of course, I couldn't tell them Hymir escaped that night because of me. Definitely a conversation for never. At least my little blunder got me one glorious battle closer to winning Odin's trust.

And it couldn't come fast enough.

I pressed my thumb to my forehead, trying to lessen the ache lurching in my head. The pain burrowed into the roots of my skull, intensifying with our return to Asgard. Whoever this Destroyer was, they would pay dearly for all this discomfort and effort.

"You all right? I've seen cadavers with better color." Thor's voice slammed against the storm in my head.

"Thanks for noticing, but I'm fine."

I lowered my hand, and sucked pine and salt into my lungs, hoping the cold air would clear my mind.

Thor gripped a double handed sword and held it out to me. The smooth steel caught the sun in white bursts.

"Will *Bastard Butcher* do for you?" Thor said. "You need something with a bit more heft than your daggers if you want to kill any Jotnar."

He grinned, as if already imagining slicing through their flesh.

"I appreciate the thought, but I don't like all my power limited to one sword."

Thor cleared his throat, as if unconvinced as I strapped my trusted set of daggers at my hips. I bent down, securing two more around my upper legs, and a collection of small throwing knives in my boots, just in case.

"I don't want to be the one strapped with lugging your limp body all the way back to Asgard."

Did he really just underestimate me?

I spun behind him, catching his thick neck behind my mother's blade *Truth*, and squeezed the edge into his pounding heartbeat. I tightened my grasp on my second dagger, pressing the tip above his liver.

"Don't forget I'm always first and last on the battlefield," I said. "I'll spill your guts and slice your throat before you can even take a breath. I'm game if you're willing to take the risk."

His muscles tensed beneath my hold, and delight rolled through me feeling the bravest of gods shiver.

"Get off me, Loki!" he gasped.

Laughter filled my ears, along with clapping. Odin came into view, and my heart rushed at his smile, though I wished it didn't.

"Like a wasp," Odin said. "Don't doubt his skill, Thor. He's been fighting longer than you."

I pushed Thor away and chuckled.

"Maybe now you understand. *Bastard Butcher* isn't my style."

Thor cursed beneath his breath and swung his scabbard over his right arm and marched off towards the others.

The wheels of a wooden cart cracked as Tyr, Njord, and

Frey dumped a collection of spears, swords, and heavy battle axes into the scarred oak.

I approached the cart, curious if any other weapon might catch my fancy.

A shadow blocked the sun behind me. I turned. Frigg's sharp face sent a rush of cold irritation through my blood. She clasped brown paper packages of food, and five wine-skins against her chest.

"I didn't realize you'd be going," she said, her voice flat.

"Did Odin not tell you? I suppose I have kept him rather busy."

I couldn't help my lips pull into a sneer.

She heaved the goods over the edge of the cart, letting them smack the steel and oak beneath. Her cheeks reddened, the shade nearly matching her crimson gown. She faced me and glared. My smile only widened.

I did so enjoy her anger.

"You wretch." She pressed the word out between her teeth. "He's my husband."

"Is this jealousy, Frigg? It's not a good look on you. It's like you've been chewing lemons."

She lifted her fist as if preparing to strike my cheek. Goodness! She was all claws and scorn today!

Unfortunately, she lowered it at her side, dashing my hopes.

"You break everything you touch."

"I cannot break what was already broken. The fault is all yours, and you know why."

Murder burned in her eyes, only diminishing when Odin stepped between us.

"Go away, Frigg," he said. "I don't want any of your poison, especially now."

Her eyes narrowed, and her lips pulled into a vicious smile.

"Just remember, husband. All things carry a price, and we will be the ones to pay it."

She cast me one last glare before turning and walking off. Odin's jaw clenched as he stared after her, his fingers curled into fists.

"What price is she talking about?" I asked.

His body immediately softened, and a smile replaced his scowl as if it never existed.

"I'd been meaning to ask, what brought you to the other side of the city last night?" he asked, ignoring my question. As he always usually did.

Sigyn's honeyed ginger hair blossomed in my memory, along with her fidelity that threatened to undo me.

"Curiosity," I said, hoping to leave it at that.

He chuckled and brushed the backs of his fingers against the side of my wrist. My lips tingled.

"You don't have to play coy with me. I saw you with that human woman."

"If you saw her, then you understand why I had to follow."

Awe glinted in his only blue eye.

"Her fidelity was like catching a butterfly in winter," he said.

"I couldn't believe it myself, but it was there, trapped in the confines of an enchanting creature." I smiled, despite myself. "Sigyn is quite the little fighter to boot."

His eye hollowed, and his hand fell to his side. Anxiety tightened the lines of his face.

"Her name is Sigyn?" he asked, unease in every syllable. He rubbed the back of his neck.

I raised my right eyebrow.

"Is that a problem? Admittedly it's not the most riveting of names, but—"

A lance of pain shot through my head. Agony throbbed as it sawed into my brain, into my core.

Odin blurred. Vanished.

The surrounding green collapsed into decay.

I stood in battlefield of scorched grass and rock. Hot air burned my cheeks. Rotting flesh seared my nostrils. Clashing metal pierced my ears, and I clapped my hands over them trying to muffle the screams.

My chaos awoke within me, spreading fire hot and wild through my blood until it escaped through my skin. Flames licked between my fingers, and my eyes filled with my internal blaze.

"Your time nears," a bodiless voice said. "Asgard will fall."

Horror surged cold and heavy through my veins, extinguishing me.

Pine and salt overtook the burnt sinew and blood. My muscles ached, and I stared at the blue Asgardian sky, gravel pressing into my back and scalp.

Odin knelt beside me, Tyr and the others circling behind him. Worry filled his expression. It didn't even compare to the fear I swallowed down.

"What's wrong?" Odin asked.

Visions were never good.

"Headache," I said. Visions were even worse to admit, especially to him.

He gripped my hand and pulled me up, and I hoped he didn't feel me tremble.

"I've never seen you collapse like that," Tyr said.

"Went down like a stone in water," Thor added.

I rubbed my temples, and I could sense myself still shaking.

This really wasn't good.

Odin's eye remained on me, as if boring into me.

"What?" I asked.

He moved his gaze to Idunn, the chestnut haired goddess who stood behind me. Fragile, innocent, and her brain nothing but trees, shrubs, and flowers. She already bored me just thinking about it.

"Idunn, take Loki to your garden and give him one of your golden apples. He needs rest."

Only six apple trees that bore golden apples existed in all the Nine Worlds, and Idunn was their guardian. They were rather miraculous things, providing mortals with immortality, and the ability to heal gods on the brink of death with a single bite. They also weren't bad paired with salted almonds, if one felt rather peckish.

She nodded her pointed face and placed a disturbingly light grip on my wrist to lead me away. A piece of me died inside contemplating listening to her discuss botany for hours.

"I don't need rest, I need to get on my horse and get into battle. Those Jotnar won't kill themselves."

Odin shifted in his heavy boots.

"Actually, I think it better you remain behind," he said.

"But you need me. You know my skills."

He reached out and took my hand, his ambition sweeping into my heart and wanting to pull me under. I wanted to drown in his dark torrent forever.

"You can't fight in this condition. It's not worth the risk of your life."

"I'm no weakling," I spat. "I'll be fine. It's happened before, and it's not slowed me down yet."

He released his hold on me, his concern melting into fear.

"This isn't the first time?"

"Well..."

Tyr coughed.

"I'm sorry to interrupt, but every second we chatter here, Hymir and his army gets closer. If we hope to win this thing, we need to leave. Now."

Odin nodded and mounted his horse, Sleipnir.

"What of me?" I asked.

Odin stroked Sleipnir's neck, not looking at me.

"You are to stay in Asgard while I'm gone."

"Stay in Asgard?" I echoed.

"And stay away from this mortal. This Sigyn." He spit out her name as if it were a curse.

I shook my head.

"This is getting ridiculous."

He finally met my gaze. Ice chilled the blue in his eye, and I knew he would not be swayed.

"Now isn't the time to take any chances."

"And still you won't tell me why." Silence surrounded us. I struck one of those nerves again.

He looked down, then back at me, his face softened.

"I only want what's best for you, Loki."

He kicked his heels into the sides of Sleipnir, and all the gods took off in a thunder of hooves and carts. Leaving me behind.

I crushed my nails against my palms.

Odin seemed to forget I never did what was best for me.

7

ROSEMARY AND SAFFRON

Midgard

Basel, Switzerland

The wind tore through my feathers as I flew in my falcon aspect towards the two red spires of the Münster Cathedral. I loved the convenience of being a shapeshifter. I could transform into any animal I pleased, and right now I chose what would get me to Sigyn fastest.

Swooping down, I glided between the lime plaster homes, their shutters of maroon, gray, and green speeding past me. And below, among the chestnut trees and sputtering fountains, Basel growled.

Wooden carts hammered cobblestone streets, fish mongers haggled over trout and eel, and women pulled their screaming offspring through the endless lanes, alleys, and steep stairways of the city.

But I hadn't come to admire the Midgardians.

Odin's little outburst about Sigyn surprised me. Jealousy, perhaps? No. I'd taken thousands of lovers and he never once blinked an eye. Hell, he often joined in. This was something else, and honestly, I didn't care. That man was a tiresome fount of eccentricities.

I knew now wasn't the best time to test Odin, but I couldn't help myself. His tantrum made paying Sigyn an impromptu visit all too delectable for me to pass up.

I continued hunting for any spark of her fidelity among the continual roar of blacksmiths, merchants, and rich men on horseback.

Nothing.

Rising higher into the air, I headed North over Basel's double stone walls and traveled along the Rhine river. The water churned and raced with a wild beauty below me. Lily of the Valley and grass filled my lungs, and at the sharpest edge of the horizon, jagged mountains cut through soft, green hills.

Blue flashed along the river bank.

My breath caught in my throat.

I descended, flying faster towards the glinting spark nestled between the trees and the water.

Sigyn stood on the sandy river bank, resting her hands against her hips as she looked out at the wilderness.

A steady rhythm of peace pulsed against my cheeks. Warmth enveloped me and serenity doused me again with that exotic sensation of hope.

My heart leapt at the newness of it all.

I flew behind the thicket of walnut, larch, and pine lining the shore and landed on the duff scattering the ground.

I stretched my arms and legs, discarding my falcon

aspect and shifted back into my usual devastatingly hand-some self.

Treading quietly through the cramped trees, I stopped once I reached where the forest butted against the rocks and silt of the river bank. Trying to get a clearer view, I gripped a branch and pushed it out of the way, ignoring the rough bark biting my palms.

I swallowed, surprised by the dryness of my throat. Sigyn stood not six feet away from me.

She walked towards the river, and a layer of grit and sand covered the bottoms of her bare feet. Lifting her slender arms to her hair, she yanked off her snood and plucked two bone pins from her coiled braid releasing a deluge of curls down her back. Taking a boxwood comb from her satchel, she pulled it through her tresses.

The sun deepened the strands of honey, and her stead-fastness drummed against my skin with her every stroke.

I breathed in the rush of her. Such a curious woman! I'd never quivered at anything so virtuous, but here I stood before Sigyn, slack jawed and not able to get enough of her.

Placing the comb and satchel on the ground, she stretched her arms behind her back and tugged at her laces. She drew the cords through the eyelets loosening her bodice from her torso. Shoving her thumb beneath the heavy fabric she pushed it off her left shoulder. Then her right.

The gown and kirtle fell to her feet in a puddle of green silk and rich brocade.

Only her thin, linen smock remained.

She removed that too.

I thought I would lose my wits, but not just because she stood naked before me.

Her fidelity veiled her skin in the most exquisite and

incandescent light. Radiance shimmered over her every dip and curve, shooting out of the tips of her fingers and toes.

Sigyn glowed in a halo of constancy, and it saddened me no one but a celestial could see the true beauty of her element, I alone now beheld.

She waded into the Rhine, and the cool water rushed between her long legs, slipped over her buttocks, sped past her waist, and finally caressed her breasts as she sank into the river.

Chaos consumed her within the roiling water.

Snap!

A twig split beneath my foot.

Her light sucked back into her chest. She spun around, crossing her arms over her breasts.

Our eyes locked.

My pulse thrashed in my ears, and I heard nothing but my own thundering blood.

Backing away, I turned and ran into the forest. Ran? Was I actually running away like a child caught red handed? This was very unlike me.

I hid behind a large walnut tree and carefully peered around the trunk. She pulled on her smock and neared the line of trees, looking through the packed branches.

"Who's there?" she asked, her tone sharp.

I stood still and my breaths burned. An odd sensation twisted my gut, rolling and heaving, fresh and new. Was this shame?

How fascinating!

Sticks and shoots splintered in the distance. She turned her gaze away from where I concealed myself, towards the crackling brush.

Three well dressed men emerged from behind the tree line, their fine leather boots crunching across the pebbles as they neared her. Sigyn stiffened, but remained firmly in place.

I recognized the one with pockmarked skin from the carnival.

Bertolf.

"Your father certainly raised a wild daughter," he told her. "Bathing alone in rivers can be dangerous, as can a mind reeking of witchcraft."

She made to grab her rumpled dress off the shore.

"I wouldn't expect you to understand the difference between witchcraft and science," she replied.

His eyes flashed with irritation, and he pulled the gown out of her grasp. He held up the heavy silk and shook his head, his eyes scanning the map of black blotches staining the fabric.

"Look at the state of this, Felix." He tossed it over Sigyn's head to his companion.

Felix caught it and clucked his tongue. His pointed goatee and small eyes begged me to punch him in the face.

"A lady of status and your gown ruined by printer's ink. You do bring shame to your sex, working like a common apprentice boy."

She tried to tear it out of his grip, but he only laughed louder. He threw it to the third man, younger and meaner looking than the first two. He lifted it to his boyish face and inhaled deeply.

"Rosemary and saffron? Smells like a dreary apothecary."

"Give that back to me," she seethed.

"And rob us from seeing the outline of your breasts? I don't think so," Bertolf said.

She ground her teeth, though her cheeks flushed as she clutched her smock closed over her chest.

They would pay for making her blush.

I made to break open their skulls, but stopped. The last time she met Bertolf she handled the situation exquisitely on her own. She was a warrior as the valkyries, and I didn't want to interfere and diminish her victory.

Besides, I was excited to sit back and watch her slit their throats one by one.

"Where's Simon?" Felix asked. He grasped the hilt of his sword, his fingers thick with gold rings. "I've nearly lost half my lands because of him and his scheme."

She took a step back.

"I am not my brother's keeper. I do not know where he goes, or who he sees," Sigyn said. "What I do know is you lot will not harass me. Leave now, or I will scream for the Watch."

Bertolf shook his head and gave a wicked grin.

"My dear, Sigyn. We are alone, and far from the city. The Watch can't hear you."

Sigyn took another step back, the gravel crackling beneath her feet.

The three of them neared her, and cold swept down my back. She had to have a plan, though. Surely she lured them to some trap.

"Two years we've waited since we shook hands with Simon and gave him our purses," Karl said. "He promised us we'd double our investments. He guaranteed wine trade between Switzerland and Portugal to be lucrative."

"And it would have been, had your brother not run away with a small fortune and left us with nothing," Bertolf added.

"We will have satisfaction in our money being returned to us," Felix said. "We do not suffer frauds."

He withdrew his sword, the sun flashing off his blade.

She bent down and picked up a large stick, her skin taught over her knuckles as she clasped it tight. Holding it out, she firmed her footing and readied to strike.

I smiled, eager for the violence to ensue.

"He's not a fraud, he's just a fool," she said. "It's your faults for believing a man with no experience capable of actually succeeding in this ludicrous plan. Leave us alone."

Her fidelity blazed, dousing her in bright white as her loyalty to her brother strengthened.

"Or what?" Bertolf asked.

"I think she's planning to hit us with that big stick," Karl said, taking out his own sword.

She swung hard, striking Karl across the face with a resounding crack that echoed through the trees.

He clapped his hand over the welt growing across his cheek and temple, and spit a mouthful of blood onto the sand.

Heat flushed deep between my legs. Sigyn was magnificent.

Bertolf charged her and gripped her stick, pulling it towards his stomach. She grunted as she arched her back and tugged.

"Since we can't find that bloated leech, you will be our sweet song bird to relay our message," Bertolf said.

"And what message would that be?"

Her arms strained trying to keep her grip.

"That deceit carries a price."

Sigyn kicked him in the groin and he cursed loudly. She released the stick, and he fell backwards. She took off at a run and clambered up the bank towards the trees, but Felix and Karl caught up to her, grabbing her ankles and pulling her back down.

My heart raced as they forced her to her feet, squeezing

her upper arms and holding her wrists. She struggled against them, but they only tightened their hold until her skin whitened beneath their stiff fingers.

Bertolf placed a bollock dagger against her flushed cheek. I didn't like the satisfied smirk on his lips. But I still believed in my little vixen. Any moment now she would give them the walloping they deserved.

Wouldn't she?

I swallowed hard.

"What should I cut off first?" he asked, dragging the sharp edge towards her right ear.

"Perhaps the ears?" He trailed the point to the crook of her eye. "Then I will pluck the eyes from their pretty sockets." He scraped the blade until it rested firmly against her nose. "That leaves the nose for last. I recall how fond you are of cutting off noses, Sigyn."

"Don't do this, Please. I'm sorry about your money, but this won't get it back," she said.

For the first time fear cracked in her voice, making fear ripple down my own back.

The others chuckled.

"I love I've finally got you to beg," Bertolf said, pressing the dagger harder into her skin. "And yes, we must do this. Nothing else seems to scare your brother into rectifying his sins, so maybe ruining his sister's pretty face will finally make it clear."

Sweat iced my skin as Bertolf nuzzled the blade between her ear and scalp, but Sigyn's scream's ground my insides.

"Let her go," I said. My pulse pounded against the leather hilts of my daggers I gripped in each hand.

Bertolf stopped and turned to meet my gaze. Shock widened his eyes, before annoyance swept it away.

"Who the hell are you?" Bertolf asked.

"The man who will decide if your deaths will be painful, or quite painful."

Bertolf cocked his head, while Felix and Karl looked at each other as Sigyn still squirmed within their hold.

Laughter burst out of their mouths.

"If you haven't noticed, you are rather outnumbered," Karl said. "Tosser."

"It seems you've opted for quite painful. Lovely. That's exceedingly more fun."

"Really? I'm glad you feel that way," Bertolf said. "Felix, take care of him."

Felix chuckled as he released Sigyn's right arm and approached me, sword held out ready to kill. I couldn't help my lips from smiling.

Unlike them, I knew not to underestimate her.

But I loved how they underestimated me.

Sigyn reached towards Karl's belt and pulled out his ivory handled stiletto. Rounding on him, she thrust the blade between the bones of his ribcage, skewering his lung.

"Oh dear," I said, looking over Felix's shoulder. "That must sting."

He followed my gaze as Karl opened his mouth, letting out a silent scream as he drowned in his own blood.

Felix ran towards his companion as his knees buckled and he fell forward, crushing the silt and pebbles beneath his dead body.

"You bitch," he shouted at Sigyn, lunging at her with his sword.

She reached down and grabbed Karl's sword, crossing it and the stiletto over her head just in time to shield her from Felix's attack.

This day was turning out to be rather exciting!

"This is all your fault!"

Bertolf growled as he cut his sword down through the air, trying to bury the edge between my neck and shoulder. I stepped to the left, letting him bury it in the mud instead.

"Please, you'll never hit me with such a sloppy method."

"I think I know how to kill a man," he grunted.

Grinding his heels into the gravel he rushed me again. I caught his sword arm between my daggers. His breath rolled hot and acrid off my face, an unhappy mixture of cheese and onion.

I rammed my boot into his solid chest, knocking him down into the bank.

"Apparently not," I said, tossing his sword into the Rhine.

I turned toward Sigyn, her grunts filling my ears like music. She cut her sword across Felix's cheek, drawing a lovely trail of blood.

A flash of steel brought my attention back to Bertolf. He gripped his bollock dagger firmly beneath his pulsing knuckles. He aimed for my armpit, but fell an inch short of actually hitting me. Not that it would have done him any good had he actually succeeded in thrusting and yanking through my arteries.

"You're such a tease with that blade of yours," I said.

Confusion washed over his face.

"You're insane," he said.

Our blades met again. Another parry. Another block.

"You have no idea."

Jerking my blades together against his blade, I snatched his dagger out of his hand, disarming him a second time. I forced his back against a twisting larch and pressed my steel into his throat.

"Let me go, please," he gasped. "Don't kill me."

"Afraid I'm not the merciful sort."

He yelped as I nicked the first layer of his sweat soaked skin. His gold buttons glinted in the light.

"I promise...I promise I won't come back. I'll leave her alone. I swear."

Chaos burned in his chest, hot and rabid as a flame. I smiled, as it revealed what I already knew.

Cheese and wood smoke thickened the air as I leaned closer to him. My lips grazed his ear.

"Liar," I whispered.

A lance of pain slid through my right side. Wedged neatly between my bottom ribs stuck out a small knife, with Bertolf's hand clenched tight around the bone handle.

Satisfaction swelled on his face.

Sadly for him, it would take more than simple Midgardian steel to kill me. Where only special blades forged in the fires of Svartalfheim could be quite serious, even deadly, my body healed relatively quickly from these inferior human weapons.

Grasping the white handle I pulled it out, trying to ignore the tickling sensation as the steel scraped my bones. My blood glistened as it slid off the tip and spattered Bertolf's boots in heavy drops.

"You are cheeky," I said.

Shock replaced his prior delight. Then came fear. I absolutely loved it when they feared.

"What are you?" he rasped.

I chuckled.

"Your end."

I made to split his windpipe.

Sigyn cried out.

I turned.

She lay on her back. Turning over, she ground her

elbows into the dirt and tried to scramble towards her sword.

Her fingers scraped the edge of the hilt.

Felix kicked it away in a gush of pebbles from her reach and stood over her. His chest heaved with every breath and his eyes showed a man possessed by want of death.

He pointed his sword directly over her heart.

Dammit.

I released Bertolf and rushed towards her. His death would have to wait.

I held my blade flat and sank it between the vertebrae in the back of Felix's neck. Tendons and muscle snapped as I wrenched the blade towards his spine, dropping him in five seconds flat.

I inhaled the thrill of his death and hungered for more. I turned back towards where I had left Bertolf ready to finish the job.

The bastard was gone.

Shit.

I shook my disappointment away, instead focusing only on Sigyn.

"Are you all right?" I asked.

She stared at Felix and Karl's dead bodies, her eyes glazed and cheeks red.

"I never wanted to...He gave me no choice."

She wiped sweat from her brow and let her fingers fall to her lips. Her hand shook.

She obviously was not accustomed to killing. I didn't like her guilt over honorable bloodshed.

"You did what was necessary," I said. "There is no blame in self defense."

She nodded, though uncertainty still hardened her expression.

"I know. I would have died otherwise."

"They chose their path. It's time to put it out of your mind. Trust me, after a stiff drink you will feel much better."

I stretched out my hand to her to help her up. Her shoulders finally relaxed and she even gave a small smile.

As she grasped my hand, I braced myself for the torrent of her fidelity as our naked skin touched.

Nothing. Not even the tiniest of tingles.

Of course.

Her element was still raw and unpredictable within her body. That's why it revealed itself through her skin, and other times, like now, it hid in her depths.

It had been the same for me before Odin transformed my chaos and made me a god.

Standing to her feet, our eyes met for the first time since the fight broke out.

Her face reddened, and she tore her hand out of mine.

"You were the one gawking at me from behind the trees!"

"A simple thank you would suffice. I did just save your neck, after all," I said.

She crossed her arms over her chest.

"I was perfectly fine on my own."

I laughed.

"Yes, that was very apparent when Bertolf was about to cut off your ear."

She narrowed her eyes.

"Wait, I know you," she said. "You're that man from the carnival. Lukas."

I smiled.

"I'm flattered you remember me."

I mean, I wasn't really surprised. I was hard to forget what with my tempting physique and fabulous hair.

Her face remained unamused.

"Why were you watching me when I was naked?" she asked, her voice short.

These humans really were peculiar about their nudity.

"You really have nothing to be ashamed of. All that swordplay of yours has kept you incredibly toned and pert. Well done."

Her mouth opened, and she shook her head.

"Typically," she said hotly. "A man would apologize after seeing a woman's breasts, pert or not."

I'd never met someone so worried over a little bare skin. But, it mattered to her, and because of that, it mattered to me. Her feelings mattered to me?

Damn, my head spun with all these new emotions.

I picked up her gown that Karl had cast among the weeds and brush along the bank.

"Then, I'm sorry." The words felt strange on my tongue. I think that was the first time I ever apologized to anyone.

I held it out to her. She let out a breath, and her arms fell to her sides. She took it from me.

"I'm the one that's sorry," she said. "My head's all a jumble after everything that just happened. I would be maimed beyond recognition, if not worse, had you not been there to stop them."

"Don't worry about it, in fact—"

Her eyes fell to my torso.

"You're injured," she said, cutting me off.

I looked down at my right side where Bertolf's blade had entered. My blood soaked my tunic, which annoyed me. Few had Elven silk of this quality, now it was ruined by a moron.

"It's nothing significant," I replied. "Just a scratch."

"That's more than a scratch," she said. "That's a serious

injury and will require stitches to stop the bleeding. I'm surprised you're standing at all. Come with me."

I could already feel my skin slowly stitching itself back together, but I couldn't have her noticing that. Humans tended to react badly to such divine happenings.

"I promise, that won't be necessary," I said. "I'm fit as a fiddle."

I stretched my arms to show her, but a fresh wave of hot blood gushed out. She raised her right eyebrow.

"I think you're afraid of some needle and thread."

Did she just call me a coward?

Wings fluttered above my head and a raven's caw rattled through the air, jolting my gut.

Daring to look up, I spotted two black figures sitting on the gnarled branch of a great walnut. Hugin and Munin, Odin's two tattletales, stared back at me.

He knew I was here. With her.

Good.

What fun would it be if Odin didn't know?

I returned my gaze to Sigyn and smiled.

"You're right. What is to fear? Please, lead the way."

8

A STITCH IN TIME SAVES NINE

We passed beneath the colossal Spalentor gate entering Basel from the East and kept straight on the narrow and steep street of Heuberg. These humans seemed to love building everything uphill.

We marched ten minutes, stopping before reaching the massive monastery of Leonhardskirche at the end of the road.

Sigyn opened a heavy door to a lime plaster faced home, just like all the others that lined Heuberg, and every street of Basel for that matter.

Another caw of a Raven clattered through the air.

Really?

Hugin and Munin landed within the jungle of ivy slipping over the top of Sigyn's garden wall. Their black eyes glinted as they stared down at us, taking in our every move.

"Are you coming in?" Sigyn asked.

Well, I better give them something of interest to report back to Odin.

I smiled and gave them a very particular finger as I followed Sigyn inside her house.

I narrowly avoided smacking my forehead against the low doorframe as wood smoke and lavender filled my nose. A large cedar chest stood shoved tight to the wall to our right.

A servant girl, perhaps all of nineteen, scurried down the tiled hall towards us. Blonde wisps of hair fell from her linen cap, and flecks of dried dough clung to her wrists and knuckles.

"Mistress! You look a mess! Whatever happened?"

"Silvia, get a kettle boiling and bring it to my study. I need to attend to Herr Lanter immediately."

The girl's gaze fell to my side, my blood drenching a good portion of my tunic. In fact, it dripped on the tiles in bright red circles.

She clapped a hand over her mouth, and her face turned slightly green.

I thought it would be gentlemanly of me to reassure her.

"It's all right, maiden. Just a touch of blood. I've endured far worse. Once in battle I got sliced open and had to fight the rest of the time clasping my side so my guts wouldn't spill out."

Her eyes widened, and she only turned greener. She stepped away and took off to what I could only assume to be the kitchens to spill her own guts out.

"Pay her no mind. She's still getting used to seeing flesh wounds," Sigyn said.

She started up the stairs, and I kept close behind her. Every step groaned beneath our feet as we headed to the main living quarters of the house.

A fireplace snapped and popped on the second floor. Lush tapestries and carpets covered the plaster and heavy oak frame of the walls. We passed two wooden doors walking the hall. She opened the third.

Light streamed through the thick glass circles of two leaded windows. Warmth hugged the room from a green tiled stove of lead-glazed earthenware standing in the corner, further condensing the scents of herbs and spices.

She walked to a solid cabinet four times her size and rustled through bottles of orange and blue glass filled with oils and dried powders. Reaching higher, she stood on her tiptoes and hunted through a collection of sealed earth.

I crossed my arms and shook my head.

So, humans remained fascinated by disks of clay and ground minerals. I remembered them from when the Romans sauntered about like they owned the world. While not wholly useless, they weren't exactly able to cure the black plague.

Thick, leather-bound volumes filled a bookcase that took up the entire opposite wall, along with some enchanting little scientific trinkets.

Moving hanging sage and basil out of my way I went over and picked up a human skull that sat atop a crisp book on anatomy. Grim. I liked her decorating style. Setting it back down, I crept through the other goodies such as a trepanning set, red coral, and mercury, all jammed between countless medical texts on animals, pharmacology, and physiology.

"I could be lost in that bookcase for hours," she said, regaining my attention. "Most of the books are from our own press. My father and I strive for what's new and revolutionary. You won't find Johann Webber reprinting copies of Galen, or other antiquated nonsense. But now, sit, I want to look at that wound."

She pointed at a chair beside a sturdy oak table with a white porcelain basin sitting on top of the oiled wood. The chair legs scraped the battered floor as I pulled it out and sat.

Sigyn brought over two small bottles and two jars all labeled in a neat hand.

"Yarrow," I read, picking up a vial of withered flowers.

The table quaked as she thumped down a brass mortar beside my arm.

"Achillea millefolium. One of the best for stopping bleeding and warding off infection," she said. "I use it often for my father."

"Really? How come?"

She squeezed her lips together, as if deciding to answer me or not.

"My father is ill. He's suffered nearly a year with his ailment," she said. "That's why I must ensure the press' survival for him. I do the books, keep the apprentices and journeymen in line, and discuss plans with my foreman. I spend my days with the business, and my nights making tinctures to dull my father's pain." She paused. "I apologize, I don't know what's come over me. I never speak of my troubles."

"That's all right, I'm happy to listen," I said. And I was, which surprised me. I rarely cared about such human trifles.

She smiled, and her brown eyes met my green ones for a heartbeat. Sigyn shifted in her shoes and looked back at her bottles and jars, opening each one.

"Paracelsus himself helped me create my little home apothecary. He's an extraordinary physician and medical thinker. His innovations and humanist philosophy have been influential to me in my work."

She emptied a spoonful each of yarrow and elder buds into the brass mortar along with a scoop of pig fat and candle wax. The table shook as she struck the mixture, pounding and stirring until a paste started to form.

I couldn't help a ripple of delight sweep down to my toes as her lips pulled into a satisfied smile squashing plants into oblivion.

"You hold quite a morbid fascination for skeletons and all the wobbly bits inside the human body."

She stopped and wiped the sweat from her brow with the back of her wrist.

"Wobbly bits?" she repeated, her tone hardening. "And my interests are not morbid."

Damn my mouth.

"I'm sorry." There was that word again. "I didn't mean to insult you."

She sighed and leaned against the table staring down.

"You didn't insult me," she said. "I get rather passionate about my pursuits. I'm so used to having to defend my every thought and action, I unfortunately forget not every word is an attack."

"Defend yourself? Whatever for?"

She arched her right eyebrow.

"Surely you can tell."

I shrugged.

"You're skilled with blades. You're tenacious in your work as a printer. You're knowledgeable in science and medicine. If something is amiss, please enlighten me. I, personally, find it all quite marvelous."

She laughed and met my gaze again.

"You are a refreshing man," she said. "Many would disagree with you about me. I'm what they call 'different,' which in Switzerland is practically akin to leprosy. Nothing satisfies the Swiss more than falling into neat and tidy rows of predetermined pegs."

She clutched a gold pendant speckled with rubies and trailed it along the black satin ribbon she wore around her neck.

"That's lovely," I said.

"It was my mother's. She's the reason I strive to share the newest medical knowledge through our press, and through my life."

"How's that?"

She stopped playing with her necklace and held it tight.

"My mother died because her doctors relied on convention. On hogwash. They refused to contemplate the new innovations being made in their own field. I swore I'd never let another suffer due to incompetence. Due to arrogance. This is why I print scientific texts, educate, and offer medical advice." She studied the pendant. "Her necklace helps me remember my vow. Knowledge is to be shared, not locked away and dictated by men with white hair."

Sigyn spoke unlike any I'd met in all the Nine Worlds before. I supposed she was different, and that's what I liked about her.

In fact, I liked her very much.

The door creaked open.

Sigyn let her necklace swing back against her chest as Silvia walked in gripping a pewter kettle. Her color remained off, as if her stomach continued to do cartwheels.

Sigyn took the kettle from her and leaned over the table, pouring a stream of steaming water into the cold porcelain basin.

"Take off your...I've never seen such a garment," she said.

I smiled.

"Yes, I am particularly fond of the embroidery along the edges."

"No, I mean, I've never seen a man wear a tunic, except for my dead grandfather in his portrait."

I didn't believe I'd ever been so highly insulted.

"I'll have you know this is the height of fashion where I come from."

Laughter danced behind her eyes, as if telling me *yes, of course it is.*

"And where exactly are you from? You have no accent, but you are definitely foreign."

I couldn't very well tell her the truth.

"The North. Aggravating place, but it's home."

She chuckled.

"Well, regardless, I need you to take it off," she said, setting the kettle down. "Don't be shy, I've seen a man's chest before. I promise not to blush."

Please.

Being shy was not in my nature.

I unbuckled my leather belt and slipped my tunic over my head. I winced from the bite of the wound, but it was more annoyance than actual pain.

She fixed on the lean muscle of my chest. She cleared her throat, and I swear her cheeks turned the slightest shade of pink. It was understandable. It wasn't every day a human saw the body of a literal god.

Sigyn dipped a linen cloth in the hot water and pressed it against the gash.

The air thickened with her scent of rosemary and saffron as she cleaned the smeared blood from my side. A stray hair from her tickled my shoulder, and I closed my eyes, silently breathing her in.

"That bastard Bertolf," she whispered. "I'm amazed he didn't kill you."

I opened my eyes, trying to regain myself.

"I told you, I am resilient."

Her brow knit together.

"Resilient? You should be dead."

She continued to inspect me and I hoped she didn't notice me tense. I was afraid of this. Damn immortality.

"Oh?"

She bent down and leaned in closer towards my injury.

"The blade went in at such an angle it should have pierced your liver. In truth, I can't see how it didn't."

"Good thing my liver is tougher than most."

Her brow knit even tighter, as if determined to figure out this riddle before her. I couldn't have that.

"What was that attack about, anyway?" I asked, wanting to get her off the trail. "It seems your brother knows how to choose sensational friends."

She wrung out my blood from the cloth and dipped it again into the fresh water. Sigyn returned to wiping my side, and I started to hate the cloth between her bare fingers and my skin.

"You don't want to be involved in my family issues."

"I got stabbed trying to defend you because of him. I think I'm already involved."

Her lips tightened, but she nodded.

"Simon creates businesses, each more ludicrous than the next, but he's charming and charismatic. People believe him and his promises for a quick return on their investments. He takes their money and then...I know I said he wasn't a fraud back there, but he is."

I tilted my head, trying to understand.

"And you protect a man you admit is a fraud?"

She looked at me as if I said something utterly stupid.

"He is my brother and my blood. He may be a con and a liar, but he doesn't deserve what they would do to him. Yes,

Simon is lost, but even the lost can be found. I won't give up on him. I can't."

Her fidelity ignited within her chest, pulsing dimly for a second or two before extinguishing completely again.

I swallowed hard.

Removing the cloth, she readied a needle and thread and knelt beside me to start her stitches. Her face twisted with confusion.

I looked down and immediately knew why. The large gash was now a thin cut, almost a scratch, thanks to my body mending itself.

"I could have sworn the wound was gaping not even a minute ago. All that blood it caused!" she said. "It makes no sense."

She shook her head and put the threaded needle on the table.

"Trust me, these things often look worse than they really are," I assured.

I grabbed my tunic and made to pull it back on, but she stopped me.

"Stitches aren't necessary, but something to prevent infection is."

She dug her fingers into the pungent grit of the mixture in the mortar. The herbs stung my nose.

"I honestly think you are making a bigger deal about this than is necessa—"

"Don't be a baby."

She pressed the salve against my naked skin.

A strike of fidelity rocked through my veins and my bones.

Sigyn's element opened to me as an inferno. And I was unprepared for the beauty of it all.

I bit my lip, not wanting to cry out as she scorched my flesh, and burned in every beat of my heart.

I inhaled her hope, rose into her overwhelming peace until I floated. My entire body chanted with her song of constancy. Of wholeness. Of overpowering joy.

She continued to skate her fingers back and forth over my ribs.

I never wanted her to stop.

Slowly, ever so slowly, I opened my element to her. The slightest sliver, almost nothing, just enough to release a single spark from my chaos.

I had to know if she could feel me as well...

She flung her hand back, ending the contact and throwing me violently back into the room of heavy herbs and spices. The warmth of the place was cold compared to her energy.

She looked down at her hand, and her breaths rose and fell fast.

"Is everything all right?" I asked, my throat parched.

She rubbed her thumb over her open palm, as if trying to smother my heat.

"What?"

"Are you all right?"

Sigyn dropped her hand to her side and gripped her skirts.

"Sorry. I felt...It's nothing. I must be light headed from not having eaten all day. Maybe put your tunic back on? Yes. I think that would be best."

I obeyed and dressed quickly, savoring the smoldering tingle on my side where she had touched me.

She walked swiftly to a side table and her hands trembled as she fumbled trying to open a ceramic jar. Sliding her arm inside, she picked out six rectangle cookies and placed them on a china plate in the center of the table.

"They're lackerli. Gingerbread with candied fruit. A Basel specialty."

I tried one, though they looked dry and unappealing. However, the flavors were delicate and sweet.

She sat across from me and ate one, and then a second. No doubt her mind raced with reasons and logic to explain away what happened between us. Perhaps I was wrong to have opened my energy to her.

Thoughtless as always, Loki!

"I've never met someone like you, Lukas," she said. She took a third lackerli now.

I chuckled.

"I'm certain of that."

"No, you don't understand." Her eyes found mine. "I don't speak of my family, of my personal struggles, openly to others. To anyone, really. But with you...and when I touched you...I thought my insides burned."

Without thought, I slowly stretched my arm towards hers beside the plate.

"Is that a bad thing?" I asked.

Uncertainty knit the lines of her face. I grazed the tips of her fingers with my own. She didn't retract her hand

My heart quickened for her answer.

The door flew open and smacked against the wall. A young man ran in, soot smearing his face and simple clothes. An apprentice.

"Dietrich!" Sigyn exclaimed, standing.

"It's on fire, my lady!" he gasped.

"What is?"

He bent over and drew in several heaving breaths.

"The printing shop." He hacked and wheezed. "It's burning."

Sigyn rushed past him and down the stairs, I fast on her heels as she flew outside and towards the rising smoke curling in the sky.

UP IN SMOKE

M en and women formed a line stretching from the fountain in the small square to the burning print shop on the corner of the street. Buckets raced from hand to hand as they heaved water in great splashes at the fire eating the entire left side of the building.

Sigyn and I ran alongside the throng all headed towards the fire. Ladders banged against the blackened plaster, and strong men lifted heavy buckets and climbed to the top, tossing a swirl of water over the spinning flames.

I appreciated their optimism, but as black clouds plumed out the windows and seeped through the tiles of the roof, I knew their tactics would yield little results against such a blaze.

Sigyn ran past me, gripping two buckets in each hand. Water sopped over the edges as she sprinted across the street and into the shop.

Gods! What was she thinking?

A single falling beam would crush her. I shuddered imagining it shatter her fragile bones.

I couldn't allow that.

I bolted inside after her.

Soot and boiling ink stung my nose and eyes. Searing heat washed over my skin as I peered through the twisting flames and ash for her.

"Sigyn!" I called.

Only the crackling of fire devouring the room to my left answered. I pushed forward through a narrow hall clogged with smoke.

Water splattered in a backroom, accompanied by the frantic grunts of a woman.

I continued towards the noise, passing beneath dry wooden beams and shelves stuffed with stacks of blank paper, books, and cotton string. My heart hammered against my chest. The entire place would go up in a matter of minutes.

Usually nothing excited me more than a woman who laughed in the face of imminent danger, but this was a touch excessive.

Why did humans have to be so damn delicate?

I nearly tripped over an empty bucket as I found Sigyn throwing a gush of water over a mammoth machine of heavy wood and iron. Lead typeface clattered to the floor, forced out by her deluge.

"Bring me more water!" She tried to scream, but it sounded more like gravel mixed with phlegm.

She had to be kidding.

Her lungs were congesting with soot. She was breaths away from collapse. Panic raged inside me with the same vigor as the fire attacking the shop.

"You need to get out of here."

I ran behind her and opened a window, letting the thick smoke escape. It wouldn't be enough.

She coughed violently, throwing her last bucket over the machine, the water crashing against every gear and beam.

Humans remained infuriatingly oblivious to the fact they only had one life, and that life was as frail as a baby sparrow.

"Leave it. You've done all you can."

She shook her head shaking the last drops out of her bucket. Her element burned hot, almost as hot as the flames now traveling towards us from the front of the shop.

"I can't—" she hacked and choked again, "—I must save it."

My heart sank for her as the truth of her words hit me. This was her life, all their lives, and it was turning to ashes.

"You must go, or you will meet your death."

Death. I didn't like that word. It was so final.

Her bloodshot eyes watered, and I wasn't sure if from the soot or her tears.

She nodded stiffly, and I wrapped my right arm over her shoulders, shielding her from the spit and bite of the flames as I escorted her back through the shop and out the door.

I breathed a sigh of relief while she coughed sharply as fresh air surrounded us again. Thankfully, two women scurried towards us to give her aid.

It kept her distracted long enough for me to slip my arm away from her.

"Lukas?"

I gave her a wink, and went back inside the inferno, slamming the door shut and locking her out.

"Lukas!" she cried and gagged, banging the door. "What are you doing?"

"Going to put out the fire," I shouted through the door. "Won't be long!"

"Lukas!"

The pop and snap of the blaze swallowed her shrill cries as I stepped over fallen and scorched beams, heading back towards the heart of the fire.

I couldn't very well let her shop burn down to ashes if I could stop it. It would be quite rude of me. Fire was part of my element, part of my very being, after all.

I narrowed my vision making my way through the heavy smoke until I reached an absolute firestorm. Flames incinerated the oak beams in the walls and ceiling, even the floor was alight as twisting and twirling yellow and orange gorged on furniture and paper.

Walking directly into the center of the storm, the sputtering flames clasped onto my skin and clothes, even licking between my fingers. I smiled as the embers danced over me, kissing me with their warm breath.

The seared floorboards creaked beneath my boots. I hadn't much time.

The fire squeezed my legs, and wrapped around my torso, squirming through my hair that fluttered the same as the inferno I now sought to extinguish.

My element grew hungry.

I took in a deep breath, inhaling the flames into myself, into my lungs and my belly. Heat, invigorating heat, filled me, coursed through my veins and sinew.

I sucked the sputtering light in through my nostrils, in through my mouth, feasting on the fire, consuming the flames faster than they could consume the wood and parchment.

The smoke started to clear. The fire quivered now. Trembled, as I devoured it down to its last embers.

My skin sizzled, and sparks snapped within my hair,

swirling around my face, chest, and feet. My chaos so bloated on pure energy lit my eyes aflame, and I could feel my pupils burning with the fire now inside me.

It was done, and I was sated.

Pale light streamed in through the broken glass of the leaded windows, revealing the charred remnants of the room. Smoke and burnt wood clung to the air.

Cheers swelled in my ears from outside. A door creaked open and steps rattled across burnt floorboards and singed paper.

"Lukas!"

Sigyn ran towards me. I closed my eyes shut. I couldn't have her see my chaos I knew still burnt within my gaze.

She wrapped her arms around me and pulled me into an embrace. I hoped she didn't notice the steam rising from my skin, or feel the heat still lingering in my bones.

"You stupid, stupid man! I thought you'd be dead for sure," she said.

"I told you I am resilient," I joked.

"However did you manage it?"

Her face told me she wanted me to recount the entire, noble feat. In vivid detail.

This was a problem.

"It's an ancient trick from the North to smother fires. I thought it worth a go," I said, hoping she'd not press further.

She pulled away ending our contact, as if remembering herself. I kept my eyes firmly shut.

"Are your eyes all right?" she asked.

Oh good. Another problem.

"Quite."

Damn. When would my eyes cool so I could open them without scaring her completely?

"Then why are you keeping them closed?"

I felt her reaching her hand towards my face. I stepped back.

"A speck of soot, is all."

"Still, I'd like to examine—"

I took another step back. Away.

"My lady, come look!" a man called. "The printing press appears unscathed. Once it dries out, we should be able to print a small amount while we repair the rest of the shop."

"That's my foreman. I must go, but I'll come back and see how your eyes are doing in a minute," she said.

"No rush!"

I let out a breath I didn't even know I held as she went to the back with her foreman.

I peeked through my eyelashes as I walked through the shop, trying to get away from the apprentices and journeymen who now inspected the damage.

Only once I was certain my element was sufficiently cooled, did I dare fully open my eyes. The destruction caught my breath in my throat.

Water dripped through the brittle rafters onto my head and shoulders. Broken and burnt plaster cracked and split to floor between the charred skeletons of desks and chairs.

Luckily, if there was any luck in this at all, the worst destruction stayed concentrated to the front, away from the back where most of the hard labor took place.

Gold glinted from within the rubble.

Bending down, I dove my fingers into the soft ash and picked up a gold button.

My heart thundered as I curled my fingers around it, recognizing the fine sheen from earlier.

Bertolf.

I clenched my jaw, anger rushing through me, at myself, that I had let him escape to only wreak more terror. I only hoped this arson slaked his thirst for vengeance.

But what did that truly matter in the end? Simon brought Bertolf straight to Sigyn's door. How many more cheated men waited in the dark to cut her throat, or sink their knives into her soft stomach, all to send a message to her brother? If not Bertolf coming back for more, it would be someone else.

Simon made her a sitting duck.

That word *death* pricked my mind again.

This was unacceptable to me.

I maneuvered through the debris, a need to keep her safe gripping my core. Sigyn knelt on the floor, bent over and picking up those scattered little lead letters. Just as when I first saw her.

My heart somersaulted. Somersaulted? Was I a ten year old girl?

Standing in front of her, I cleared my throat.

"Sigyn, there's something I want to speak to you about. I'm...I'm planning on lengthening my visit to..."

Her posture slumped. Ink and soot stained her finger-nails as she carefully gathered the pieces and dropped them into a wicker basket.

"It will be months before we can be up and running again," she said, not listening to me at all. "Thank God the press itself was spared. At least we can produce something to bring in coinage."

Pity rolled in my gut. I knelt down and helped her collect the metal cubes, my own fingers getting stained black.

"Take heart knowing it can at least be repaired," I said.

She sighed.

"But our clients expect their orders. We promised the printing of a new anatomy book for the university by September. I'm overwhelmed by what all needs to be done this summer alone. And then my papa..."

She clutched at the pieces, and for the first time she appeared vulnerable. Unsure. I wanted to pull her into my arms and tell her it would be all right, but I didn't.

She sat back on her heels and put her hands on her waist. She looked at the smoke stained walls and knowing tugged on her features.

"This was intentional, wasn't it?" she whispered.

I grimaced. I held out the incriminating button to her, confirming her suspicions.

"It appears that way," I said.

"Bastard," she spat. "He knew where to strike hard and deep. If he couldn't take my face, he'd take what I loved. If he ever shows up here again, I'll gut him."

She returned to picking up the final pieces.

"Which brings me back to what I wanted to talk to you about..."

She met my gaze.

"Yes?"

My words stuck in my mouth. I knew them immediately to be foolish. She was not a woman to accept a man's protection. She would laugh and refuse me. Then laugh again.

I smiled.

"The rebuilding of your shop will be an overwhelming undertaking, Sigyn. Let me help you repair. We will make your shop rise from the ashes like a phoenix."

She chuckled.

"You make everything sound so theatrical," she said.

"But you've done more than enough for me already. I can't accept your help anymore."

Stubborn woman. I loved it.

"You like going it alone, don't you?" I asked.

"It's how it's always been for me. I'm used to it."

"You are a strong woman, Sigyn, but even you can't oversee both the rebuilding and the printing, not to mention caring for your father. That's too much for any one person to handle. I'm offering you my help as a friend."

Silence.

More silence.

I thought my hair would turn gray any second.

She drew in a breath.

"Where are you staying?" she finally asked.

A sharp caw cracked through the open window. Peering behind her those two black beasts of Odin's sat on the windowsill, clucking and growling at me.

Munin's right eye turned a vivid blue.

Well, this was new.

I told you to leave Sigyn alone, Odin's voice warned me from within my mind.

He spoke through raven's now? He was getting uncomfortably good with his charms.

"At *Les Troi Roi*," I lied, ignoring Odin. "It has a sufficient view of the Rhine."

Her eyes widened.

"That's the most expensive inn in the entire city."

I shrugged.

"Well, when you want a water view."

She chuckled.

"If you find it tolerable losing your river view, I have a spare room. If I'm to take your help, then I insist I feed and house you. It's the least I can do."

Lovely.

I know you're scorning me, Odin's voice echoed again in my mind. *Punishing me for leaving you behind. I've given you time to traipse around and have your fun, but the novelty has worn off, Loki...Come home, now.*

Oh dear. Whatever would I decide?

10

POISON AND A PRAYER

Odin and his flying rats could piss off.

Did he think he could clap, and I'd come running back to him? Odin rendered me useless in helping him and the gods fight to protect Asgard from this Destroyer. From this threat that continued to pound in my brain.

I would not abide being made useless, especially when I was needed here. Until I was assured of Sigyn's safety, Odin would have to wait. It would all have to wait.

I struggled to shake off the chill in my spine as my head throbbed harder, as if telling me I was being extremely foolish.

Thankfully, rebuilding Johann Webbers proved a delightful distraction. I labored with the workers lifting heavy beams in place, slapping fresh lime plaster over the walls with the journeymen. The snarl of saws and striking hammers created an unceasing chorus of progress as we rebuilt Sigyn's shop.

I enjoyed the novelty of manual labor. Especially the opportunities it provided for me to remove my doublet, giving me a chance to show off my firm chest beneath my half open undershirt.

The maids blushed when they brought me my afternoon ale. Sigyn rolled her eyes at them.

But, from time to time, I caught Sigyn watching me drive iron nails into fresh timber, her eyes following down my arms that glistened with sweat. I wasn't sure if it was because of my devilish allure, or the fact she wanted to make sure my work met her standards.

Either way, it made me smile.

Days turned into weeks and the shop finally started to function.

In the back, the acrid aroma of ink soured the air as she covered typeface with the sticky ooze. Once the machine squeezed the ink into the plain paper, she'd carefully take the wet pages and hang them to dry on cords strung across the ceiling.

Our evenings I cherished the most, when we returned to her home on Heuberg and sat down to a simple dinner of bread and potage rich with chicken and a pinch of ginger. We talked late into the night, discussing science, history, and which apples produced the best cider. How any one being could contain such passion and intelligence dazzled me. I wished to listen to her talk always.

I gifted her a dagger made from quality steel with excellent balance. If one of those rogues found her alone...I refused to see her defend herself with the shit blades she favored.

She hugged me for that.

I wished for her to hug me again.

However, as her father's health worsened, I increasingly ate alone. Her foreman took over watching the apprentices place the type correctly.

Purple circles grew beneath her eyes and her skin dulled.

She remained more and more upstairs tending to his needs. She wouldn't speak of what ailed him, only that he must remain clean and comfortable. The man continued to exist as only a ghost to me.

Concern for her wellbeing ate me from within.

"Let me help you acquire a nursemaid for your father," I said, during a rare moment we breakfasted together in her small, but richly furnished dining room. "You bring him tinctures and salves at all hours. You can't continue on like this."

Her lips flattened as she spread a thick pat of butter over her dense bread stuffed with grains.

"I appreciate your concern, but a nursemaid can't replace the care and love a daughter provides."

She dug her silver knife into the raspberry jam and slathered it over the butter. Taking a large bite, she chewed forcefully as if already anxious to be done with eating.

"I'm not speaking of replacing, just letting someone sit with him for several hours at night so you can actually sleep for once."

"I can manage."

She took a swig of ale, washing down her mouthful of bread.

"It's draining you."

"Leave it. I'm fine. Please."

I laughed at that.

"You always are," I said, perhaps with a bit too much scorn in my voice. "I hope you feel the same when your fatigue causes you to fall ill."

She dropped her bread onto her china plate, sending

crumbs scattering across the oiled wood. Her face tightened as she drew in a breath.

Her fidelity ignited in her chest.

"I know I'm tired. I know I look a mess," she said. "I also know what can happen when you entrust a loved one to the care of another. I won't allow it. I won't let him suffer as my mother did."

"But—"

She stood, her chair screeching across the oak floorboards. Her element shined white, forcing me to almost narrow my gaze. She clasped her pendant, running it up and down the black ribbon.

"Haven't you ever done anything difficult out of love for another?" she asked.

I leaned back in my own chair as Odin's face sharpened in my memory, and I fell back to a time I tried to forget.

Odin stood on the beach looking out over the Asgardian sea, the ocean wind tearing through his russet hair. I stood beside him, overcome by his strength, his danger...

Tell the king it is the only way, he said to me. The waves crashed and filled my lungs with salt. *Tell him what he wants to hear so he will finally concede. Only your silver tongue can achieve what I desperately require, Loki. I need this of you.*

He turned to me and cupped my face, letting his icy ambition bleed into me through his fingertips as he asked this evil of me.

I didn't want to do it, but he knew my love for him was greater than my resolve. I hated him for it.

Odin and the ocean dissolved, and I found myself back in Sigyn's dining room, the clatter of horses and carts rattling through the windows.

"Once, a long time ago."

Bitter regret coated my mouth. Guilt pitted my stomach.

"Then you understand?" she whispered.

I shook my head, unable to stop my lips from pulling into a sneer.

"Oh, I do," I said, rising out of my seat. "What's more, I understand what it is to sacrifice everything we are."

Her right eyebrow raised.

"That's what love is," she said. "Love is sacrifice."

I chuckled darkly crossing my arms. Dear innocent little Sigyn.

"Love makes us fools and monsters."

I stopped, realizing I didn't speak of Sigyn and her father anymore.

I spoke of Odin and myself.

"I…I don't want you to get hurt."

Her gaze searched me, and I braced myself for her heated objections. She smiled softly instead.

Had she not heard a single word I just said? I would have slapped myself across the face had I been her.

"I'm going to the apothecary to purchase some more calendula to make a new batch of ointment. Come with me. There's something you should see."

* * *

WE WALKED across the large open square of Münsterplatz towards the red cathedral that stood as a lone giant beside a small grove of chestnut trees. The Rhine raced behind the church. Fishermen on weidling boats fought against the strong current as they pulled in nets loaded with salmon and trout.

"I love the Münster," Sigyn said. "It's lasted seven centuries, and the great earthquake of 1356. Now there are whispers protestantism will overtake it soon." She looked up at the two spires touching the blue sky. "It's a reminder to me. If this building can survive so many changes and bumps, then I can, too."

Curiosity gripped me noticing a carved sandstone knight fixed to the outside of the Münster. He sat on a rearing horse, his spear plunging into the open mouth of a dragon.

"Who is that supposed to be?" I asked, standing directly beneath it.

"St. George," she replied. "Legend says he saved a woman from being devoured by a dragon. Apparently the dragon had an appetite for young maidens and required them daily as a sacrifice."

Dragons were odious with their quirky demands. Bunch of vexatious divas.

"I love the story," she continued. "The heroism, the daring risk! It's a shame such myths are only fiction. A world where gods and monsters were real would be fun."

A lance of pain struck inside my skull. I swallowed and rubbed my temples forcing the sensation away.

"One would think that," I replied.

She walked up to the immense door and pulled on the handle, the wood groaning as she heaved it open.

Panic filled me. I'd never entered a church before. In fact, I made it a strict rule for myself to never do so. This God had been known to be quite ruthless in His younger days.

I'd spent a lovely week in Sodom and Gomorrah before He had the indecency to destroy it.

I wasn't certain if He'd view my presence here with the same contempt.

"What are you doing?" I asked.

"Going inside, of course."

"I thought you'd needed to get to the apothecary?"

"I always make a stop here first. Come along."

"But—"

She slipped in behind the door.

I remained outside, tapping my fingers against my upper leg, thinking. Pouting.

Dammit.

What were rules for if not to break them?

My stomach lurched with awkwardness entering the silence. Incense thickened and sweetened the air as it swirled within the light shining through the stained glass.

My boots snapped against the red sandstone as I walked down the nave, passing pews of richly carved, dark oak. Sandstone pillars rose above my head fusing into arches lushly painted with saints and angels.

But all the beauty couldn't compare to the sacred stillness of the place. The thoughts constantly running in my mind quieted, and my heartbeats softened as if my soul had been given a gentle hush.

Sigyn entered the right transept populated by brightly colored statues and a small, marble altar. She stepped before a votive stand, and light from around thirty beeswax candles bathed her in gold.

I loved how the soft luster made the honey in her hair glow as if she wore a halo.

I stood beside her, and she dropped two coins into a metal box and picked out a pair of thin candles from a tray.

"My mother always brought me here as a little girl," she whispered. "She'd let me light two candles, one for my papa's patience with the new apprentices."

Hovering the wick over the twinkling flames she smiled, as if thinking back on the memory until her candle ignited with a small orb.

She placed the candle within the sand among the others.

"And the second for my brother, that he'd grow out of playing pranks on the maid. I can still hear poor Elsie scream when that toad hopped out of her potage."

She lit the second candle and stood it beside the first.

"Of course, my prayers have changed since then. I now light a candle for my papa to finally be freed from his pain, and for Simon to reclaim his life. For all our sakes."

She bore her hand into her purse and pulled out another coin and dropped it into the box. Sigyn picked up a third candle, clasping it firm in her hand.

"And who is that for?" I asked.

She met my gaze, and sincerity filled her eyes.

"For you."

My breaths tightened.

"Me? I don't know if that's a good idea, I—"

She reached out and gripped my upper arm and squeezed reassuringly. My throat dried, and I nearly melted, but this wasn't right. She shouldn't do this for me. For someone *like* me. I was hardly suitable for such hallowed things.

"Shhh..." she whispered.

"But I don't deserve to be included in something so intimate. I don't belong here."

She smiled wider.

"I think you deserve a candle more than anyone I've met."

My pulse thrashed in my chest and my ears.

She let her hand fall away, and I wished she hadn't. I felt terribly and wholly unsteady in everything I knew or was.

Sigyn tilted the candle towards the sea of fluttering flames, each one a prayer, a hope.

I didn't breathe anymore.

"Love is a funny thing," she said. "It can harm, but it can heal. Give us pain, and give us joy. But what I've discovered is that no matter what, when love does make us fools, it also makes us better."

Light erupted from the wick, and with it, set her own fidelity ablaze.

I thought I would die as her element burned bright and hot, soaking my skin in warmth. For the first time, it burnt in constancy for me.

"Perhaps this candle can chase away the ghosts I see lingering in your eyes, Lukas. That is what I will pray for you."

She pressed my candle into the sand, standing it equal to the rest.

Tapping her forehead, chest, and both shoulders, Sigyn folded her hands together and closed her lids.

My eyes stung as her whispers swelled in the silence as she prayed to one God for another.

For the god of lies.

The evil-doer.

The trickster.

I knew then my heart was lost to her.

* * *

WE HEADED down the famed Totengässlein. Death Alley. A very fitting name for a very inconveniently designed street of narrow slopes, steps, and landings.

Entering an apothecary at the end of the alley, my sinuses revolted as herbs and acidic solutions stung my nostrils from the vast collection of porcelain vases, jars, and jugs all crammed in bending oak shelves and cupboards.

Despite the pungent smell, I enjoyed the taxidermy alligator hanging over a copper still. It made the entire shop gloriously creepy.

"Grüezi Mitenand," the shop owner said, his red nose and straining buttons showing a man with a healthy appetite for beer and sausages.

He stood behind a dark wood counter littered with marble and brass mortars.

"Grüezi Herr Burgi," Sigyn said.

"The usual satchel of calendula?" he asked, already roving over a wall made entirely of small drawers.

Sliding one open, he took a metal spoon and scooped out the shriveled orange flowers and stuffed them into a leather pouch.

"I can always count on you to remember," she said. "I also need pearls and amber to make a new tincture of opium. Father can't bear without it, and I'm nearly out."

He smiled.

"Of course."

Heading towards the opposite wall, he maneuvered around an immense bellow and ducked below a set of hanging brass scales. Thick shelves bowed beneath pewter bowls and clay pots.

"I hope your partiality towards Paracelsus' potions is wise," he said, reaching for a painted box shoved far in the right corner. "I find the man exceedingly arrogant. He screamed at four medical students he caught reading Avicenna yesterday. Called it 'old fodder'."

This Paracelsus seemed a feisty sort. I approved.

"Trust me," I said. "It takes the arrogant to bring about the new and fresh changes the world needs. Otherwise, you'd all still live in caves."

Sigyn chuckled, but quickly stopped when Herr Burgi did not share our amusement.

He counted out three pearls in his thick palm and emptied them into a small vial.

"Anything else?" he asked, wrapping a chunk of amber in brown paper. "Or does your friend here have more words of wisdom he'd like to share?"

"I'm always happy to oblige."

I winked.

He narrowed his gaze and his stony face grew stonier, reminding me of Tyr when I told him lewd jokes. It almost made me feel back home in Asgard.

Sigyn leaned over the scarred counter towards his ear.

"I need hemlock juice. The smallest vial. His pain increases to where the laudanum only takes the edge off," she whispered.

His eyes widened.

"That is dangerous," he said. "Is he really going that downhill you have to resort to poison?"

"It's the dose that makes the poison," I replied. He glowered at me now. "Well, you said if I had anymore words of wisdom to share."

He sighed.

"Please," she said. "Hemlock is the only plant strong enough to give him a few hours rest. It's my only recourse to stop his writhing."

He chewed the inside of his lip, thinking.

"I don't like this," he said. "If the amount isn't exact, the consequences can be dire."

"I know what I'm doing," she said. "Now, will you sell it to me, or do I need to take my business to Ramseier's Apothecary on Marktplatz?"

Sighing, he dropped his shoulders.

"I will give you only enough for one, small draught, and not a drop more," he said.

He disappeared into the back of the shop, grumbling beneath his breath the entire journey.

"Truly a delightful man," I told her. "We must invite him to dine with us."

She laughed softly.

"Sigyn, my dear," a woman's voice came from behind us. "I've not seen you since the St. John's bonfire."

Sigyn stiffened, and her laughter died away.

Whoever this woman was, I hated her already.

Turning, Sigyn curtseyed to a long faced woman with small eyes and bony frame. A set of fine, white teeth made her appear more horse than woman.

"Frau Annen," Sigyn said.

Frau Annen curtsied back.

I made the mistake of catching her gaze and swallowed hard. A glint of lust sparked deep in her eyes for me.

Damn my accursed allure!

"I don't believe I've had the pleasure of an introduction." She put out her hand to me.

"Herr Lanter."

I kissed her hand and her aged skin slipped over the brittle bones beneath my lips. Her cheeks flushed. I wanted nothing more than to wipe my mouth on my sleeve.

"So this is the man you've been hiding from us?" she asked Sigyn.

Frau Annen's cheeks remained pink, and she cooled herself with a white lace fan.

"Herr Lanter is helping with the repair and rebuilding of my father's shop because of the fire. I'm sure you heard that news."

She grimaced and lengthened her posture.

"Yes, terribly tragic. It pained me deeply to hear of such horridness happening in our city."

Chaos ignited in her chest.

She lied.

My fingers curled into fists at my sides.

Herr Burgi cleared his throat returning to the counter with a small bottle wrapped in cotton cloth. Frau Annen looked over Sigyn's shoulder as she quickly placed her ingredients into her satchel.

The woman tutted, and I fantasized about hitting her over the head with the taxidermy alligator.

"Your poor father," she said. "Does he not improve?"

"Obviously," I whispered, unable to control my tongue.

Sigyn shot me a look. I closed my mouth.

Sigyn slid over several silver coins to Herr Burgi, turned, and walked for the door.

We exited back out onto the empty Totengässlein. Frau Annen followed. Why was she so driven to talk to Sigyn?

"I remember what a proud man he was," she huffed, losing her breath as we climbed the steps back towards Heuberg. "He nearly had a dynasty with your family. A third generation printer with the birth of your brother. Your father had such high hopes for Simon."

"He is still a proud man, and our hopes remain high as the press continues to succeed," Sigyn said. "Once we finish the repairs, we will be more modern than before."

Frau Annen smirked.

"I can't imagine the added stress he suffers knowing the shame that now infects your family name he so strived to build."

Sigyn stopped. Frau Annen took the chance to draw in several deep breaths.

"Shame?"

Eagerness pulled at the lines around her eyes and lips. She neared Sigyn, like a weasel cornering a chicken.

"I'm told on good authority your brother sold land to the magistrate's friend that did not exist, and now the Watch is looking to arrest him," she said. "Horrid boy. If ever a neck needed the axe...well, I'm sure you agree. Look what he's made of you."

Sigyn rubbed her thumbs against her fingers.

"And what's that?" I asked.

Shock twisted her brow as if confused why I would ask such an apparent question.

"Why, an unfit woman."

She turned back to Sigyn.

"No man will take you as a wife, what with your associations with your brother. Simon has polluted your name and tarnished your reputation. You will curse any house you enter."

I started calculating how much force I would need to throw her from the stairs to split open her skull.

Sigyn ground her teeth.

"Then you better not speak to me, in case someone might see the company you keep."

The nasty spark of glee in Frau Annen's eyes boiled my blood.

"At least there is still some good breeding remaining beneath all that black ink staining the creases in your fingers. Such a great family the Webbers once were, driven into the dirt with pigs."

My sight went red.

Heat broiled my skin and my chaos crackled inside my core as my rage overtook me.

I stepped towards her, forcing her back against a plaster faced house. She kept trying to step back, but her heels only skidded and clopped against the wall preventing her any hope of escape from me.

"You venomous snake!" I yelled. "Sigyn is the kindest, most generous heart I've ever witnessed, and you dare scorn her?"

She trembled violently, and her mouth bobbed like a fish out of water.

"I..." she stammered.

Excitement rolled through me watching this proud lady collapse into fear.

Sparks flew and snapped in my vision as my element strengthened with my growing anger.

Did I dare?

Making sure Sigyn remained behind me, I allowed my chaos to blaze through my eyes. I turned my irises into embers and my sclera into flames. This miserable human would know what I truly was.

Reckless? Perhaps. But I found it easier to not worry about such things.

She clapped her hand over her mouth and screamed, but her terror seized her throat closed and she only gasped.

Frau Annen tried to scramble away, but tripped and landed on her backside. I laughed as she dug her nails into the cobblestones, trying to flee.

I knelt down over her, keeping my gaze firmly on hers, letting her see my inferno burning with all my wrath.

I couldn't help smiling in great delight as she quaked with fear from me.

I could be very convincing when I wanted to be.

"The next time you utter a foul word against Sigyn I will find you, I will cut out your tongue, and I will feed it to those very pigs you spoke of."

"Lukas!" Sigyn cried. "Leave her alone."

She gripped my wrist and pulled me back. I sucked the fire back into myself and cleared my eyes as she spun me around to face her.

"Stop this! You're frightening her."

"That's the point."

Disappointment in me filled her gaze. It made my stomach churn.

She let go of my wrist and stepped next to the trembling Frau Annen. She remained staring out in shock, as if the image of my face remained branded in her mind.

Sigyn took the woman's quivering hands and helped her back up to her feet.

"I will make sure she gets home safe," she said. "I think it best you don't follow."

11

ALWAYS EXPECT THE UNEXPECTED

I remained in that alley a good twenty minutes, my mind spinning in a chorus of astonishment and confusion.

She left me?

Left me to escort that hateful dried prune home?

I expected a thank you, or even a kiss on the cheek. Not a scowl and a slap on the wrist as if I'd been a naughty child.

I thought I'd been rather gallant, myself.

Somehow Sigyn didn't feel the same, and I found it all extremely vexing.

I grumbled the whole way back to Sigyn's house, only stopping once I banged on the door.

Silvia answered.

"Is your mistress returned?" I asked, pushing in past her.

"Yes, sir. She came back ten minutes ago."

A deep and methodical banging echoed down the stairs from Sigyn's study. What on earth was she doing now?

I immediately climbed the creaking steps towards the racket. Usually I would avoid an angered woman. Eons of experience taught me that was always the best method, but I had to speak to her. I needed to understand.

Swinging open the door, I found her standing at the heavy table furiously crushing pearls in her brass mortar.

"Hello," I said, the word clipped and short.

She didn't answer.

She kept her eyes on her work, her forearms flexing as she now stirred and ground the pearls into a fine powder.

So this is how it would be?

The sun fell below the tile roofs, dissolving the final pink and orange hues into shadows. She kept working in the dark. This was ridiculous.

I picked up the metal tinderbox and struck the flint, sending a fan of sparks over the charcloth. Or, at least I pretended to do so.

Keeping the box hidden from her view, I touched the charcloth with my fingertip, sending a spark directly into the dry fiber. A flame instantly burst to life, allowing me to light a reed.

I lit two candlesticks by the window, chasing away the darkness and letting her actually see what she was doing.

"I'm sorry if my defense of your honor offended you earlier," I said, with perhaps a touch more sarcasm than I should have.

Sigyn continued to mill her pearls, and the persistent thumping and pulverizing started to grate my nerves. Would she really not answer me?

"Fine," I said. "I know I've irked you, but how can you blame me for what I did? I could not stand idly by and allow that vicious woman to abuse you."

Silence.

I lit a third candle on a maple stand beside an embroidered chair, more light swelling the room with gold.

"It's not your defense of me that angered me, it's that you acted like a brute," she said.

"Brute?"

I neared her, lighting the final candle in the middle of the table.

"Yes. Brute. She spoke only words. Not threats."

"Words *are* threats. You best believe that."

Her face tightened, and she pounded the pearls harder.

Sweat glistened on her brow in the warm candlelight, and a curl of her hair escaped her snood and skated over her shoulder. It bobbed in front of her face, and I wished to brush it away.

But I didn't dare.

"Frau Annen didn't deserve to be terrified and intimidated out of her wits like that," she said. "She trembled the entire way back to her home. I instructed her maid to give her some wine and let me know how she is in the morning."

"That's more than that scornful hag deserves."

She flattened her lips into thin ribbons.

"Instilling such fear in someone harmless like her is unkind. Unnecessary. If you attacked every scandalmonger in the city, there'd be no one left. Frau Annen is only a gossip, echoing the tales she hears in the street. Trust me, Simon makes plenty of it that follows me around."

I leaned against the table.

Sigyn was right.

My anger against Frau Annen was misguided. She wasn't the source of the poison. That honor fell purely on Simon. He was the one dragging his sister down into the muck with him.

Or worse...

I swallowed as the reality of it all set in.

Any second she could be taken from me, without warning, without decorum, just cold and cruel and finite.

Panic set in.

If Simon and I ever crossed paths...

"You need to end this," I said.

"End what?" she asked.

"Any relationship you have with Simon. You must distance yourself from him. Disown him if you have too," I said. "He's a man whose exploits will rip you apart."

"Ridiculous."

I gripped her arm, forcing her to stop her incessant pummeling and listen to me.

"He's dangerous to you, Sigyn. Bertolf nearly disfigured your face and practically destroyed your printing press because of Simon. Don't let him also damn your reputation as he continues to steal and cheat from vicious men. You'll be a pariah and you'll lose everything you've built."

She pulled out of my grip and crossed her arms.

"You're taking that bitch's side now?"

I shrugged, smirking.

"It is funny, isn't it?"

Sigyn's eyes widened as she fumed.

"I don't care what Frau Annen thinks, and I sure as hell don't care what anyone else thinks, including you."

I pushed off the table and stepped right in front of her.

"That's a lie," I said.

"Is it?"

I leaned into her and she held her ground. Her breasts rose and fell against my chest. I tried not to think how I felt her skin heat through her dress.

"Yes," I said. "Everyone cares. We tell ourselves we can be strong, that words are just words, but every hurtful utterance cuts us, every snide remark brands our flesh. We drown in the criticism of others, all the while pretending we can swim."

"And what makes you such an expert?" she snapped.

"Because where I come from I am despised," I hissed. "I don't want the same fate for you. I don't want you to be crushed beneath their boot heels."

I paused and my heart thundered in my ears. There was only thunder.

I never said it before, but it was the truth. The first truth I ever admitted about myself.

Her eyes searched me deep, and something like pity reflected behind them.

"I'm sure that's not true," she said.

I chuckled darkly.

"Well, let's say relationships in my family are complicated."

Her features softened, and she took a deep breath.

"I know what Simon is," she whispered. "I know the price of believing in someone like him."

"Then let him go. If the people think you sullied by his disease, they will scatter your dreams among the coals."

Mist coated her eyes.

"You don't understand. We share not only the same blood, but the same past. The same memories." She took in a ragged breath. "When Mother died, my grief turned into perseverance. Simon's turned into recklessness. But I know who he used to be, and still can be again. I won't give up on him."

Her fidelity erupted in her chest, almost unraveling me as it pulsed hot through my doublet.

I swallowed, forcing myself to remain focused.

"It's obvious the boy you once knew isn't coming back.

He made a choice, and now, you must forget him. He only brings you heartache."

Our faces were mere inches from one another. Her breath curled across my cheeks and neck.

"I won't ever forsake my brother," she said. "Yes, he is a leech, a fraud, a cheat, but beneath the deceit still exists a good man. Any goodness must be fought for, even if it comes at my expense."

A lovely thought.

"Some souls are lost, Sigyn."

She shuffled two steps back.

"I will never believe that."

Her element blazed, and light flowed out of her pores and swathed her face and arms in pure radiance.

The truth twisted my gut and emotion hit me hard.

I asked of her an impossible thing.

Sigyn *was* fidelity, the very essence of loyalty and love, and I pushed her to do what went against her very force. She was a prisoner to her virtue. To her element. She was incapable of anything but loyalty.

"I'm...I'm sorry," I said. "Forgive my words. I spoke them out of fear. I just want you safe."

She took my hands in hers, sucking the air out of me. I wanted to wrap her in my arms and hold her tight. To protect her from her own goodness.

"I know," she whispered.

We held each other's gaze and quiet thickened around us. I felt her heart beat through my clothes, matching the frantic rhythm of my own.

I pulled her closer, falling into her light.

She slid her hand behind my waist. My skin burned beneath her touch, and I cursed the clothes keeping our naked skin apart.

Sigyn wet her lips waking a hunger deep in me for them. Touching my forefinger beneath her chin, I lifted her mouth towards mine.

Our lips skated across one another. I closed my eyes...

A scream splintered like porcelain above our heads.

She pulled away.

"Papa!"

* * *

"MAKE THE PAIN STOP. Please. I'll give you anything!"

Her father twisted his fingers into his sweat drenched sheets, and a web of blue veins rose to the surface of his arms and hands. His eyes sank deep into his protruding sockets, and his yellow cheeks dipped into the hollows of his jaw. He looked ghoulish.

Sigyn mixed three spoonfuls of laudanum into a goblet of claret and sat beside him on his massive bed thick with wool blankets and stuffed with feather pillows. She lifted the potion to his lips. He clamped them shut.

"This will take away the worst of it," she said.

"My stomach heaves so," he moaned. "I can't drink a drop."

"If you want to lessen the pain, you must."

He scrunched his wrinkled face and took a sip. Then another.

"I promise it will be better," she said as she dabbed his chin with a cloth.

He answered her by closing and opening his eyelids.

She rose and placed the goblet on a table shoved against the back wall. Cloths, bottles, and candles littered the beautifully inlaid surface.

"This is ghastly," I whispered to her. "How did this illness start?"

She poured a stream of water from a pitcher in a porcelain basin.

"He only complained of some fatigue at first." She submerged the cloth in the water. "Then he started to lose weight despite me feeding him enough for two men. The pain followed, growing in his left hip and spreading. I knew what it meant when a mass swelled beneath his skin."

I chilled, knowing the disease she described.

Cancer.

"I've had every surgeon come to look, but it's impossible to remove the malignant tumor. The only option I have is to care for him and ease his discomfort as much as possible."

She gripped the cloth tight and wrung a delicate waterfall into the bowl.

Sigyn returned to his bedside and wiped the sweat from his forehead. He turned his head towards me as she cooled his neck with the damp cloth.

Our eyes met. A faint smile spread on his gray lips.

"Simon, you've come home."

My stomach pitted.

I turned my gaze to Sigyn, not sure what to do.

"It's the opium," she said to me. "It sometimes makes him see things that aren't there."

She looked at her father.

"Simon is away at university, remember?"

She lied, of course, but it was a kindness to a dying man lost in a haze of pain and laudanum. Why remind him of the truth in his final moments?

Confusion filled his face, as if every word falling from her lips was gibberish. Understanding descended over his eyes like a curtain. Disappointment followed.

"I wish your brother were here," he said.

She took his hands in hers and kissed them.

"I know."

He squirmed and tossed beneath his blanket, grunting as another wave of pain overcame him.

"Please," he begged. "The pain. I'll give you anything you want. Make it quit."

She squeezed his hands harder. My insides burned as emotion overcame me. As empathy swelled in my chest.

"There's nothing else I can do, papa. I'm sorry. I'm so sorry. I failed you, as I failed Mother."

Tears ran down her cheeks.

I laid my hand on her shoulder.

"You've not failed," I said.

She shook her head.

"I have! Look at him!"

He pressed his head back into his pillow, stretching and contorting his body while a series of horrific expressions twisted the lines of his face.

I never felt so useless.

I was a god. I could wield fire. Magic flowed in my veins.

But none of it would let me heal him. None of it would let me take away his pain.

However, it would let me make it appear so.

I went to the table covered in bottles and picked up her tincture of opium. I poured the final dose into his claret.

"Give him the rest of the laudanum," I said, handing it out to her. "It will hold him over enough while I make your hemlock draught for him."

Her brow knit together.

"You? No. I don't think...I don't let anyone make his tinctures but me."

Her father cried out again, writhing and thrashing.

"You can't leave his side now," I said. "You said the laudanum only takes the edge off, which is plain to see. That hemlock is what he needs now for any relief. Let me make it for him."

She bit her lip.

"Dammit," she whispered. "You must follow my instructions exactly."

"Of course."

She took the goblet from me and lifted it again to his lips.

"Add one spoonful of hemlock juice, just one, to three spoonfuls of willow bark and three spoonfuls of turmeric. Place them all into a small pot and boil for twenty minutes."

I nodded and sprinted for the door.

"Lukas," she called. "I'm trusting you with this."

I smiled at her, turned out into the dark hallway, and ran down the stairs towards her study.

Midgardians still didn't understand disease. A human in this much pain meant the cancer ate at his bones and organs.

Hemlock would do little for him at this stage.

But I wouldn't let her think she failed her father.

Even if that meant tricking her.

I entered her study and opened the large cabinet. Pungent herbs and spices hit me in the face, forcing me to hold my breath as I rummaged through bottles and jars of cumin, thyme, and cinnamon.

Finally finding willow bark and turmeric, I took them to the battered oak table where the bottle of hemlock juice already waited beside an iron kettle.

Perfect.

Taking a silver spoon, I measured three level spoonfuls of willow bark and turmeric and emptied them into the kettle. A frightful aroma of parsnips and mice seized my windpipe shut as I unstoppered the hemlock juice.

The things I did for this woman.

Lifting it to my gaze, I carefully poured a single spoon and dumped it into the kettle.

Now where to boil this dredge?

The green tiled stove in her study would hardly do. But the massive fireplace in the main sitting room would work marvelously.

Heading down the hall I entered the lavishly furnished room of wainscot chairs, tapestries, and a heavily built desk shoved between two leaded windows.

I walked across a Persian rug towards the raging fire and placed the kettle on an iron rod inside the hearth.

Running my hand through my hair I sat on the richly carved oak settle and rested against the high back. I twisted the fibers of the sheepskin beneath me and watched the flames lick the iron kettle, lost in what I intended next.

The door handle jiggled.

I stood, expecting Sigyn or Silvia.

A man stumbled in, a mop of brown hair curling around his ears. He seemed no more than thirty, with a thin nose and angled features. His clothes were fine, and though he didn't look a thief, his small eyes were those of a liar.

I bristled as realization washed over me who this maggot was.

Simon.

12

PRETTY LIES

He looked at me, and pulled out a bollock dagger. It flashed in the firelight as he approached me and pressed the point directly at my chin. I smiled.

Really?

"Waiting in the shadows to kill me?" he seethed. "Christoph gave me until Tuesday to get the money."

He yelped as I grasped his wrist, forcing his dagger effortlessly out of his hand and to the floor.

Sigyn's fidelity and innate goodness made it impossible for her to cut this leech from her life. But for me? A delightful shiver of anticipation rolled the length of my spine.

"I've been so looking forward to our meeting, Simon."

"Wait, you aren't one of Christoph's men." He tried to pull free. "Who the bloody hell are you?"

His breath stank of ale.

I released him, and I couldn't help a twisted smile from pulling on my lips. The fun we were about to have!

"A friend of your sister," I said. "A very concerned friend."

His anger melted into amusement.

"Ah, so dear Sigyn has taken a lover," he said. "Well, cheers to her for finally breaking a rule for once in her life."

He took a leather flask out of his coat pocket and drank deeply as he dropped into the Dante chair beside the settle. Plopping his heavy boots on a footstool, thick sheets of mud and shit slid off his heels onto the Persian rug.

I crossed my arms and leaned against the mantel, imagining smashing his head into the sharp edge.

I hated him coming back to this house.

"Tell me, have you run out of idiots to recruit for your schemes that you've a sudden need to return?" I asked.

He chuckled and took another swig of ale from his flask.

"I see they've told you of me."

"Yes, you are quite the envy of every family."

He clenched his jaw and dug his fingernails into the oak armrests.

"I'm growing wearisome of you," he growled. "Where is my sister?"

"Why do you care?"

"I'm her brother. It is my duty."

I sneered at that.

"Duty? That's a laugh," I said. "Especially when you leave the burden of your father on her shoulders."

Amusement overtook his features and he scratched the side of his face.

"Dear papa," he said wistfully. "Is he still an overbearing asshole?"

I pushed off the mantel and braced myself against his armrests, leaning into him.

"He's on his deathbed, you ungrateful git."

Fear overtook his smug, horrible little face. He melted into a terrified boy.

"Deathbed?" he echoed. "Sigyn never told me he was ill. But then, I've made myself scarce these last eight months, and...God...I hate this house. Being back here..."

He got up and pushed past me, going straight to a table against the far wall. He trembled as he cracked open a bottle of claret, sending a splash of crimson spilling over his fingers.

"I...I can't see another parent die like that...I can still see my mother's sunken face. Waxed and gaunt. A hollow shell."

He drank from the bottle. My body started to heat and the tips of my fingers tingled.

"Sigyn told him you are at university," I said. "I think it best it stay that way."

He nodded, wiping his mouth on his sleeve.

"Good...good," he whispered. "I can always count on Sigyn to make an excuse for me. She always keeps those nits guessing when they come round trying to find me."

Outrage split open and pulled through my veins and my core. He went too far rejoicing in her risks.

I rushed him, curling my fingers into his coat and jerked him against me. His bottle flung out of his grasp and shattered against the floorboards at our feet.

"Get off!" he cried.

"Yes, Sigyn is awfully good at making excuses for you," I spat. "Your friend Bertolf nearly disfigured her face because of it. She nearly died in a fire he started in your father's print shop."

He shrunk as concern filled his expression. Perhaps he had a heart after all.

"He almost did what?"

I shoved him back hard, sending him crashing against

the wall. He moaned as he slid down and landed on top of a sturdy oak chest.

Perhaps he needed an example.

I pressed my dagger against the side of his nose and pricked the paper-like tissue below his eye. The faintest line of his blood trickled along my blade towards the hilt. He hissed.

"He was going to cut off her nose. He was going to gouge out her eyes. He was going to burn down the shop. Because of you. Because she wouldn't betray you."

He trembled like a wet rat.

I removed my blade. He touched the fine line I slit and paled seeing his own blood covering his fingertips.

He curled his hand into a fist and glared at me.

"Don't put that on me," he seethed. "It's Sigyn's choice to protect me. I don't ask her to. Whether she gets maimed is not my fault."

"Not your fault?" I asked, baffled. "You brought that bastard right to her. She could have died because of you."

The word was bitter on my tongue. Even he shivered from the thought.

Clutching his coat again, I lifted him off the chest and threw him to the rug. He choked and wheezed trying to catch his breath.

His dagger glinted to his right. He stretched for it, grasping the hilt in his sweaty palms.

Naughty boy.

I crunched my boot into his wrist, a lovely crackle filling the night. He ground his teeth, and beautiful beads of sweat glistened on his forehead like morning dew. I gorged on his fear.

"Don't do that," I said. "I rather this not get messier than it has to be."

He winced letting the dagger slip from his fingers.

"If you're worried about Bertolf, Sigyn won't have anymore trouble from him," he gasped. "He's dead. I killed him myself last Saturday. Well, Christoph killed him, but I would have had I gotten the chance."

"You think his death enough for her safety?" I shouted. "You are a fool."

Anger stiffened his flushed face. He grasped the tip of my boot with his free hand, trying to lift me off.

I chuckled. It was adorable, really.

I struck my heel into his wrist, and a satisfying crack rang out. He screamed, and it sent a deep thrill through me to my toes. No one could hear us in this corner of the house, not with Sigyn's father's own screams to disguise his son's.

I smiled wider.

"You broke my wrist!"

I wanted to break so much more, but something stopped me. A voice in my head imploring me to cease. It wasn't mercy for this rat, but for Sigyn. For her trust in me.

Gods. I couldn't believe I was going to do this. I was thoroughly disappointed in myself.

Leniency was not my style.

"You need to leave and never return, or I will make you hurt more than giving you a measly fractured wrist. If you have any love at all in that putrid heart of yours, you will stay out of her life."

His lips quivered as the pain and shock started to work on him.

"You're insane!" he shouted. "I'm not going anywhere."

I shrugged. He didn't know how insane I could get.

I ground my sole into his hand, snapping the fan of delicate bones. One, two, three, four, five! I breathed in the rush of each.

"I'd think very hard if you wish to keep testing me," I said. "Unless you want your arm to match your wrist and hand, you will leave this house."

His breaths were quick and shallow. He narrowed his eyes and tightened his lips. I tutted as I positioned my heel over his forearm, ready to fracture his radius.

"Wait!" he shouted. "I've only returned tonight for the necklace. Give me that, and only then I will go."

"What necklace?"

"My mother's necklace! Sigyn received it after her death. It's exceedingly valuable. Why should she get it simply because she was a daughter? It's only fair to sell the necklace and split the profit between us."

Hatred boiled in my gut for this weasel. I almost broke his arm for the hell of it.

"That necklace means everything to her," I said.

He shook his head and his eyes misted.

"I don't like hurting her. I truly don't. I love Sigyn, but selling the necklace is my only choice to save my neck."

"You will take what she loves most to fix your mistakes?"

"If I don't get the money by Tuesday..." He stopped. "What Bertolf wanted to do to Sigyn was nothing to what Christoph will do to me."

My mouth soured seeing the only choice before me.

At least I tried.

I removed my boot from his broken bones and he grunted. He cradled his bent wrist and twisted fingers.

"Bastard! Look what you've done to me!"

"You have more to worry about than one little hand," I said. "There is only one solution to this problem, and it isn't giving Christoph the money."

His brow twisted with confusion.

"What do you mean?"

I walked to the door.

"As I've already said, you need to go away."

It sounded more eloquent this way.

"Away? Like flee to Italy?"

I smiled.

"Something like that."

Grasping the brass handle, I closed the door.

He nodded.

"Perhaps you're right."

A smile tugged at his lips, as if already thinking of sun soaked terracotta tiles and fresh burrata cheese.

"No, you are right," he said. "Papa's death changes everything. I have possibility now. I can disappear. I can purchase a villa in Naples with my inheritance. Sigyn might protest when I sell the printing press, but it's for the best to break free from this godforsaken city."

He would even take that from her.

Resolve beat in every strike of my heart.

I locked the door.

"Then, I can finally and properly care for Sigyn as I always should have. I will become the man she believes I am. We can start over, her and I."

Maybe he meant it.

Maybe he could start over.

But this was about her.

I rested my hand on his shoulder. He looked up at me, and I hated how he and Sigyn shared the same eyes.

"A pretty thought," I said. "But that's all it will ever be."

Confusion stiffened his face.

Stepping behind him, I locked his neck in the crook of my elbow and squeezed. He wheezed as he dug his fingers into my arm, clawing, thrashing, fighting for his life as I squeezed tighter.

"Let me...go!" he rasped.

I covered his mouth with my other hand and pinched his nose shut. Simon's pulse thundered in his neck as he strained to suck in any infinitesimal breath between my fingers.

I crushed my hand harder against his lips.

"I know she loves you. I know she believes in you," I whispered in his ear as he continued to struggle. "But I can't let you destroy her."

He tugged at my arms until he weakened. He lost his footing. We dropped to the floor and I cradled him in my arms, keeping my clasp tight over his nose and mouth.

His pulse slowed. Shades of blue tinted his face.

"Shhh," I breathed. "It won't be long now."

His brown eyes, Sigyn's brown eyes, turned glassy.

If she ever discovered what I did...

His body loosened. His arms fell slack at his sides.

His heart stopped beating.

It was done.

And she was safe.

* * *

CLUTCHING a glass vessel filled with the finished hemlock draught, I returned to her father's room.

His cries filled my ears as he twisted and thrashed in his bed. Sigyn paced across the bright rugs, gripping her right elbow tight against her chest as she chewed her fingernails.

"I have it," I said.

She met my gaze, and relief dissolved the anxiety in her irises.

"Thank God," she said, snatching the vessel from me. "What's taken you so long?"

I scratched the back of my ear. I hoped she didn't notice the mud on my boots.

"I had to stoke the fire," I lied. "Damn scullery maid let it dwindle to its final embers."

She gave an exasperated sigh and walked to the cluttered table, clearing a space. Her hands trembled as she tried to pour a spoonful of the draught, sending drops scattering over the wood in beads.

It hurt seeing her so distressed.

I reached out and held the bottom of the vessel, helping steady her hand.

"Sorry for snapping. I'm...I'm so afraid," she whispered, her voice cracking.

"You won't go through this alone," I said.

For a heartbeat, a quivering smile stretched across her lips before sinking back into a worried frown.

She poured the draught into a goblet of claret and stirred the mixture well as she went to her father.

"This will ease the pain, Papa," she said.

Sigyn lifted it to his lips, which were white and cadaverous now, and tilted the goblet to him. He sipped slowly as streams of crimson flowed down his wrinkles and chin, soaking into his pillow.

He finished, and the liquid gurgled in the base of his throat as he took in labored and shivery breaths.

She clapped her hand over her mouth and turned to me.

"It will ease the pain, won't it?"

Suffering hardened every line of his face as he gripped his sheets, twisting his fingers into the linen.

It would do nothing.

"It will," I lied again.

But was it truly a lie if the draught appeared to work to her?

I couldn't have her notice what came next.

I handed her a wax sealed letter.

"A messenger came with this for you," I said.

Her brow knit with curiosity.

"At this hour?"

"Apparently it's quite urgent. I think you best read it."

She took it from me and cracked the seal, opening the letter.

Her curiosity faded into shock.

"It's from Simon," she said. "I've not heard a word from him for near nine months."

Her eyes darted from left to right across the parchment, reading what she saw as her brother's hand, and not really my own. A simple charm, but effective.

"What does he say?" I asked, as I sat in the chair beside her father.

I needed her eyes to remain on the letter. I couldn't risk them wandering for this.

"He's joined the French army as a mercenary," she said.

I took her father's hand in my own. The delicate bones flexed beneath my touch as he writhed and moaned.

In my mind, I started to paint a portrait of him. The strained muscles of his face relaxed. The pain in his gaze melted into peace.

"He's fighting against the Habsburgs in Italy."

"Really?" I replied. "Tell me more of what he says."

I envisioned her Father's every line, his every wrinkle and breath calming.

Her words now floated somewhere in the distance as I concentrated harder on sharpening the picture of him I wished. Every detail a brush stroke.

I took in a breath, and pushed it out of my palm, dousing her father in the image I painted. In the illusion I crafted.

It flickered over him, of a man tranquil and serene.

It stopped.

Damn.

Casting illusions over other people was a challenge in the best of circumstances, but this one would take all my skill as he fought against me.

"He said when he learned of what Bertolf had attempted, he couldn't continue placing me in danger. He decided this was best for both of us."

And when she inevitably would never hear from him again, she could tell her friends he had died honorably in battle in the Italian countryside.

"I told you," she continued. "Good is always worth fighting for."

My throat dried, knowing the truth. That as we spoke, eels happily feasted on Simon's fingers and toes as he floated down the Rhine.

Her father moaned again.

I focused harder on the rigid muscles of his arms and legs loosening.

On his lips curling into a soft smile awaiting heaven.

I forced the image stronger onto him, bathing him in what Sigyn wished most to see. I shook.

A quiet face fluttered over one of agony. A man content in death, a good death with no pain, sparked and sputtered over a man in torment.

My heart raced.

Her father's cries hushed into silence as my illusion finally held.

But I shivered hearing him continue to scream beneath the image. That didn't matter, though. All that mattered was Sigyn couldn't hear his screams.

Couldn't see his pain.

"Sigyn," I said, "Look. It worked, as I said it would."

She gazed over her letter at her father, a gentle smile pulling on his lips. His eyes contained no hint of discomfort.

The letter fell from her fingers as she rushed over and kneeled at his side. Her eyes rimmed in red.

"Thank you, Sigyn. You've given me peace in my final minutes," he said.

She smiled through her sadness, combing her trembling fingers through his hair.

"I'd do anything for you," she whispered.

He took her hand, and she brought it to her lips and kissed it.

But really, he writhed beneath my illusion as she kissed him.

"I will tell your mama how clever you've grown. How strong you've become. I am proud of you."

Tears streamed down her face at his beautiful words.

At *my* beautiful words.

"I love you, papa."

He let out another loud wail.

She only heard a sigh.

"And I you."

His eyes closed, and his chest fell as it released his final breath.

His final scream.

13

THE COMING STORM

The funeral was bleak as all funerals are.

Incense spiraled within the colored light of the stained glass windows, and music, rich, dark music, of the Requiem mass filled our ears. As they lowered her father's body beneath the church floor into the crypts, I embraced Sigyn, letting her violent tears soak into my doublet.

I couldn't help the bite in the back of my throat.

While she suffered from the grief of losing her father, I grieved from being reminded of the frailty of human life. At the frailty of *her* life.

I'd feared for her when she rushed into her burning print shop. When Simon and his goons threatened her body. But this...This made it too real.

I couldn't accept the idea of losing her, of her element rushing back into the ocean of the universe. Forgotten.

The inevitability of it all sickened me to my depths.

Why did she have to be human?

I decided not to think about it.

I tried not to think about it.

And when we finally left the church beneath the weighted tones of funeral bells, I held her tight to my chest as my gaze found two black ravens watching us from a chestnut tree.

Odin's patience was wearing thin.

And my head throbbed.

I knew I should return to him, return to Asgard and end this threat that continued to pound in my brain, but I still couldn't leave her.

Not now.

Not yet.

* * *

THE FIRE SNAPPED and popped in the fireplace as we sat in the sitting room, a new routine the past week since the burial.

I read through Sigyn's favorite anatomy book, enjoying the beautifully grotesque engravings of the vessels and chambers of the human heart. The details and angles captured in the ink strokes impressed me, as in ages past such renderings appeared more like blobs than organs.

However, I had to stifle a snicker when I turned to a page discussing humorism and the correct proportions of yellow and black bile. I guess humans still had ways to go in their understanding of basic concepts, the poor darlings.

Closing the book I tossed it on the Dante chair and got up from the settle and stretched my back.

Sigyn sat hunched over the massive desk squeezed between the two leaded glass windows, writing furiously in a thick leather book. She had released her hair from her snood, and now it fell between her shoulder blades freely, capturing the warmth of the fire in the honeyed strands.

A need to run my fingers through her soft spirals woke in me...

Curling them shut, I walked towards her across the patchwork of Persian rugs where I'd killed Simon. I tried to ignore the rosemary and saffron filling my lungs as I leaned over her shoulder to see what engrossed her so fully.

Her eyes roved the ledger filled with numbers and figures in neat little lines. She bit the end of her quill lost in concentration.

"What are you doing?" I asked, surprised how my blood raced.

"The books for the shop. I need to ensure all monies are accounted for."

She scratched another series of numbers onto the page. Humans really liked making themselves miserable.

"How frightfully dull," I said. "All that calculating would put me out cold."

"Excuse me, it's the farthest thing from dull," she replied. "Nothing gives me a greater thrill than when all the numbers at the end of the ledger equal zero. The satisfaction!"

Raising my eyebrows, I laughed loudly.

"You really should get out more if you consider that a thrill."

She chuckled as she put her quill on the desk and leaned back in her chair. Another wave of rosemary rose into my nose.

"Father loved doing the books. He was so meticulous. Nothing was unaccounted for, even down to the last rappen," she said. "It's shocking how fast life speeds past us. I can still see him at this desk, and now..."

Her words cracked.

"I miss him."

I didn't like the pain in her voice. I hated it and wanted to make it go away.

My heart raced as I slowly, ever so slowly, reached out my hand to her and let it hover over her shoulder. Holding my breath, I allowed myself to touch her. To comfort her.

"It will get easier," I said.

"I know."

Without thought, I stroked her shoulder, making small circles on her skin with my thumb. Her hair softly tickled my fingers, and a flush of heat seared every vertebrae of my spine.

My lips tingled, remembering our almost kiss.

She turned her head, her eyes falling where I touched her.

I stopped.

What's wrong with you? This isn't the time.

I withdrew my hand letting it fall to my side, yet fire continued to char my veins.

"Sorry," I blurted.

Going to the window I opened it, pulling the chilled night air deep into my lungs to obliterate the rosemary from my nostrils. I rubbed my mouth forcefully, trying to remove the desire still prickling my lips.

Lightning flared within the dark florets of storm clouds, washing the sky and city streets below in white. Thunder rumbled in the distance.

Chair legs scraped against wooden floorboards as Sigyn rose to her feet. She came beside me and leaned against the window frame.

"Is everything all right?" she asked.

I cleared my throat.

"Quite," I said. "I needed some air, is all."

She nodded.

"It did seem to get suddenly stuffy in here."

Sigyn gripped her skirts and twisted the fabric in her fingers.

"Are *you* all right?" I asked.

My chest constricted with a thousand reasons she should be so anxious.

"There's...there's something I feel compelled to tell you," she said.

Obviously that I overstepped touching her shoulder as I did.

"I apologize for forgetting myself—"

"I want to thank you," she said, with a smile. "You might annoy me at times, but beneath your constant quips and fervor, you are a good man. Truly."

I chuckled darkly at such a strange thought. Me? A good man? If only she knew the truth.

"You will make me blush," I jested, rubbing behind my ear.

Her gaze deepened with sincerity.

"It's been a great relief having you here through these hardships. Everything you've done for me...I can never repay you."

A small flame of fidelity ignited in her chest, its warmth beating against my chest in a gentle pulse, making the distance between us feel like a great ocean.

"I do it only for your happiness," I whispered.

Silence surrounded us, except for a roll of thunder clattering the tile shingles. I could smell rain in the breeze now.

"You were right about me, you know," she said.

A gust of wind blew streams of her ginger hair across her nose and lips. I feared shattering into a million pieces.

"What do you mean?"

She passed her fingers back and forth over the top of her

bodice, her nails grazing her breasts. I was grateful for the cool air coming through the open window, as another flush of heat tore through me.

"Remember the fire?" she asked.

How could I forget? I almost lost her that day. I shivered, forcing that thought away.

"Of course," I pushed out.

"You told me how I liked going it alone after I refused your help to rebuild. It infuriated me, because it was the truth. You really do have an irritating knack for always exposing the truth behind the pretenses."

She crossed her arms and looked out the window. Lightning cast the city in crackling flickers of white. It flashed off the hilt of the dagger I gave her. She always kept it by her side. It made me happy, like a piece of me was with her always.

"I took pride in doing everything myself," she continued. "I wanted to prove to the world I was strong and capable. I didn't need anyone, and so pushed everyone away until I was alone."

"You made that very clear to me on more than one occasion," I said.

She smiled and stepped towards me. My breaths tightened.

"The fact is, I was afraid."

"Of what?"

She laid her hand on my chest, trailing her finger along the stitches of my velvet doublet. She might have well flung me onto a pyre.

"Being hurt," she whispered. "Relying only on myself was the only way to shield my heart."

I swallowed.

I knew the fear she spoke of. After Odin had crushed my

heart, it was far easier to hide behind my scorn and indifference than face the reality.

She cupped my cheek.

"I don't feel that fear with you," she said. "Somehow you disarm me, and I don't want to be anywhere else but by your side."

I lifted my hand on top of hers

"Then don't go anywhere else."

I sank my fingers into her thick hair.

I moved closer to her lips.

Her mouth parted.

My blood thrashed in my ears.

And our lips met in a torrential kiss.

Lightning split the night, throwing us in and out of silvers and blues.

Our tongues wove together, sending a shock of heat flooding my entire body. Thunder rocked overhead, and rain bounced off the windowsill, pelting us.

I believed myself burning.

Everything Sigyn was lived within our kiss, and she threatened to engulf me whole. My blood sang with the hope sparking through her veins. My soul shook as her constancy scorched my flesh.

The overwhelming beauty of her made me think I would lose my wits as we deepened our kiss.

I tasted fidelity on her lips.

I tasted salvation.

And I needed her love as one needed breath.

Remember the price of falling in love with a human, Loki. You will lose her.

She pulled back, her cheeks crimson and eyes black. She tore at my laces, pulling me out of my doublet. All thought but one vanished from my mind as she tugged at my shirt and I yanked at the dozens of knots and cords of her gown and kirtle.

"How many damn layers must I rip through?" I asked, trying to liberate her breasts.

She laughed, slipping out of her smock as a flash of white illuminated her finally bare flesh. Any further words I had died in my mouth.

Damn she was beautiful.

Thunder quaked the floorboards, shaking into the soles of my feet. I ran my hand along the curve of her naked back and I drew her to me. I slipped my fingers over the rain covering her skin, and I groaned as her breasts pressed against my chest.

Lowering my lips to the crook of her neck, I tasted the raindrops on the pulse of her throat.

I loved how she quivered with every open mouthed kiss I scorched into her. But we were just starting.

And I had a reputation to uphold.

Gripping into her damp skin, I lifted her and plunked her on the desk sending pots of ink flying and books crashing to the floor.

She braced herself, clutching her fingers on the rounded edges of the desk. Wind blew her hair wild about her forehead and cheeks as lightning lit her eyes and lips in a flickering blaze. My pulse raced at the absolute chaos of it all.

"What are you waiting for?" she breathed.

Leaning into her, thunder roared again as I grazed my mouth over her collarbone and along her shoulder.

"Has no one ever told you that patience is a virtue?"

She trembled beneath my lips as I engulfed her nipples, savoring the swell of her breasts.

Savoring the salt on her skin.

Still, I went lower...

"I'm not the patient kind," she rasped.

She moaned as I worked my way slowly down her stomach. She whimpered as I thoroughly explored every dip and curve of her heated skin. She bucked and twisted as I kissed her hips, her thighs, her calves.

...Until I knelt before her.

"Really?" I asked, my breath curling over her kneecaps. "Then let me correct my grievous error."

Placing a hand on each of her knees, I spread her legs and gave her a little devilish smile before burying my head between her inner thighs.

She gasped for air when I closed my mouth around her, loving her utterly and completely.

She rocked against me as I kissed, consumed, and revered her. With my entire being I venerated her for the goddess she should have been.

If only...

Thunder shook the room, drowning out her screams as her release quaked through her.

I had many talents, but giving pleasure was the one at which I excelled.

Sigyn seemed to agree as she bent forward and pulled me up between her legs. Her eyes were even darker now, and my own need twisted deep in me for her.

She caught my lips, urgency and hunger filling our every kiss as we moved in a frenzy towards the oak settle, knocking over a side table and shattering a vase in our wake.

She pushed me down onto the thick sheepskin and straddled me with a coy smile of her own that made me shiver myself.

This woman was truly magnificent!

"Are you ready?" she asked, her breaths ragged.

The heat from the fire dried the rain from her back as she gripped into my shoulders. I throbbed against her.

"Always."

I skated my open palms over her breasts, over her waist, branding every inch of her into my memory as she slid hot and slick down onto me. Digging her fingers into the flexing muscles of my back, she hissed as I stretched and filled her.

Her eyes rolled back into her head as I gripped her hips and moved within her heat. Her breaths deepened as I kept the pace agonizingly tender, holding her tight, never wanting to let her go.

Not wanting to believe that she was but a heartbeat in the vast universe. A spark that would extinguish.

But right now, as I loved her, she existed eternally, and she was mine.

To hell with the price.

Sheets of white doused us as she bucked her hips faster against mine, taking more of me into her, surrounding me in her softness. Pleasure coiled in my depths, nearly sending me to the edge.

Another roll of thunder vibrated through us as our pace quickened into a frantic need. Sweat rolled down our chests, and I tore at the seams as she rode me, coiling the heat in me tighter and tighter.

We careened towards the end, lost in a fog of ecstasy and racing hearts.

She scratched her nails into my shoulders as she cried out in release as my own roared through me.

In that slice of bliss, time stopped. Ceased. She was immortal, and I her willing slave.

I wrapped my arms tight around her, wanting to feel her every spent breath rise and fall. She kissed me gently.

We dropped to the warm Persian rug in front of the fire.

Laying her head on my shoulder, she ran her fingers languidly through my hair.

"Don't ever leave me," she whispered.

"I won't."

I pulled her tighter against me, hating the bitter truth of my words.

It is you who will leave me.

14

BITTER MEDICINE

Sigyn slept on my chest, her hair fanning over my right shoulder as we laid on the Persian rug beside the crackling fire. I skated my fingers over her upper arm, drawing languid circles as I refused sleep to take me. I didn't want to miss a single heartbeat with her huddled in my arms.

Especially as the storm outside strengthened in ferocity.

Lightning doused us in sheets of garish white.

My skin prickled as a violent and sharp crack exploded within the sky. I gripped her tighter against me as every stone and timber in the city rattled.

This was no Midgardian thunder.

This was an entrance, and only one god would ever be so *subtle*.

At least Thor was incredibly hopeless with directions, and cities only confused him further.

I forced my heart to calm. Yes. There was a better chance of him ending up across the border in France than ever finding me within Basel's twisting streets.

Bang! Bang! Bang!

Of course he'd get it right this time.

Annoyance flared in me hotter than the lightning blazing outside as Thor continued to pound at the door downstairs.

I nestled my face in Sigyn's hair, breathing in her scent of rosemary, determined to go nowhere. I closed my eyes.

Bang! Bang! Bang!

I ground my teeth.

"Loki! I know you're in there!" Thor shouted. "Open up before I break down the door. Nothing would delight me more than wringing that scrawny neck of yours."

Sigyn stirred, mumbling beneath her breath still in sleep. Now this I couldn't allow.

I couldn't have her wake and be forced to explain to her why the literal god of thunder was splitting through her door. It would make for a horribly awkward conversation.

Slipping from beneath her, I pulled the sheepskin from the settle and laid it over her shoulders and legs. The fact I had to resort to a pelt covering her naked body instead of myself was abhorrent.

I would seriously tear out Thor's throat for this.

Grabbing my shirt, I ran down the stairs to shut him up before he woke the entire damned city.

Wrenching open the door my heart pounded as Thor *and* Tyr stood in the pouring rain, their beards and trousers soaked through.

Now it made sense. I knew Thor couldn't have found his way here without help.

"I'm afraid I'm terribly busy." I crossed my arms and leaned against the doorframe. "Maybe you could come back, oh, I don't know, never?"

Thor set his jaw as he and Tyr shoved past me and entered the foyer. Streams of water slid off their cloaks, and mud squelched beneath their boots as they tracked it over the stone floor.

"Yes, by all means, please make yourselves at home. It's not like it's the dead of night or anything."

Tyr rolled his eyes, flinging his cloak over the banister. He glanced around and gave a hard, judgmental sniff.

"So, this is where you've been this whole time?" He fingered the corner of a tapestry. "Rather domestic for you. You've called places far nicer than this a 'shit hole'."

Keep your cool.

"It's so nice the two of you dropping by," I said. "You're always a delight."

Thor pressed Mjolnir against my chest.

"This isn't a social visit," Thor growled.

"Damn, and I had a cake prepared."

Thor's gaze brightened with a need to crush my skull. Envisioning my murder always brought out the color of his eyes.

"Listen you..."

His voice quaked the plaster and even shook the timber. I couldn't have our voices carry up the stairs to Sigyn.

I put out my hand to him, interrupting his huff.

"Actually, if you don't mind, I rather we do this in the kitchen. You always make such a racket."

Thor's skin achieved an even deeper shade of red, but Tyr nodded. Thor grumbled as he removed Mjolnir, and I breathed a sigh of relief.

I led them to the kitchen and latched the door shut behind us.

Wood smoke and animal fat saturated the room, and the final smoldering embers glowed orange in the fireplace beneath a giant iron cauldron. At least tucked away in this part of the house no one could hear us.

A basket filled with yellow and red spotted apples stood on a sturdy oak table in the center of the kitchen. My mouth watered as I picked through them until I found the firmest. Lovemaking always left me famished.

Spinning around, I sprung my backside onto the table and sat beside the basket, letting my feet dangle.

The annoyance on Thor and Tyr's faces gave me great satisfaction.

Tyr cleared his throat, running his only hand through his blonde hair.

"We need to talk—"

"Let me guess," I interrupted. "You are about to tell me how Odin wishes me to return to Asgard. How he has sent you two to fetch me and bring me back kicking and screaming. Correct?"

I cleaned my apple on my shirt as several expressions swam across their faces.

"Odin has been more than generous in accepting this defiance of yours," Tyr said. "He's...concerned."

I nodded as I bit into the firm fruit, my tongue prickling from its acidic sweetness.

"How benevolent of him," I pushed out through a mouthful of apple. "But, I'm afraid it's quite impossible for me to return just yet. I'm needed here a bit longer than I initially thought."

Annoyance melted into amusement as laughter rumbled from their guts.

I dug my nails into the wood grain of the table.

"What possible need have you to remain in Midgard?" Thor wiped a tear from his eye.

"You wouldn't understand," I said.

Tyr walked to me until my knees almost touched the tops of his muscular legs. I could smell the Asgardian forest and salt on his tunic and furs. Home.

"I'm sure I wouldn't, because there is no reason to act as you are," Tyr said, looming over me.

"And how is that?" I asked. "Reckless? Insolent? How kind of you to notice."

I took another bite of apple, holding his gaze. He ripped it from my grasp and threw it into the fire.

"That was rather uncalled for."

"Do I have to remind you of the oath you swore to Odin?" he asked. "He is who needs you."

I was sure he did.

"I am quite conscious of my oaths. You don't have to remind me," I spat. "But an oath doesn't require I be chained at Odin's hip. Trust me, he quite enjoys the chase."

I pushed him back, hating how his solid build made it like pushing a boulder out of my way. I slid off the table and walked away from him.

"Odin wants you to know he isn't angry with you." Thor started in on me now.

"Just disappointed?" I finished. "Please. I've heard it all before. Odin's silver tongue is only second to my own."

Thor sighed, scratching his heavy beard.

"He understands you need your time away. You've had your fun with your whore, but now it's time to come home."

I bristled as anger swept through me.

"It's funny he's sent you both to collect me and not come himself." I dripped with scorn. "As he's so concerned..."

"You know the weight on his shoulders."

A shock of pain, of that maddening warning, sparked in my head.

"Yes, I'm well aware of the weight you all seem to suffer." I rubbed my temples, easing the sharp coil of pain.

"Loki..."

"He never liked getting his hands dirty," I said, spite drenching my every word. "Much rather have other people do it for him."

Thor waved me away and picked up a porcelain pitcher from the mantel. It looked ridiculous in his thick fingers as he eyed the vessel upside down and sideways. I wouldn't let the buffoon break Sigyn's possessions.

Rushing to him I snatched it out of his hands and placed it back over the mantel with care. It was then I noticed my fingers shaking.

"Don't touch what doesn't belong to you," I snapped.

Surprise lit Thor's face.

"What's gotten into you?" he asked. "It's not like you to be so preoccupied with humans. I thought they didn't interest you?"

I forced a smile, trying to calm myself.

"I'm able to change my mind, aren't I?" I asked. "And she isn't a whore. She's..."

My words left me, and my silence said everything.

Their lips straightened and a grim look tightened their features.

"She's what?" Tyr asked, danger in his voice.

"Nothing."

His brow shot up.

"That's the weakest lie you've ever told," he said. "I see it in your eyes."

"And what do you see?"

Pity softened the lines of his face and he put his hand on my shoulder.

"Gods cannot love what will last mere seconds to us.

Humans are as a rose, decaying from their first bloom. This woman will die."

The fear I forced deep down inside of me spewed out. A terrifying chill trickled the length of my back.

I shook his hand off me.

"How poetic, but you won't sway me."

"She will die an old crone before you even finish a blink," Thor added.

Did they have to keep saying it?

"You think I don't know this?" I said. "This is why I must stay in Midgard. She is too fragile. I...I have to ensure nothing happens to her."

I scrubbed my face with my hand, lost in grief and desperation. In truth. In inevitability.

I would lose her.

Porcelain shattered against the stone floor. I shot my gaze to Tyr, who stood over the broken pitcher I had returned to the mantel.

"A human is no different." He crushed the pieces beneath his boot with each step he took towards me. "She will shatter into a thousand shards and you won't be able to piece her back together. A mortal's fate is inescapable and staying here will make no difference."

I stared at the sharp slivers.

He was right. Staying here would make no difference.

How didn't I see it before? It was so simple.

I smiled.

If the issue was her being a mortal, then I'd just have to make her an *immortal*.

Unlike the rest of the fated Midgardians, Sigyn contained an element within her. That made her singular. That made a solution to a problem.

Once we too were beings with untamed elements in us

like hers, until Odin plucked us out of mortality and transformed us into gods. She could be metamorphosed into a goddess the same way. Easy peasy.

I tapped my finger against my lips. Only one hiccup stood in my way.

I didn't have a bloody clue how to do it.

But Odin did.

I doubted the idea would thrill him, but I knew his lust for collecting all the elements of the universe like some divine china set. He would not turn away such a perfect specimen of fidelity. His greed would be her salvation.

I met Tyr's gaze.

"All right, you've changed my mind," I said.

Tyr's brow twisted with shock and confusion.

"Really?"

Thor clapped and rubbed his hands together, a great oafish smile spreading across his lips.

"Don't question him, Tyr. Best we get a move on before he flips again," he said. "I was giving him two more minutes before I broke his legs and dragged him back. This way I don't have to listen to him moan the entire journey home."

My stomach churned at the thought.

"Yes, let's quit wasting time," I said. "You've reminded me just how much I miss Asgard. I haven't been decently drunk the entire time I've been here. Midgardian ale is horrid, watery stuff."

Tyr's mouth fell open, but he shook his bewilderment away.

We grabbed our cloaks, and I couldn't help but throw a final glance up the stairs where Sigyn still slept thinking me beside her.

Part of me knew there was a risk in returning to Odin,

but what choice did I have? Besides, nothing they could do would keep me from returning to her.

That's what I told myself as I left with Tyr and Thor back out into the driving rain.

That's what I told myself as Odin's ravens followed us, their caws resounding through the night like laughter.

15

A LINE IN THE SAND

Asgard

S alt filled my every breath and the ocean mist clung to my skin as I watched Odin throw stones into the breaking waves. Pinks and blues softened the night sky as dawn approached, and I could just make out the pines on the surrounding cliff tops.

Memories rushed over me as the waves beat against the rocky coast.

My stomach tightened.

He would choose here.

Bastard.

I couldn't recall how many hours we'd spent over the millennia talking deep into the night, casting pebbles into the ocean as he did now. What hit me harder were all the times we didn't speak at all. I could still feel the heat of his breath, and smell the sage and clove on his skin...

I wiped my face with my hand, wanting to remove any trace of him. Of our past.

Water rippled and clacked through the smooth stones as

another wave crashed against the shore. Surf foamed around Odin's leather boots. He picked up another rock and tossed it into the churning sea.

Best get this over with.

I walked to him and my heels sank into the gray pebbles. I hated how familiar it all remained to me. Like I'd been here only yesterday, even though it had been far, far longer.

I cleared the dryness from my throat.

"It's been ages since we both stood here together," I said. "Are you trying to awaken sentiment in me?"

He didn't answer.

Wind raced through his russet hair and flapped his blue tunic around his broad shoulders and trim waist. He hurled an oval rock at a small boulder standing beyond the breaking waves.

He missed it by a good six feet.

"I see your aim is still dreadful."

He picked up two more stones and spun them in his palm as he stared out at the Asgardian sea.

"I had hoped respect for our friendship would have been enough to bring you back to me," he said.

He threw one of the rocks, this time missing the boulder by only three feet.

I moved closer until I stood right beside him, killing the urge to pick up a pebble and join him like the old days. He kept his gaze firmly on the horizon. Or I guessed he did, I only saw his eyepatch covering his right eye.

"You have my respect," I said. "I have returned to you as you wished."

He chuckled darkly.

"You always did think you could lie to me, Loki."

I crossed my arms. I didn't have the energy for his games.

"If you have something to accuse me of, then come out with it."

The lines of his face tightened and the corner of his lips drew into a frown. He angrily flung the final stone into the black roiling ocean.

"I told you to stay away from that girl," he snapped. "But you always love to disobey me."

I admit, it was vastly entertaining. I particularly enjoyed his annoyance when he found me out. It always brought a pretty color to his cheeks.

As it did now, but I knew better than to tell him that. I might be rash, but I wasn't an idiot.

"Then why are you acting so shocked? I warned you long ago not to command me."

He finally turned to me and met my gaze, his only crystal blue eye searching me. His displeasure thawed into a frosty sorrow.

"I only wish for once you would understand. The position you've put me in with this thoughtless impulsiveness of yours. Put us all in..."

My head started to throb at the base of my skull, and I tried to ignore that always accompanying shudder of danger.

"And what position is that?"

His lips flattened.

Of course. What else did I expect from him but silence?

I pressed the ridge of my brow above my nose trying to dull the sheets of white pain. He stepped closer to me, unease etching his face.

"Are you still having headaches?" he asked.

I forced a smile.

"No, I've never been better. Don't I look a picture of health?"

His eye narrowed.

"You need to stop meddling with this woman," he warned.

Did I?

I dropped my hand to my side, curling my fingers into a fist and glared at him.

"I can't."

"You mean you won't."

He got me there.

"I refuse to let her die, Odin."

He nodded stiffly as he bent over and picked up a gray stone. He rubbed his thumb over the polished surface.

"And so you've come to me," he said.

"Well, yes."

He threw it, watching as it hurdled in a fantastic arc towards the frothing waves.

"Say it, Loki," he hissed. "Say what you've come here to ask me. The true reason you've returned at all."

I think this was a dare, and I never passed up a dare.

"How did you make me a god?" I asked. "How...How does it work?"

"You play with fire."

"Stop evading and tell me how, or I swear, I will leave and never return to you."

I loved the flicker of fear I lit behind his eye, though indignation took it over.

"You so desperately want to make so much of this girl," he said. "Her existence is a mistake. Humans are not meant to hold elements within them. Let this dream of yours die."

Shock flooded me, surging with anger through my veins.

"A mistake?" I repeated. "You, yourself said her fidelity was like catching a butterfly in winter."

He scoffed, staring back out across the sea and ran his fingers through his short beard.

"I'm done talking," he said.

The hell he was.

I marched into the surf and stood right before him, forcing him to meet my gaze.

"And I'm done with your continual avoidance," I said. "You only grew upset about her once you learned her name. What is Sigyn to you? What aren't you telling me?"

Silence pressed down on us making my headache pulse deeper into my brain.

He sighed, and pity softened him as he looked into my eyes. I hated I couldn't tell if his pity were genuine or not.

"If you would do what you wanted, you would give her a death sentence."

My throat tightened.

I searched for any spark, any glint, of chaos in his chest to prove his lie. It had to be a lie.

I found nothing.

But then, he was always impenetrable to my sight.

Did I have to resort to trusting him? The man no one could trust?

"Explain."

He crouched on the shore, the stones scuttling beneath his boots as he looked out over their expanse. His eye deepened with thought, with mystery and with knowledge.

"The universe is a collection of elements, of energies, much like this shore is a collection of rocks and pebbles," he said. "Certain beings are gifted with these concentrated forces within them, such as yours of chaos, Thor's of thunder and strength, and Freya's of beauty and fertility."

He ran his fingers over the top of the stones, smiling as if enjoying some secret only he knew. Only he could understand.

"Let's move this lesson along."

"Even though an element lives within Sigyn, she is not a strong being like Jotnar or Aesir. She is a Midgardian. Human. Weak."

He dove his hand beneath the rocks and grabbed a fist of sand. He let the granules slip out his curled fingers in a stream.

"She would never survive the transformation into a goddess," he continued. "We are rock, and she is sand. That is why she is a mistake. Her energy is trapped and destined to disperse back into the universe, as this sand will be washed back into the sea."

How did he speak these things so easily? So indifferently?

"I don't believe you," I said, though I trembled from his words.

His eye cleared as he returned from drifting I knew not where.

He rose to his feet and faced me.

"This is ancient power we are speaking of," he said. "It could kill her."

Hope sprang in my soul.

"*Could*," I said. "A possibility is not a certainty."

He shook his head.

"But it remains a risk," he said. "Don't let your cleverness with words blind you to the truth. You would damn her to a death of agony and torment. You would lose her by trying to save her."

Dread bit the back of my throat as the truth washed over me.

"Surely there is a way…That can't be it…"

But it was.

Sadness deepened the creases of his brow, as if my pain was his pain.

He leaned in and caught my face between his hands and stroked my cheeks with his thumbs. Sage and clove flooded my nostrils as he leaned his forehead against my own.

"Are you so unhappy?" he asked. "Do you really not love me anymore?"

A single drop of his ambition rushed cold through my arteries, pulling and tugging me down into his depths. I wanted to lose myself in the darkness, in his unslakable hunger for more. Always more.

I gripped his upper arms and squeezed into his firm muscle.

"I will always love you," I whispered, letting my lips graze his cheek. "But I am returning to Sigyn. If she must live a short life, I will not miss a single heartbeat of it."

I pushed away from him and stepped back, letting the sea breeze flutter between us. Sorrow creased his beautiful face, grinding my heart raw.

I turned and walked away, leaving him again on the shore where I had once left him long ago.

"I suppose I cannot compete with such a pure creature as Sigyn," he mocked.

"Don't waste your breath on melodramatics," I said, refusing to look back. "It doesn't suit you."

He let out a cold laugh.

"I think you are denying the facts of this little infatuation of yours."

I stopped. Clenching my jaw, I turned and met his gaze.

"Am I?"

He approached me, my every muscle stiffening the closer he got.

"Every element has a complimentary force. Such as you and I. Your potential allows my ambition to realize heights otherwise impossible. Together we take kingdoms and conquer entire worlds."

I rolled my eyes and started off again.

"I'm well aware."

He grabbed my wrist, tugging me back.

"I don't think you are," he said, tightening his grip on me. "Otherwise you'd know chaos and fidelity are incompatible. At odds. You will destroy one another."

Cold rolled down my spine, bitter and raw. It was perplexing to be attracted to an energy that was steadfast, when mine was anything but. However, this was madness.

Wasn't it?

"I think your jealousy is showing." I wrenched free of him.

Earnestness hardened him.

"You know I'm right," he said. "You will raze her hope. You will shatter her loyalty. You will betray her constancy and hurt her again and again when you inevitably fall short of the mark."

I scoffed.

"This is utterly ridiculous. How can I hurt her when I only have her best interests at heart?"

A devious smile tugged at his lips.

"I wonder if she would feel the same if she ever found out you killed her brother?"

A threat hid behind his words, each striking me in the chest.

"How do you know about that?" I growled.

He chuckled.

"It's your fault you always underestimated Hugin and

Munin. The tales they told of your misadventures. I must commend you on creating a superb drama."

Damn his ravens. If I ever got my hands on them, I would impale them both on a spit and roast them for supper.

I wiped the sweat from my brow.

"Are you resorting to coercion to make me not return to her? I never pegged you as the blackmail type."

"No, I want you to come to the right conclusion yourself. Blackmail is only a patch to a problem, but a decision is permanent."

It was my turn to laugh now.

"Good luck there."

He stared at me like I were the grandest fool he'd ever witnessed. For two seconds I considered punching him in the face, but it wasn't worth bloodying my rings.

"She wants faithfulness and truth," he continued. "You broke into her world and only wreaked havoc."

"I protected her."

"You've done nothing but trick and lie to her."

My heart dropped from the bitterness of this unfortunate fact.

"I only did what was necessary for her benefit."

"Her benefit? That's a capital joke," he replied. "If you truly have her best interests at heart like you claim, you will let her go before your nature harms her."

"I refuse to believe that."

"You never were perceptive about yourself."

"Excuse me?"

"Have you ever once stopped to think how you being, well *you*, has ruined the lives of so many others?"

I shrugged.

"What are you talking about?"

He sighed.

"You gave Prince Fafnir cursed gold, which caused him to lose his mind and kill his own father..."

It wasn't my fault Fafnir couldn't handle his curses.

"You almost lost us the sun, moon, and Freya on a bet gone wrong."

Ok, that I was partially guilty of. But no more than fifteen percent.

"You traded Idunn to Thiazi without a second thought, almost resulting in my own death..."

My mouth dried.

He continued, laying charge after charge at my feet.

Blood rushed in my ears as what I didn't want to admit started to ensnare me and squeeze.

"These are all rather extreme examples. I am capable of goodness."

I grasped at any straw I could. Anything to keep believing what I wanted.

He laughed again.

"Capable of goodness?" he asked. "Like when you instructed the king in what he must do for me? Stop running from the truth. Innocent blood stains your hands Loki, as it stains my own."

I bristled and clenched my teeth as guilt doused me, cold and wicked.

"We agreed to never speak of that day again," I said. "That child...I begged you..."

"I know, but you need to be reminded just what you are *capable* of."

My stomach churned as his words sank into my core, my resolve fading into a ghost.

"You're conning me," I said, so weakly I didn't even recognize the voice that spoke as my own.

He raised his left eyebrow.

"How can I con you when I speak only facts?" he asked. "You are a father of wolves. A father of literal monsters. You are a trickster and a liar, as I am a killer and a deceiver. This is what we are, and we cannot change what is our very essence."

A sickening and terrible truth attacked me like venom, destroying any remaining residue of hope in its wake.

My arguments suddenly felt stupid.

They *were* stupid.

I believed myself noble when I only ever deceived Sigyn wholly and intimately, in every way a person could be deceived.

I lied to her about who I was. *What* I was.

I lied to her about Simon joining the army to live a decent life, when I still felt his last breath curl through my fingers.

I lied to her about granting her father peace in his final moments, when his screams still filled my ears.

I lied to her about never leaving her, as I now stood far away in another world.

I drowned in my lies and my tricks, and I would only ever feed her beautiful fables rather than the truth she needed.

Odin was right, and it destroyed me.

I loved Sigyn, but my love would only hurt her.

And I wouldn't do that.

I braced my knees, forcing myself to remain standing tall though everything in me threatened to buckle and sink into the cold sand.

I can't break

I will not break

The sun peeked over the horizon now.

Pebbles rushed beneath Odin's boots as he stepped behind me. He reached out his arm and laid his hand on my shoulder.

"She would never accept you fully, love you as deeply, as I do."

My every muscle tensed. He really was a bastard.

I shook him off and moved back, having to get away from his scent and his need and his love.

"You astound me," I said.

His eye searched me as if confused.

"How so?" he asked.

I scrubbed my face, trying to keep myself from fracturing.

"You think we can just pick up where we left off?" I asked. "That I will forget her with a snap of your fingers and fall back in your arms?"

He smiled softly as he picked up a gray stone. Compassion bled from his eye. I didn't want his compassion. I didn't want any of this.

I only wanted her.

"I don't expect you to forget her, but when you're ready, I will be waiting. As I always have."

He handed me the stone, and its chill spread into my palm as bitterness filled my mouth.

Was this truly it?

Clasping the rock tight, I turned and walked towards the ocean. Salt filled the air as I stepped into the surf, foam and froth slipping across my boots.

I looked out. The sunrise filled the sky with bright oranges and yellows, and I knew those same rays now fell through Sigyn's window and warmed her skin.

I blinked away the sting in my eyes, knowing she would soon wake to find me gone.

I gripped the stone until my knuckles turned white and my arm shook.

This was it

I had to let her go.

I threw the stone hard into the crashing waves, sending it sinking beneath the heaving ocean into its depths, the future I planned with Sigyn sinking along with it.

I turned slowly back to Odin, though I couldn't meet his gaze.

"When I'm ready," I replied.

But I never would be.

16

ROCK, MEET BOTTOM

"This is the first I've caught you lurking outside your rooms these last eight months," Frigg said. "I thought maybe we were lucky, and you'd finally died."

"Trust me, I'm as disappointed as you are," I replied.

I opened an oak cabinet in the kitchens and rummaged through the alcohol stores. I needed something with a sharp edge to keep me decently inebriated. If only the blasted letters would stop spinning, perhaps I could make out these labels...

"All that reminds me you're even around anymore are the servant's whispers about your dismal state," she said. "I'll admit, what I've heard has made me curious. Could it be the lie-smith has really been broken?"

Her voice scraped across my nerves, making my already infuriating headache throb even deeper in the base of my skull. I wished whatever this danger was that threatened Asgard would get on with it and strike. At this point, I welcomed whatever would put me permanently out of my misery.

"Is there anything stronger than bloody claret in this place?" I asked, knocking over bottles of mead and wine as I rifled through the shelf.

A crooked smile twisted her lips as she turned and opened the mahogany cupboard across from a massive fireplace where a wild boar roasted.

She reached to the back and pulled out a bottle of amber akvavit, a drink that curled the hair of even the burliest of men.

Sweet salvation at last.

My heart raced with anticipation as I stretched for the bottle, but as I grazed the glass, she pulled it away.

Really?

I shouldn't have been surprised. She never failed at being delightfully vicious.

"As much as I enjoy these nasty little games of yours, can we postpone this for another time?" I asked. "I'm teetering dangerously close towards sobriety."

I reached for the bottle again. She tightened her thin fingers around its neck and took a step back.

"Not just yet," she said.

"And why not?"

Her eyes fell slowly from my gaze to my chest, and then lower still.

Oh.

Of course. The akvavit came at a price.

"It's true what they've told me, you are much thinner than you used to be," she said. "And your pallor...so ashen. You haven't even combed your hair for weeks from the looks of it. And is that a chicken wing stuck to the side of your tunic?"

She was a true romantic.

"You know how to set my blood ablaze," I said, struggling to unbuckle my belt from around my waist. "Is the table good for you? Let's get this over with before you speak anymore honeyed words."

She raised her right eyebrow.

"Is that what you think I want? You?"

"Isn't it?"

She laughed, the tone of her voice shredding my nerves even further.

"Definitely not."

I clapped my hand over my heart and breathed out in relief.

"Thank the gods. Sleeping with you would have truly been a low point for me," I said. "Yeah, that one would have hurt."

She curled her fingers into her purple, silk skirts.

Maybe now was my chance.

I rushed her, trying again to snatch the bottle from her grasp. And again, she pulled it away causing a wave of dizziness to lurch in my head. Losing my footing, I fell against the tiled floor.

"Ow," I said, rubbing my left elbow.

Pure amusement lifted every line of her face.

"The servants mentioned never seeing you quite this self destructive before," she said. "How completely that girl wrecked you."

I bristled at the mention of Sigyn. I still couldn't bear the thought of...It all remained as fresh and raw as the day I decided not to return to her.

I glared up at Frigg as she stood over me. I would not give her the satisfaction of rubbing salt in my wounds.

"I'll give you until the count of three to hand that akvavit over, or..." I hissed.

She tilted her head.

"Or what?"

"Or I'll...I'll...oh bugger. I'm too tired for this. Just the usual threats of violence, blah blah blah, you know how it goes."

She laughed again, making my muscles tighten.

"You used to strut these halls so freely with your tail in the air."

"Don't think I still can't bite," I spat.

Her blonde braids slipped over her shoulders as she bent towards me, our faces an inch apart.

"But your teeth are dull now, Loki."

I wanted to say something devastatingly cruel. Something that would chew at her for months. Something the old me would have rolled off my tongue without one missed breath. But now, it didn't seem worth the effort.

That was a lie.

The truth was, I didn't have the will anymore.

And she knew it.

Her lips stretched into a wicked smile, and my insides twisted as pure enjoyment sparked in her gaze.

"This is what I wanted," she said. "Since I first heard the servant's gossip I wanted to see this new you. I wanted to see you broken. To see how pathetic you've become. For the first time, you've not disappointed me. The lie-smith has collapsed in on himself, and Asgard is safer for it."

Safer? What nonsense did she talk about?

A lance of pain shot through my head again, sharp and deep.

I needed to get away from her. I didn't want her to see how my hand shook as I kneaded my forehead to quell the hardening tension. I didn't want to give her anymore pleasure at seeing me look like some doddering fool.

Rising to my feet, I wrenched the bottle from her and took off for my private apartments.

I sped through the great hall and library and shielded my gaze from the sun as I rushed across the main courtyard. Why did it always have to shine so damn bright? All it did was sting my eyes and promise another tomorrow.

I didn't want anymore tomorrows.

Especially when I couldn't ever leave my yesterdays. I lived in those weeks I spent with Sigyn as if I were trapped in an unforgiving loop. Guilt tore out my guts as I played through it all over and over again.

I made her a victim of my poisonous nature. I made her suffer a disgusting love from a disgusting thing.

I hurt her.

And there I went again. Thinking. Remembering. The standard self loathing.

I uncorked the akvavit and lifted it to my lips and swallowed a large mouthful of liquid fire. It seared my nose and throat and pricked my tongue with caraway.

Exquisitely revolting stuff.

I took a second swig, trying to dissolve Sigyn within the fog of alcohol as fast as I could.

Pulling open the door to my rooms I took in a deep breath, safe once more inside the gloom, closing out the light, closing out the world...It was wonderful, until the stale and sour air clamped my lungs and sent me into a hacking fit.

I grumbled as I walked across a mishmash of rugs and furs, only stopping to curse as I accidentally struck my toes against an empty wine bottle, sending it rolling beneath an inlaid table.

But it was what sat on top of the table that made me groan.

Not another one. Dammit Odin.

A silver bowl overflowed with ripe oranges and pome-granates all piled around a pineapple nestled in the center. What the hell was I supposed to do with all this fruit? Eat it? I was on a strict alcohol only diet.

He was seriously starting to vex me with these gifts he continually sent me. This had to be the eighth one this month alone. Did he really think I could be pampered back into being his whore?

A pineapple would hardly cut it.

Sighing, I walked to the far corner beside my closed drapes and I fell into a divan. Sinking into an ocean of silk cushions, I tried to kick off my boots, only to realize I hadn't been wearing any to begin with.

Whatever.

Leaning back into the plush pillows, I guzzled more akvavit, not caring as thin streams of alcohol ran over my cheeks and into my hair.

I hissed as a fresh shock of pain struck inside my head again. This danger pulsed harder and stronger than it had in months. How much more of this must I endure?

Putting the akvavit on the floor beside a collection of lacquered wine stains, I dug into my pockets and pulled out a small, gilded box. Obviously I needed something stronger for relief, and this would do the job. Nothing in all the Nine Worlds allowed one to drift quite so far away in a tranquil haze as Poppy of Alfheim.

I shoved my thumbnail between the clasp.

Absolute agony split through my skull.

I rolled off the divan, knocking over a small table as I fell to the floor grunting and rasping quick breaths into the dense fibers of the sheepskin rug. I dug my fingers into my hair, clawing into my scalp desperate to stop the shooting torment driving deeper and deeper into me.

The entire room spun.

The pain stopped.

And I was no longer in my rooms.

I was elsewhere.

Scorching air swept over my face, and the jolt of metal striking metal filled my ears along with the screams of dying men and women. My stomach rolled as burning flesh and blood stung my nostrils.

Shit. Not this vision again.

Rocks and grit pricked my palms as I pressed into the dried earth and rose to my feet. Smoke and cinders blew through the breeze as I found myself back on that battlefield of brown grass that stretched far beyond the horizon.

However, this time I was not alone.

A figure shrouded head to toe in fine, white linen walked towards me through the red haze. If a man or a woman, I couldn't tell, but every step they took filled me with unease, and stranger still, woke the chaos within me again.

Fire spiraled through my veins making my skin sear my clothing, while sparks and ash rippled through my hair. I didn't like how this place made my element behave as an unstoppable lust in my body.

In fact, this was getting extremely irritating.

I stepped towards the figure, ready to have it out.

"Who are you?" I demanded, my breath as hot as the wind.

It tilted its head, its veil whipping behind its shoulders making it appear as a ghost. Perhaps it was a ghost.

"Inevitability," it answered, its tone definite. Haunting.

How awfully humble.

"I see," I said. "And what is this place?"

Anticipation rocked through me for the answer.

"Vigridr."

"Is that a type of soup?"

The figure stared at me in silence. Definitely not the chattiest of spirits I'd ever encountered.

"I'll take that as a no."

It took a step towards me, and a fan of heat rushed down my spine making me grind my teeth.

"Vigridr is fate." Its every word was like bellows feeding my flames. "Vigridr is this glorious battlefield where what the Destroyer promises will commence."

Destroyer?

My heart raced. This is what I'd been waiting for. To finally know.

"And what is the Destroyer?"

Flame and brimstone blazed behind my eyes as fire rushed wild and wicked through me, fighting to get out. Fighting to play. To consume.

"The Destroyer is not a what, but a who."

"Is it you?"

It stared at me again, not giving me any answer.

I clenched my hands shut, embers cackling and snapping between my fingers. I would not be robbed of finally finding out the answer to this maddening riddle.

"Answer me!"

It laughed.

"And I thought you were the cleverest of the gods."

The ground quaked, and a firestorm roared over the field engulfing everything in a blaze. We both stood amid flame and scorching winds, remaining unharmed as fire licked at our skin.

The land shifted and flickered as another image, another realm, overtook Vigridr like a painting.

My throat went dry.

Asgard surrounded me, burning and collapsing into rubble. Fire raced across the green hills towards the mountains, leaving Odin's great halls nothing but charred and broken remnants.

"A great reckoning nears." Eagerness lifted its every word.

The land fluttered and jerked again, Asgard giving way to Vanaheim. Razed palaces, wrecked homes, beaches coated with blood.

Another twitch and shudder.

Jotunheim surrounded us, nothing remaining but cinders and smoke, followed by Alfheim, Svaltalfheim, Niflheim...All the same horrors. All the same splitting and crumbling into an absolute inferno.

Into absolute death.

My heart thrashed in my chest and my blood frosted despite the fire in and outside of me. And while terror filled me at the carnage spreading out behind and before me, I admit I thought of only her.

"Is Sigyn in danger?"

It laughed again.

"My dear boy, every *one* is in danger. Every *thing* is in danger."

Another sputter, another flash.

Midgard surrounded me now, blistering and broiling as a great conflagration decimated Sigyn's world into ash.

Dread sped through my veins. This couldn't happen. I wouldn't let it.

"I must stop this," I said. "Tell me how to stop it."

The figure sighed, as if disappointed in me.

"You can't stop what has already started."

"And what exactly is it that has started?" I asked.

It paused.

"You cannot stop inevitability."

More blasted half answers. I guess I had to do this the old fashioned way.

"We will see about that," I said.

I lunged at the figure, trying to capture it and force it to tell me how to avoid whatever this coming death was. I grasped its solid frame. It and Vigridr dissolved.

Soft wool cradled my cheek as I gasped for breath, finding myself back in my rooms.

Dammit!

Anger and panic as I'd never known churned in my gut, and fear rushed down my back. Fear? Oh, this Destroyer would pay dearly for making me feel that particular sensation.

This was worse than I ever imagined. This threat, this reckoning, didn't include only Asgard, but the entire damned Nine Worlds!

It included Sigyn.

And that just wouldn't do.

I stretched my neck, letting the bones crack neatly down the row. I combed my fingers through the tangles in my hair, feeling my familiar wry smile pull at my lips again.

I was back, more invigorated than ever before. Nothing beat the absolute thrill when death was on the line, and I had someone to crush.

But how to stop this, whatever this was?

I tapped my finger against my lips.

Obviously seeking Odin's help was out. Already been there and done that and went down spectacularly in flames. Besides, I didn't like how oddly nervous he got from me having a little headache. If he found out I'd been having actual visions...No, best leave him out of it.

That left me only one option.

Her.

Maybe a fiery death would be preferable after all?

17

A LITTLE KNIFE PLAY

Jotunheim

The Ironwood Forest

S hards of sunlight glinted off the pine duff as I hiked through the dense spruce and larch. Moss and bark filled my lungs, and I enjoyed calculating my every move as I navigated over and around the thousand gnarled roots jutting out of the ground.

The things that lurked in the shade waited for one errant step, and I wouldn't give them the pleasure.

While beautifully ethereal, this wasn't just any old forest, this was the Ironwood. And depending on who you asked, they might describe this place as "risky," "dangerous," or even as "certain death."

I just called it a damn good time.

But I supposed people got nervous after a few gods went mad in the maze of pine. And if the madness didn't get you, the excessively large and always peckish demon bears would.

Yes, the Ironwood was quite treacherous, but none of these risks compared to the woman who ruled the forest.

Angrboda.

Dearest Angrboda. Excellent at knives and swords, more excellent in bed. She was a terrifying and relentless woman, and I couldn't get enough of her.

I often snuck into Ironwood to spend long summer days with her when Asgard turned dull, or when Odin left me for the hundredth time to go on some blasted quest. She was always there and always up for a spot of fun, or better yet, trouble.

I would say it was a type of love we shared, if that love were a violent and salacious storm. Until she and I agreed to never see each other again after...well...

This reunion promised to be interesting.

The fine mist wet my skin making me delightfully clammy as I trekked deeper into the woods, towards her fortress that lay south of the mountains and east of the sea. I passed a boulder, and behind it, nestled within the tightly packed trees, a massive structure of gray limestone rose before me.

Finally.

I hated how my palms began to sweat as I neared the great oak doors, something I'd done countless times before. But I never was one to let my nerves get the better of me.

I gripped the heavy iron knocker and gave it a bang to see if anyone was home.

A knife whizzed past my ear, the sharp steel lodging neatly in the wood grain.

My heart raced as I turned, another flash coming at me as a second blade pierced my tunic below my left wrist.

A third followed, striking not even an inch above my right forearm, pinning me to the door.

I smiled.

She was happy to see me after all! Otherwise, she would have aimed directly for my head.

"I see your skill remains legendary," I said to the spruce, unsure which tree my little forest nymph hid behind.

"As does your impertinence," a husky, yet sultry, voice replied.

She stepped out of the shadows and into the small, fluttering streams of sunlight. Warmth spread throughout my chest, fond memories rushing back to me.

I wasn't sure if she experienced the same butterflies as I did, though.

She pulled another knife from one of her many belts that cinched her waist. Twigs snapped beneath her boots as she approached me, her black hair pulled back tight, sharpening her already severe features.

She was gorgeously terrifying.

"What has it been, Ang?" I asked. "Five? Maybe six centuries?"

She glared at me, her bright gray eyes beaming with murder as she twirled her blade within her experienced fingers. A flush of heat rippled down my legs.

How I missed this.

"Nine."

"Oh, well, regardless, you don't look a day over five thousand years old."

With a grunt, she threw her dagger, the point impaling the door a centimeter below my groin.

Ok, this wasn't fun anymore.

"Don't try to charm me, Loki," she growled. "You aren't supposed to be here. We agreed."

I nodded.

"I know...I know...But, certain circumstances have arisen and...I need your help."

Her eyes flashed and laughter burst out from deep in her throat.

"Are you serious?" she asked. "After everything you dare come back, trespass on my lands, and ask for my aid? You have enormous balls to think I'd ever do such a thing."

"I'm flattered you remember at least that about me."

Her red lips flattened. She unsheathed another knife, a *bigger* knife, the steel catching the splinters of light. Sweat beaded on my temples and I cleared my drying throat.

"I know seeing me again stirs up old wounds..."

She scoffed and pressed the knife edge into my neck.

"It's not seeing you. It's you showing up here and acting like all is forgotten."

My mouth turned bitter. She went too far.

"How else should I act?" I spat. "You think I suffer any less pain than you about what happened?"

"It appears that way to me."

I struggled to free myself, but she pressed the steel harder into my thrashing pulse.

"Watching them be sent away nearly destroyed me," I hissed, hating speaking these truths I worked centuries to bury deep inside me. "Not to mention the tears you shed for their fates. I swore that day I'd never father another child. I couldn't bear to have it happen again."

She stared into me, and I watched her desire to tear out my guts wane. Sighing, she backed away and lowered her blade, letting her shoulders relax.

I breathed out, not realizing I'd stopped breathing at all. Although, I'd prefer she hadn't left me pinned to the door.

"I know," she whispered, looking at her feet. "I've spent these years lost in intense, focused hatred and...I'm so angry.

I'm angry every day because we let ourselves be talked into letting them take our children from us. We both stood there and let it happen."

She spun around and threw her knife at a nearby stump covered in mushrooms, screaming several unsavory curses. Strands of her black hair fell out across her flushed cheeks.

I wanted to go and console her, but perhaps it was for the best I remained stuck to the door. Comforting her was like comforting a bad-tempered cobra.

"We did what was best to protect them from everyone," I said. "They were monsters, and they would have been hunted and destroyed for simply being what they were. At least this way we could give them some sliver of a life. Safety. We gave them their best chance."

She turned and faced me again, grimacing.

"But did we?" she asked. "Did we really do what was best?"

I didn't like her questions. They were too plausible.

"I have to believe that. Anything else is too horrible to contemplate."

She crossed her arms, chuckling darkly.

"That 'anything else' is precisely what's been filling my thoughts since we parted."

"What do you mean?"

Her gaze grew distant.

"When Odin came to us and spoke of the dangers our children faced, I believed him. Few would understand they were only monsters by appearance, but not by heart. We could send them away from those who would seek to harm them as threats, or for trophies. Odin made complete sense. But what if we made a mistake in listening to him?"

I shook my head.

"No. Odin gave us his word it was for their benefit. We can trust him."

She smirked.

"But who can trust Odin, really?" she asked. "What if by agreeing to let him banish them, we really agreed to something that benefited him alone? What if that's what he wanted all along, and we damned Jormungand to the sea, Fenrir to an island, and Hel to rule the dead?

My skin crawled at the thought. Odin was a masterful con, but what reason would he have to go to such lengths? Our children were nothing to him.

I didn't want to speak about this ridiculousness anymore. Not when I was running out of time.

"As fun as these theoretics are, I need you to put all this conjecture aside, and kindly remove your knives from my clothes," I said. "There's something significant coming."

She neared me, her scent of primrose and burdock filling my nose as she searched my gaze.

"There's a spark of fear behind your eyes," she said, pulling out the knife above my right forearm. "I don't think I've ever seen you afraid. This must truly be dire."

She tugged the knife away that fastened my left wrist, freeing my hand. My skin prickled already as blood flowed back to my fingers.

"You have no idea. A great reckoning lays at our doorstep."

Her lips pulled into a wide smile, as if I'd presented her a gift.

"Ooo! This sounds absolutely marvelous! Tell me everything. You know how I enjoy the disastrous."

I scratched behind my ear, unsure how to start. This was a bit more than disastrous.

"I've been having visions."

"Excellent! Only the best calamities start that way."

"Yes, well, except they showed me terrible things," I continued. "Utter devastation and slaughter by war and flame, and a mysterious figure at the center of it all called the Destroyer. I saw Asgard burning and crumbling to ash."

Delight sparked her features.

"Good," she said. "Asgard needs to crackle in fire until those stuck up Aesir learn a thing or two about humility. They really chap my tits, thinking they are better than everyone else. Maybe this will teach them a lesson."

Fair points, but she wasn't getting it.

"That may be, but I must learn what this reckoning is that approaches. I must find out what it all means. All I know is what these visions show me, and it isn't enough to stop this Destroyer."

Her brow knit with confusion. Disappointment.

"Stop them? Why would you want to stop them? I want to go get my knives and help! This is what I've been longing for. Recompense for what everyone back in Asgard took from us."

I sighed, shaking my head.

"You don't understand, it's not just Asgard. It's every thing. It's every one. All the Nine Worlds will fall, including you. Including our children. Including..."

I stopped. I couldn't say her name.

Saying it would make it real.

"Including who?" she asked.

I met her gaze. I didn't like all the sensations suddenly gripping my heart. All these bloody emotions that threatened to make me weak. I could not abide being vulnerable.

"There is a woman. A human. I won't have her harmed if there's some way I can stop it."

She nodded, knowing filling her eyes.

"You've found someone else, then?"

My chest tightened, and I pulled in a shivering breath. If only she knew.

"I thought I had, but...it's complicated."

"By complicated you mean Odin got involved?"

I didn't answer.

She sneered.

"I'll never understand what you see in him that makes you stay by his side," she said. "Why don't you go to him with this concern of yours?"

"Bastard is always busy," I lied. "Besides, your advice on the matter will be loads more entertaining than his anyway. You're the most cunning and steel hearted woman I know."

She smiled, but not because of my flattery.

"He doesn't want you knowing about this, does he?"

Shit. For being the god of lies, I was losing my edge.

"No," I growled. "Odin, all of them, have been keeping this threat a secret from me. They know I know, they know I know they know, but they still won't trust me to help them for whatever reason," I said. "The ironic thing is, I don't trust them to not muck this up. I love my life, and the lives of the ones I cherish, too much to have it be placed in their hands like a fragile bird."

I stepped towards her and reached out, taking her cool hands in mine. "This is why I must know what this reckoning is. I must know how to stop the Destroyer, and I need your aid to do it."

She nodded slowly, as if considering my words carefully.

"If Odin found out what you are planning, what with going behind his back and all, would this anger him?"

I smiled.

"Most definitely."

Her eyes glinted with a lovely deviousness. She laid her

hands on my chest and traced the delicate gold embroidery of my tunic with her fingertips.

"Then how can I refuse you?" I shivered, her delectable coolness sinking through the silk. "How can I refuse helping the cleverest of the gods steal Odin's glory? Nothing will give me greater satisfaction than when you rip it out from beneath his boots."

I pulled her against me, sinking into the primrose and burdock rising from the crook of her neck.

"I love when you speak like this," I said.

Her lips curled into a coy smile.

"Odin is a collector," she continued. "He travels to the ends of the realms for any crumb of knowledge, any scrap of wisdom. He's insatiable in his hunger for more. The secrets that man has found!"

"Yes, his vices are quite dull."

"But not even Odin understands everything he learns. What is one of the most wise of the Nine Worlds to do if he can't figure out one of those puzzles or riddles he picks up? Hmmm?"

I drew circles on her back, thinking as I skimmed her gown of heavy wool and leather.

"Well, usually he comes to me and drones on about this unknowable rune, or that lost poem while I get drunk to tune him out. Bloody aggravating. Who cares!"

She rolled her eyes.

"He finds someone who can discern it for him." She curled her fingers into my tunic and leaned into my right ear. "I've heard whispers of a völva. A seeress."

I laughed.

"You can't be serious."

"You asked for my help, don't discount me so quickly. To keep myself from growing stiff with boredom in this forsaken forest, I entertain. Gossip thrives within my halls, and with gossip comes information. Tales."

"Odin has no need of a völva. His wife is a witch, and I know he practices the dark magic of seidr in secret."

She raised her right eyebrow.

"But what if his skills weren't enough?" she asked. "You know his talents lie purely in charms, and not in divination. Same for his bitch of a wife who prefers fiddling with curses rather than figuring out the future. She's the most worthless völva I ever met."

I had to admit, she had a point.

"True, but..."

"Think," she said, her breath rushing hot over my chin and cheeks. "A völva is the only one who can decipher visions and torment. Riddles and puzzles. Who can unravel destiny. Since he and Frigg aren't capable, he would have had no choice but to pay her a visit."

"Does this witch have a name?"

She paused.

"They call her Golda."

"Not the most terrifying of names for a witch, is it? I'm disappointed."

Her face grew serious, and she uncurled her fingers from my tunic, letting her hands fall and rest on my forearms instead. Holding me.

Was she afraid for me?

"Be sure this is what you want. No knowledge comes without cost."

My lips drew into a grin, as I stroked her cheek with my thumb.

"I would hope not," I said. "If this wasn't high stakes, this wouldn't be any fun."

18

AN UNFORTUNATE PROPHECY

Midgard

(Somewhere deep in the mangrove swamps of La Florida)

Why did she have to live here?

Sweat trickled between my shoulder blades and dripped off my nose as I scrambled through the sludge and mire of an immense swamp. Small crabs fell like rain from the mangroves as I pressed forward, pushing the jumble of branches out of my way, desperate to reach Golda before the tide rose and submerged what little miserable terrain I had.

Actually, miserable didn't even begin to describe it.

If it wasn't the branches hitting me in the face every other step, it was the swarms of mosquitos stinging my skin. And let me not forget about the endless supply of golden orb spiders, whose sticky webs kept getting stuck in my hair.

This völva better be worth all this aggravation. As it were, I doubted I'd ever get the stench of mildew, rot, and reptile out of my nose.

I stopped, having to get my bearing again for the hundredth time thanks to there being no path and little visibility. Right. I still headed North.

Mud squelched beneath my boots as I trudged forward again, water snakes and deadly cottonmouths slithering away as I passed them by.

I stopped again. A small channel cut off my way. Of course it would.

Cursing under my breath, I clambered between the mangroves and sank into the brackish water until it reached my chest. Crocodiles vanished into the tangled mess of branches and roots like apparitions.

I tried not to think about them as I pushed off the silt and swam against the rushing current to the opposite bank.

Pulling myself up onto the other side, I found higher ground, thankfully more sand than mud. The mangroves were spread out, and I could finally see more than ten feet ahead.

And in the near distance stood a wooden shack covered in moss. The roof sagged towards the crooked foundations. One good gust of wind and the entire structure would collapse.

Having no time for knocking or politeness I opened the door. Damp and decay entered my lungs, and I blinked several times trying to adjust to the gloom inside.

"Hello?" I asked.

No answer, save the flickering of the myriad of candles placed on cupboards, chests, and tables.

I walked in. The floorboards bowed beneath my every step as I moved aside hanging ropes and nets. Geckos scurried under the molding furniture.

"Hello?" I called again.

No answer. Again.

"Figures," I whispered to myself, wiping sweat from my brow.

Perhaps she died and her corpse rotted away along with the rest of this hovel? I would seriously be put out if I came here and destroyed my best boots for nothing.

I turned to investigate behind a stack of crumbling books, when my heart jumped.

A woman stood in front of me.

Her canvas dress hung from leathered, sunburnt shoulders, and a belt made of alligator skin cinched her sturdy waist. Tattoos of ancient runes and symbols ran the length of her muscular arms. She knew hard labor.

Her lips cracked as she smiled at me, crinkling the lines around her coal rimmed eyes.

"Loki the Sly One. I've waited eons to meet you." Her soft, but weathered, face lifted with joy. "Five minutes late, but at least you've finally made it, you tricky devil."

She gave a raspy chuckle, and her spirit pulsed with the rush of primeval knowledge.

"How creepy," I replied. "That being the case, I hope I'm not a disappointment."

"I seriously doubt it, my sweet," she said. "Your arrival at my door calls for a drink."

Golda went to the cupboard behind her and grabbed two clouded glasses and a bottle crusted in dirt. Moving to the battered table in the center of the room, she set the glasses down and poured out something that seared my nostrils.

She held the glass out to me.

"I think I'm good," I said.

She frowned.

"But this is a moment to celebrate!"

Her gaze fell to a roach scuttling across the table. She

brought down the glass on top of its back, crushing it with a firm twist.

Satisfaction filled her features as she scraped the squashed remnants of legs and antenna off on the edge of the table and then pressed the glass into my hand.

My stomach lurched.

"As lovely as this all is." I forced down what threatened to come up. "I'm afraid I'm in a bit of a rush."

I put the glass down, wiping my fingers on my trousers.

She clucked her tongue.

"They always are. Never even give me a chance to bring out the pickled leopard frogs. You're missing out on a great delicacy."

I closed my eyes and counted to ten. Did her horrible hospitality have no end?

"Tell me..."

"...What your visions mean? What this terrible thing you see coming is?" she finished. "What dearest Odin doesn't want you to know?"

I smiled. She was good.

"Can you?"

She gave me a coy smile, then guzzled her putrid gut rot as if water.

"I'll never understand. For being gods, you are all quite anxious when it comes to the future. Always asking me to figure it out," she said. "At least you are much calmer than Odin was, I'll give you that. Nearly cracked his jaw clenching his teeth together so tightly."

That sneaky bastard. Angrboda would be pleased to know she was right. He had paid Golda a visit.

"So he needed the help of a witch after all. He always was rubbish with magic. I will have to rub this one in his face," I said.

She leaned over the table, pressing her calloused knuckles into the grime covering the surface.

"I am the only way for the desperate," she said. "And how desperate he was when he came to me long before you even mixed your blood. As desperate as you are now to learn who the Destroyer is."

A wave of excitement rushed through me.

"And who are they?"

She covered her mouth with her hand and snickered, tears streaming over her greasy cheeks as if I told her a fantastic joke.

I pressed my thumbs into my fists. She toyed with me.

"You are adorable to think I'd just tell you!" She wiped her eyes, smearing her black eyeliner. "Odin sacrificed much for wisdom, even plucking out his right eye."

"Your point?" I snapped.

"Nothing comes without a price, Loki. The only question is, what are you willing to sacrifice to receive the wisdom you desire?"

Now we were talking.

"If body parts can be avoided, that would be greatly appreciated," I said. "I'm afraid eyepatches aren't me."

She nodded, twisting her finger in her hair packed with braids.

"I rather agree," she said. "You don't have Odin's bone structure to pull it off. But, I'm sure we can come to some other agreement."

Golda came around the table and grabbed my wrists, pressing her rough thumbs between the bones of my forearm. Her chipped nails dug into my skin as she squeezed harder until I could feel my own arteries pulse.

She sucked in a shivery breath through her yellowed teeth.

"You beauty" she said. "You're everything I hoped you'd be. Chaos vibrates within your every heartbeat, and your fire hungers to explode out of you."

This was getting weird.

"What do you want from me? My blood? A bit of my hair? Name your price."

She let go of me, and I rubbed my wrists trying to erase the red marks she left.

"That is a dangerous thing to say to one such as myself, sweetie," she said. "But, I want nothing so cliche." Her eyes fell to my mother's blade at my hip. "I want your dagger."

I stepped back.

"My dagger? Why would you want that?"

She shrugged.

"Mine broke," she said. "I need something to gut the fish I catch."

I never was one for sentiment, but now it struck my insides. Hard.

"I'd much prefer if we did the blood thing," I said. "This dagger is all I have left of my mother, and I don't know if I can stomach the thought of you gutting fish with it."

She scoffed and shook her head.

"A dagger is hardly comparable to an eye, wouldn't you say?"

Point made. Still difficult.

"Are you sure you wouldn't rather prefer a bar of soap? What about a lovely broom?"

"It's your dagger, or no deal."

Nasty shriveled fig.

My spine ran cold as I slowly took the dagger out of the sheath at my side. I couldn't remember a time I'd ever been without it. It was a part of me.

I stared at the blade, gripping the leather wrapped hilt

my mother once also gripped. A connection. A connection to her I would no longer have.

"Nothing worth anything ever came easy," she said. "Best be making up your mind, before I change my own."

I stomped my emotions into my depths. I wouldn't let memories stop me from learning what I came here to know. I'd give anything to keep Sigyn safe.

"Take it," I hissed, handing the blade to Golda.

Her eyes widened as she grasped the hilt, the steel flashing in the candlelight. Absolute euphoria lifted every line of her face as if reunited with an old lover.

For two seconds, I felt like I had done something extraordinarily foolish.

She wove between the cramped furniture towards a bookcase of bending shelves filled with jars and minerals. All the things any decent witch would have. Reaching high, she pulled down a small, cedar box with metal fittings and opened it.

"I would've thought choosing to live so isolated would be bad for business," I said, taking a seat on a rickety chair. Placing my hands behind my head, I tilted back in the chair, balancing on the two back legs.

Her body stiffened as she placed the dagger inside.

"I didn't choose to live here," she growled. "It was chosen for me."

She shut the lid with a bang and locked it closed.

"I've given you what you asked for, now tell me what I want," I said.

Her shoulders relaxed as she turned and faced me, her features pleasant once again as if whatever had bothered her never existed.

"Of course, my sweet! A deal is a deal."

She arched her neck, the bones cracking beneath her sunburnt skin.

"In the beginning, there was only the nothingness of Ginnungagap. Potential. Ymir, the first giant, was born of this and roamed freely, until Odin and his brothers saw fit to slay him and use his body to build Midgard."

She stepped towards me, and a rush of her power iced my flesh.

"Odin was content taking his seat as Allfather of the gods, and the entire Nine Worlds quivered beneath Aesir might. How he loved realizing his ambitions! But he wanted more. He needed knowledge, and so he stole poetry, consumed language, and killed for wisdom. Still, it was not enough."

I put out my hand to stop her.

"Can we skip this history lesson?" I said, growing impatient. "Trust me, Odin loves to tell these stories, and I've endured them a hundred times over."

She raised her right eyebrow, bending over the table again.

"But has he ever told you the true reason for such unslakable thirst?"

"I always assumed he just wanted to be the universe's biggest asshole."

She dropped her head and sighed.

"It's to stop his fate," she said. "Odin never much liked the concept of fate, you see. It's what he fears most of all. It's why he sought me out and gave me his eye."

She lowered her voice to almost a whisper. I leaned forward, the chair legs striking the floorboards.

"The same visions plaguing you tormented Odin. And like you, he begged me to tell him what they meant."

The hair on the back of my neck rose, as pure anticipation inflamed my cheeks.

"And what did you tell him?" I asked, scooting to the edge of my seat, needing to get closer.

She gave a crooked smile.

"The truth. That the Destroyer walked among the worlds, and would bring Ragnarok to Odin's door."

My blood ignited from the very mention of the word, though I'd never heard of it.

"And what is Ragnarok?" I asked.

She chuckled standing over me, tall and supreme.

"Inevitability."

Inevitability, the shrouded figure from my visions echoed.

My throat dried recalling the smell of scorched earth and the clash of metal ringing in my ears.

The fire in my veins crackled.

"Come again?" I asked, shaking it all away.

"Ragnarok is inevitability. It is the end of all the worlds. The end of all the universes. All will collapse in searing wind and flame until all cease to exist."

Terror flooded me.

Absolute terror.

I wiped my face, not realizing how much cold sweat beaded on my temples. My hands shook. My entire body shook.

This wasn't just war, this was utter annihilation.

I rose to my feet, needing to do something. Anything.

"I can't allow this," I said, hating the quiver in my voice. "I must find a way to stop it. Tell me witch, how..."

She laughed, a vicious, rolling sound from deep in her gut.

"The first sign has already come to pass," she interrupted. "It's already begun and there's nothing you can do."

"What sign?"

She looked at me as if I were a sweet fool.

"Why, Sigyn of course," she said.

My heart dropped to my stomach, and my mouth fell open. Not much had been capable of shaking me so deeply in all my millennia, but this...

I paced back and forth, twisting my tunic between my fingers.

"Impossible," I said. "How can she be involved in any of this? She's just a human."

She smirked.

"You know she's so much more than that," she said. "Odin knows it too. He learned of her in his visions. Sigyn carries his failure. Sigyn carries tidings that all he ever did was for naught."

"I don't understand."

"Isn't it obvious?" she asked. "She will bear the sign that instigates Ragnarok."

I clamped my teeth together. It all made sense now. Why Odin seemed so afraid once he learned her name. Why he didn't want me near her.

"Odin should have told me about this," I growled. "He should have told me about her. We could have figured this all out together."

She gripped my arm, stopping me and forcing me to face her.

"Why would he tell the Destroyer himself?"

My heart stopped.

"What?"

She reached for my hands and grasped them in hers. My

fire immediately woke, spiraling up through my arms and down my legs, filling me. Fighting me to get out.

"You've been given the greatest of gifts. Of burdens," she said, her voice coming from outside me and from within. "Fire burns in you for a reason. You are chaos, and you are potential."

I shook my head, hating the firestorm she seemed to call inside me against my will.

"I don't understand," I said, my breath hot. "This can't be possible. I'm just Loki the Trickster."

She strengthened her grip on me.

"You are Loki the Breaker of Worlds!" she yelled. "You are a harbinger of death and destruction. Chaos consumes and purges the universe of the past and makes way for the new. As it was in the beginning with Ginnungagap, so it shall be in the end. You are the Destroyer."

She squeezed my hands even tighter. I cried out as that familiar pain I knew so well split through my skull, peeling me back until everything was raw and throbbing.

I was back in Vigridr. We both stood there, surrounded by anguish and death as ash and cinders twisted through our hair. Flames raged in my veins, wanting to be free to cause destruction.

I struggled to keep them inside me, but I no longer could. They escaped out of my fingers and my pores, spiraling into a cyclone of fire. A great conflagration raced across the battlefield, making a world of embers and brimstone.

I always prized myself on my control over my element. Fire was wild by nature, yet I wielded it with ease. But now...my element was more than me. I was no longer its master, it was mine.

"It's beautiful!" I heard Golda exclaim over the screams of the dying, as the wall of flames soared into the sky.

She kept hold of me, even though I seared her skin beneath my touch.

"This is ludicrous!"

I pulled away from her, forcing it all to be extinguished. My headache stopped. Vigridr vanished. We stood back in her infested hovel. I chilled, seeing red blisters bubble on her palms and fingers from where I had burned her.

I knew then it all to be true, but I could not accept it.

She shook her head, as if shocked by my reaction.

"No, this is to be," she said. "You will descend upon the Nine Worlds, and your children will end the reign of the gods in a final, glorious battle on Vigridr."

I stepped back, but she took one towards me. And another. Until she backed me up, and I fell back into the chair.

"My children?"

"The children of Loki are who the gods fear above all others. They are their undoing."

"How?"

"Your daughter, Hel, will sweep through the worlds with her army of the dead, while Jormungand will douse Thor in venom, killing him with one, single bite. And as for Fenrir, the great wolf...he will crush Odin between his jowls. This is the fate Odin wants to escape."

Angrboda's words rippled through my mind.

What if by agreeing to let him banish them, we really agreed to something that benefited him alone?

Anger tore at me, racing hot through my blood. They made my children prisoners because of some stupid prophecy. Odin told me it was for their benefit, when it only ever was for his own. How could he have done this to us? To them?

I shook my head as it all slowly sank in, chilling my bones.

"I thought Odin loved me," I said, my voice rougher than I liked.

She leaned into me, her face inches from my own.

"How could he love the man destined to destroy him?" she asked. "He's only ever feared you. They all fear you. They hate you for what you will do to them."

My chest tightened.

I ground my nails into the grain of the wood, my gut twisting with pain and truth and other lies. It all threatened to crush me beneath the weight of what it all meant.

"They've all known," I hissed. "And they kept it from me. Thought me capable…"

The words died in my mouth. I couldn't say it.

"They've all known since the very beginning."

That one particularly hurt.

Especially thinking of halfwit Thor knowing something about myself even I didn't know. But the worst was having been conned by Odin all along. Wholly.

Completely.

Pain bit the back of my throat.

"Why would he bring me to Asgard if he feared me? Why go through all this risk?"

She dropped to her knees and looked up at me, sympathy welling within her eyes.

"Everything Odin's ever done has only ever been for himself," she said. "You were his enemy, and he did what it took to trap you in a pretty cage, hoping you'd never notice."

I shivered as rage overtook me. It was all too unacceptable, but I refused to live in the lies they wove for me anymore.

She reached out and stroked my hair, as if to calm me.

"Don't despair," she said. "Your path is the most noble of all, and you've finally found your freedom in truth. Your headaches, your visions, have all been Vigridr calling to you. Waking the fire within you so you can do your good work."

She stood and walked back to the box that contained the dagger.

"Surtr, the fire giant, awaits your command," she said, shoving the box high on a shelf. "And only then will Surtr rise from the depths of chaos and Muspelheim with a sword of fire in hand and smite every galaxy and universe. The cleansing death that awaits all will be enacted, and the circle will begin again."

As horrified as I was, I heard a strange noise bubble up from within me. It was laughter.

I was laughing.

Laughing at literally being told I would raise an army and destroy every living organism for the fun of it.

That seemed like an awful lot of work.

I suppose I should have hated being told I was the Destroyer, but I actually only felt utter relief. If I was the one to summon Ragnarok, I just never would. Problem solved!

I stood from the chair.

"You forget one thing in this interpretation of these visions. Choice. As I am the Destroyer, I have no intention to annihilate anything, especially the woman I love. This horror you speak of will never come to pass."

She flattened her lips.

"Odin believed the same when he didn't like what he learned," she replied. "I will tell you what I told him. You cannot escape your fate. You cannot escape the destiny that has been cast for you. No matter how long you put it off, how long you run, it will win. Entropy is inevitable."

That word again.

My laughter faded. Unease gripped me.

I approached her.

"No one decides my fate but me."

She chuckled darkly.

"A word of warning, then, my dear," she said, placing her palms on my chest as if I were her son.

"Please, go on," I mocked. "I love a good omen."

"Odin believes he found a way to stop Ragnarok," she said. "But when he learned what must be done to the Destroyer, to you...well, he found another less extreme method."

She clasped my wrist again and rubbed her thumb across the scar where he and I had blended our blood.

"It was quite clever of little Odin, but in the end, useless. As if he could have actually prevented Ragnarok," she said, every word thick with scorn. "The Destroyer cannot be prevented from his purpose, but that doesn't mean he can't experience an unpleasant delay or two along the way if he isn't careful."

I scoffed.

"And what, exactly, must be done to me?" I asked.

Her lips twisted into a smile, one that iced me to my last cell.

"Tread lightly Sly One. You know the truth now, and the truth is a dangerous thing."

19

WHEN THE TRUTH HURTS

Asgard

Everything I knew was a lie.

The more I thought about it, the angrier I grew. Their every fib, their every deception swirled together in my head, repeating and repeating like a chorus until a kind of madness descended over me. A peculiar viciousness that wanted nothing more than to strike them down.

But I think the irony enraged me the most. The god of lies and tricks fell for their fantasy hook, line, and sinker.

They would pay dearly for that one.

No one tricked me.

I marched towards the feast hall, where drums pounded and roasted lamb saturated the air.

I smiled.

They celebrated. I would make sure this was a party they'd never forget.

Squaring my shoulders, I burst open the doors and

walked into a crowded banquet filled with some of the most important beings of the Nine Worlds.

Dignitaries all the way from Vanaheim reveled in the lavishness of wine and song alongside representatives from Jotunheim. Even the snobby Elvish ambassador, who rarely lowered herself to attend any Aesir function, chatted amiably with Frigg.

This wasn't any old little shindig, this was a feast intended to impress our neighbors, and all the gods were present.

Well, all the gods except Odin.

He'd just have to catch my encore later. I couldn't miss this opportunity to mix venom in their mead.

I sauntered between the two long oak tables stuffed with game hens, meat pies, and exotic fruit.

The thin strings of the lutes jerked to a stop. Freya dropped her goblet, spilling ale over her honey cakes. Several dwarves from Svartalfheim pointed at me and chortled.

I supposed I didn't look my best slathered in swamp muck, and my hair ratted with sweat and spider webs. But at least I had their attention.

"Why so silent?" I said, unable to control the anger shaking in my voice. "I was hoping to catch everyone here. It's time we had a little chat."

I grabbed a chicken leg off of Balder's plate and took a bite. The finely dressed ladies beside him leaned away from me, furiously fanning themselves.

Balder pulled his tunic up over his nose.

"Get away! You smell like alligator piss," he said.

"Swamps tend to leave a bit of tang on one's skin." I pulled a clump of moss off my shoulder.

Tyr tilted his head.

"Swamp?" He put his elbow on the table and leaned forward. "What were you doing in a swamp?"

He seemed nervous. Good.

"Visiting an old friend of Odin's in a lovely place in Midgard the humans call La Florida."

I tossed the chicken leg behind me as I turned on my heel and walked to Njord and Idunn. They jumped out of their chairs and backed away until out of my sight. Smart move.

"She and I had the best time together," I said. "She told me the greatest tale. Really opened my eyes to what's been confusing me so much."

My lips curled into a coy smile. I plopped down in Idunn's empty chair, slamming my feet on the table sending dishes clattering and mud sloughing off my boots.

Thor tightened his grip around his turkey leg, pulling his knuckles white. He sat at the table across from me.

"I couldn't give a blasted newt what's been confusing you," he growled. "Not when Aegir is providing us with all the best ale we can drink. I won't have you spoil this for me."

Wrong thing to say to me.

"You're worried I will spoil your good time?" I laughed. "That's a joke. If anyone here is apt at spoiling feasts, it's you. Remember what happened in Jotunheim with Thrym?"

Everyone turned and stared at him. He crossed his arms and swallowed.

"You speak madness."

I clucked my tongue.

"Did your own wedding mean so little to you?"

Whispers raced throughout the hall. Thor went red, and anxiety blossomed in his tiny eyes. He made me swear to never to tell a soul, but it was such a great story...

"Be quiet..."

"You should have seen him," I said to the others, ignoring him. "He pretended to be Freya and thought no one would notice him eat an entire ox and wash it down with a barrel of mead. Unfortunately for Thor, this only heated Thrym's blood all the more."

Darts of giggles and chortles sprung from the crowd.

I picked up a fork and used the prongs to dig out the thick lines of dirt from beneath my nails.

"He's only joking," Thor said to them, reddening even deeper. "He's always weaving crazy and improbable tales that would never, ever, ever happen."

He turned and locked eyes with me. Shielding the left side of his mouth with his hand so only I could see his lips, he mouthed "I will kill you."

Tease.

"You shouldn't be so shy, Thor. Thrym found you absolutely stunning in your silk dress, and with orange blossoms in your hair. You made such a beautiful bride, you can't blame him for trying to kiss you. Oops...did I just let that slip?"

Laughter exploded out of the guest's lungs, several having to wipe tears from their eyes. Even the Elvish ambassador let out a guffaw that pierced my ears.

Thor crushed his turkey leg in his grip, shooting split bone and meat into the hair of his dinner companions.

I loved it.

"Loki." Sif's voice.

I locked eyes with hers.

"It would be best if you leave," she said, petting Thor's hand to calm him.

Brave Sif. Foolish Sif.

Had she not been paying attention to how this game worked? She should have better kept her mouth shut.

I clapped the fork on the table and stood. My right eye twitched. Hoots and snickers continued to skip around the room as I walked between the tables.

Standing in front of her, I ground my fists into the gnarled oak and leaned in. She pressed herself into the back of her chair, trying to escape me.

Too late for that.

"I never got a chance to ask, but do you always sound like a small dog when you get excited?" I asked. "Because I don't know how Thor can concentrate making love to you with all that yipping you make. I know I found it damn distracting."

Two of the Jotun dignitaries spit out their ale and gripped their sides, cackling. Laughter filled the room quaking the dishes and goblets.

Thor stood up knocking over his chair and lunged at me, sending an avalanche of buttered potatoes rolling along the tables.

Tyr and Bragi grasped at his tunic and leather belt, holding him back.

"I really will kill you now!" he shouted.

I rolled my eyes.

"Shut up, Thor," I said. "I'm done with your whining."

I turned to face the crowd.

"I'm done with all of you."

The roar of laughter dissolved into a hush. No one had ever dared speak to the god of thunder in such a manner. The outrage electrified my blood. This was a long time coming.

"What insolence has gotten into you?" Frigg asked.

Her face tightened, and she dug her nails into her arm rests.

I shrugged.

"Am I not allowed to be slightly wrathful now and again?"

"We've done nothing to wrong you," Freya said.

Others echoed her sentiments, their voices just noise to me.

I smiled, spite burning my blood.

"Really?" I asked. "My new friend Golda might disagree with you."

Fear filled Tyr's eyes. Feared filled all their eyes. Except Frigg's.

"Turns out there's a rather delicious secret you've all been keeping from me. No wonder you didn't want my help with this threat facing Asgard. It would have made it terribly awkward."

Frigg chuckled.

"Am I amusing, Frigg?" I asked.

She rose from the table and walked towards me, her purple skirts slipping between her long legs.

"I've waited for this moment," she replied. "To see your face when you finally knew."

Dark anticipation flashed behind her gaze, as if daring me to keep going. How could I refuse?

A rustle of clothing. The snap of boots against marble.

Tyr pushed through the crowd rushing towards me. The apprehensive determination in his face told me I was in for one of his dull appeals for peace.

I sighed as he laid his hand on my shoulder and pulled me towards him. Lowering his head to my ear I could feel the heat of his breath.

"Loki, say no more," he whispered. "Forget all of this. For your own sake."

Oh Tyr. Always looking out for me. Always trying to stop the fun when it was just beginning.

"You always were a dear, but this is one time I need you to stand back."

Frigg stood right beside us.

"Yes, get away from him Tyr. He has something he wishes to get off his chest."

"You have no idea," I said.

Her lips twisted into a smile, sending a rush of disappointment to my toes. I didn't want her to be happy about this. She should be furious.

Looking at me, Frigg pulled Tyr off my shoulder and stepped closer. She stunk of licorice and rose petal.

"Say it."

I ground my teeth. She enjoyed herself too much. This wasn't how this was supposed to go.

"Say it!" she screamed.

"I know," I spat. "I know about Ragnarok. I know I am the Destroyer."

No one moved. No one in that hall even took a breath.

They just stared at me without a word, striking me to the ground.

I lowered my chin, fighting the deluge of emotions rocking deep in my gut.

"We've celebrated together. We've fought together. We've mourned together." I lifted my eyes, facing them. "I can forgive much, but there's one thing I cannot forgive. That you believe it. After everything. You believe it."

My chest tightened saying those words.

Satisfaction filled the lines of Frigg's face.

"Loki…" Tyr said, regret weighing on his voice.

No. He didn't get to be sorry.

I curled my fingers into fists. I hated them.

"Did you really flatter yourselves that I'd destroy you?" I

snapped. "That I'd want to watch the worlds burn? Please. I have better things to do."

I turned away from them and walked towards the doors.

"Are we having a tantrum?" Frigg mocked.

"Don't test me," I warned.

"No, don't test me," she spat. "What did you hope to gain by embarrassing us with this pitiful performance? An apology? Honey cakes and a kiss to make it better?"

I stopped and faced her again, sneering.

"Honey cakes would be a decent start," I said.

She snickered. What else was she concocting in that warped mind of hers?

"Get on your knees."

"Excuse me?"

"On your knees."

Of course. Humiliation. Two could play that game.

"I don't do that," I said.

Several gods and guests stood, putting their hands on their sword hilts. I guess insults were fine, but they drew the line at outright defiance.

"If you value your health, if you want a lesser punishment, you will bow."

She pushed me too far.

"I kneel to no one, Frigg," I said. "Especially to a woman who lied to her husband that she loved him."

The other half of the room stood, steel flashing like lightning as they unsheathed their blades.

She narrowed her eyes, and her entire face sharpened.

"How dare you," she snapped.

"He loved you deeply. Made you his queen. You were enough for him, but he wasn't enough for you."

"Of course he was!" she shouted. "Odin has always held

my heart and holds it still, even though I lost him because of you."

I scoffed.

"Is that the fable you tell yourself?"

"He was my husband. Mine! And you took him from me."

"I didn't take him away, you pushed him away. Out of your arms and into mine."

Silence.

She ground her teeth.

"You don't understand what he and I had," she seethed. "What we shared."

I laughed.

"Not your bed, I know that much," I said. "After he gave you the son you craved, you tensed when he touched you. You closed your door in his face when he knocked. You didn't want him anymore, because you had no further use of him."

She lifted her hand and tried to strike me, but I gripped her wrist, stopping her.

"You go too far."

Her breath curled hot across my neck.

She couldn't imagine how much farther I would go.

"Balder became your only concern. You anticipated the power he would give you. How great that day would be when Odin finally died." I tightened my grasp. "Your son would rule, and you held the reins to a weak boy." Her tendons rolled over her bones beneath my fingers. "You only ever loved the prestige and power Odin offered you, but you never loved the man as I did. You couldn't."

I released her.

Hurt riddled her features. I hit something deep. Dark. Some truth she knew, but hadn't admitted to herself.

Finally it was my turn to enjoy.

"That's the true reason you hate me," I continued. "It's not the prophecy, not me having your husband, but that I threatened your ambitions. You're only capable of loving power, and you'd destroy for it. If the Nine Worlds are to be destroyed, it won't be because of me, it will be because of you."

Her eyes burned into me, and her cheeks glowed crimson. I'd never seen such rage in her before.

The doors bolted shut.

She reached into the leather pouch of runes tied to her belt and pulled out a smooth square of bone. The rune Isa, ice, was carved into it.

Shit.

Frigg was one of the few whose magic equaled my own. I hated admitting how beautifully talented she was, even if her magic only worked through her runes. Unlike her, I didn't need any special tokens to channel my magic. Caveat or no, it didn't make her any less formidable.

I tried to run, but she threw the Isa rune at my feet. Ice spread across the marble floor, fusing the soles of my boots to the stone.

I fell, my shoulder hitting the ground. The rune flew back to her hand, and she put it back in her pouch.

I stretched out my arms, grasping into the grooves of the floor, trying to pull myself away. But her rune magic was faster. Isa worked its way through my body, smothering my fire, knitting my muscles stiff and rigid, until I couldn't move.

All the gods, dignitaries, representatives, and even the stone faced Elvish ambassador, surrounded me. Jeering. Heckling. Encouraging her on.

This wasn't good.

Frigg stepped over me and knelt by my right shoulder. I hated her smug expression.

"Still need your runes to get any decent spell out of you, I see," I mocked. "Maybe one day you'll finally be able to cast something without straight up spells."

"Say what you like. Soon your words won't have quite the same punch."

She pulled out a needle and a spool of thick, black thread.

Interesting choice. I hoped for something bigger and sharper to make this at least slightly scary.

"Move it," Tyr shouted.

He pushed the Vanir dignitaries out of the way, stopping next to Frigg. His eyes fell to her fingers as she threaded the needle.

"What are you doing?" Tyr asked.

"Ensuring the god of lies has told his last," she snapped. "I will not tolerate such slander in my court."

"Oh, I am terrified," I said.

The needle glinted, twisting between her thumb and forefinger.

"You should be."

I chuckled.

"You have no authority," I said. "Odin won't permit whatever twisted torture this is."

She squeezed my chin with a firm hand, driving her nails into my jaw until my bones cracked.

"If you haven't noticed, Odin isn't here."

She thrust the needle into my bottom lip, shooting a raw, lance of pain down my body.

I struggled against her curse to free myself, but I could not move. I could not escape and she tugged the thread through my delicate flesh. Stabbed the needle into my upper lip. Jabbed it back through the bottom.

Sharp. Relentless.

Blood ran down my chin.

And she continued to dig the needle into my swelling mouth. The fibers stung with every yank of the thread she forced through my skin.

White agony gnawed into my bones.

"End this," Tyr bellowed. "You're severing his lips clean off."

Her face lit with exuberance as she split through my skin again.

I groaned with each searing bite of the needle point. Copper rolled hot over my tongue.

"He needs to suffer for what he said!" she screamed.

"Stop this wife, or so help me. Your punishment will be a thousand times worse."

Another voice.

Odin's voice.

20

WHEN PUSH COMES TO SHOVE

I stared at myself in the full length mirror, taking in the damage.

Black thread criss-crossed my lips shut. Blood crusted where the string tore into my flesh. I ran my fingertips over the tight stitches, wincing as I counted them.

Ten in all.

The door to my rooms clicked open. Odin appeared in the mirror's reflection.

I turned to shout at him to get out. I only achieved tugging on the threads instead, cutting them deeper into my skin. A fresh wave of pain seared through my already throbbing flesh.

He walked towards me, taking advantage of my silence, forcing his company on me. Oh. This was cruel even for him.

"She will never lay a hand on you again," he said. "I've ensured it."

I didn't care. I only cared about getting these blasted stitches out so I could have the satisfaction to tell him to go to Hel.

Shoving past him I rushed to my wardrobe and fumbled through the shelves. Silk tunics and fine leather boots fell in heaps to the furs beneath my feet. Where the bloody blazes did I put that knife?

"Looking for this?"

He pointed at a delicate, silver blade laying beside the bowl of pomegranates he had sent me. His smug grin made me want to punch him in the face even more.

I sprung for the blade, but he grabbed it before I reached the handle.

"The veins bulging across your forehead tell me you're in no state to handle sharp objects," he jested. "Let me do it for you so you don't cut yourself."

Fat chance.

I snatched the knife from him and placed the razor edge against the stitches and cut across them.

My flesh stung as I opened my mouth. The threads stretched apart along with ropes of saliva. My eyes watered. Shoving my finger behind the strings, I caught them all and pulled them out in one go.

I returned to the mirror, poking at my lips. Ten red puncture wounds surrounded my mouth like a halo.

"All that work to achieve the perfect complexion, wasted," I grumbled.

He stepped behind me.

"They will heal," he reassured.

I looked at him as if he were mad.

"She used Dwarven steel. That doesn't tend to mix well with immortal flesh," I snapped. "Frigg wanted to ensure she left scars to always remind me. And of course, she had to go for the face."

He rummaged through his pocket and pulled out a small, tin jar and slid it across the inlaid table towards me.

"It's aloe mixed with honey. At least it can help fade the worst of them."

He had to be joking. I needed a shit ton of aloe if I had any hopes of diminishing the mutilation done to me. At least the pain already started to subside as my body healed what it could itself.

"If you wish to do me a favor, stay away from me for a good century or two."

His forehead wrinkled.

"You expect me to abandon you in this state? Your lips are crusted in blood, and muck cakes your clothes...is that a gecko squashed on your backside?"

I twisted my torso and looked down at a flattened, beige creature stuck to my trousers. Must have accidentally sat on the poor thing between the swamp and here.

"Hadn't you heard? It's a new fashion trend."

I walked away from him and entered my bathroom of clean marble and bright tiles. Heading to my alabaster tub, I turned the gold faucet until hot water poured out of the mouth of a swan. Steam slowly filled the room.

My skin tingled with anticipation of soaking myself in jasmine and vanilla.

Odin came in. I bristled. Could he not take a hint I wanted to be alone?

"Stop being stubborn and let me help you," he said.

I lifted my tunic over my head and threw it down. Bits of moss and mangrove leaves sprinkled across the marble.

"I don't want your false concern," I snapped, slipping out of my trousers.

He cleared his throat and looked away, rubbing the back of his neck.

"False concern? What are you talking about?"

I rolled my eyes.

"See yourself out."

Stepping into the tub I slid into the scalding water, loving the heat sinking into my aching muscles. I draped a hot cloth over my face, shutting out the world.

He pulled off the cloth and threw it to the ground, forcing me to stare at him.

"Explain."

He was insistent.

"It's all been an elaborate con since the beginning," I said. "I want no more of it."

I grabbed a bar of Castile soap and rubbed it over my body and face.

"Con?" he asked. "What's gotten into you? The last several months you've been in a drunken stupor, and now your spitting fire and venom."

He chose to play.

"I guess you did miss the main event earlier. You know, before your wife made me a living pin cushion."

I splashed water over myself, rinsing away the soap and dirt, dissolving any remnants of Frigg's attack.

He crossed his arms and arched his right eyebrow.

"Missed what?"

I drove my fingers through my wet hair and glared at him.

"Golda."

The color drained from his face. I enjoyed his shock. It was a rare sight with him.

"Then everything has changed," he whispered.

I sneered.

"Indeed."

I stood, rivets of water running down my bare chest and legs. Stepping out of the tub, I took a clean, linen cloth and dried myself off.

"Why didn't you tell me the truth?" I asked.

He dared to look at me again.

"I was protecting you."

"Don't lie to me." I wrapped the cloth snug around my waist. "You've only ever cared about protecting yourself. From me. Because some stupid prophecy told you I was a harbinger of death and decay."

I barged past him again and walked back to my bedroom, the sheepskin rugs soft against my toes.

He followed.

"Loki…"

I turned and faced him, close enough to…I hated how my blood still heated from him.

"Why did you bring me here," I asked. "Why did you really bring me here?"

He sighed, and sincere misery filled his single, crystal blue eye.

"It was the only way to avoid the fate cast at our feet. Yours, and mine."

I laughed.

"You are hilarious," I said. "Always trying to make it sound better than it is. Like you did me a favor."

He gripped my wrist and pulled me against his chest of hard muscle.

"You have no idea how this could have gone," he growled.

His hot breath spiraled over my naked shoulders, and his heartbeat pounded against me.

"Enlighten me."

He bared his teeth and gripped me tighter, sending a heated thrill down my spine.

"When I first learned of your existence from Golda, I hated you. All you were disgusted me to my very core. You were destined to kill me. To destroy what I broke my back to create. I decided to kill you first."

"How pragmatic."

He held my other arm now, squeezing above my elbow sending shocks of pain to my fingers. Despite myself, each lit my blood.

"I found you in Jotunheim. Alone by the river bank, hungry for your life. All I needed was a second to snap your neck, and I'd be free of you."

I shuddered at the thought of there being no more me.

"And what then?" I asked. "I'm still standing. What changed your mind?"

I felt my pulse thunder beneath his hold, and a darker part of me wished he'd dig his nails even harder into my skin. As he used to do to me. As I had used to do to him.

What was wrong with me?

I didn't want him anymore.

"You did," he whispered. "You were unlike any other I'd ever met. Clever. Exceptionally gifted. The chaos in your veins bewitched me. I couldn't take your life."

How kind of him.

His chest rose and fell against my own like the ocean waves against the shore outside my terrace. Our breaths deepened. I remembered a time I wanted nothing else than to feel him in this way. To steal soft moments in the dark.

Memories of us rose like ghosts.

I did want him. Still. After everything.

"Was any of it ever real?" I asked. My voice rasped.

He stared into my eyes. He loosened his grip and slid his hands down to my own. He skated his thumb across my knuckles. I prickled.

"All of it was real."

I never wanted any words to be so true.

But I knew...

I pulled away, shaking my head.

"I see what you're doing," I said. "You want to confuse me until I can't recognize what's up or down. Make me a victim of gooey memories and salacious sentiment."

"That's not true."

He tried to take my hands again, but I stepped back.

"You just said you tried to murder me. Sorry if I find that idea a mood killer."

He took in a breath.

"What matters is I fell in love with you. I had to discover a way we could be together and escape this wretched curse. Why do you think I'm always off searching for knowledge? Wisdom? The lengths I've gone to gain the answer."

"Apparently you didn't go far enough."

"I traveled to Yggdrasil."

I stiffened.

"The world tree? Men don't survive who visit its branches."

"They don't."

"Yet here you stand."

A sad smile tugged at the corners of his lips.

"It promised me a solution," he said. "I sacrificed myself to myself. I hung from a rope for nine days, dead to all the worlds just to learn what I most wanted to know."

My stomach tightened.

"How to stop me."

He nodded.

"It showed me terrible things. Horrors. What must be done to the Destroyer to escape Ragnarok."

I swallowed what felt like hot sand.

"And what is that?"

His face turned grim. Dark. Haunted.

Frost raced within my bone and sinew.

"It doesn't matter," he said. "What does, is that the tree showed me another way. Not only what I must do, but what I *could* do. A loophole."

He took my hand and turned it to show the mark on my arm from our oath. From when he made me his brother.

"Our blood oath was the loophole."

He nodded.

"You would be forever bound to me. Both of us locked together in fealty to one another. It was a failsafe."

I should have been grateful he sacrificed his very life for an answer to our little problem. But I felt only anger.

I thought he wanted me to be a god because he saw beauty in me. But it was one more fable he fed me with a silver spoon.

"I didn't know when I agreed to be your brother, I really agreed to be your tamed monster."

"I could never tell you the truth of my motive," he said. "It was better you stayed in darkness. As long as you remained by my side, bound to me by our oath, Ragnarok would never come."

"As long as I was controlled, you mean."

He shook his head.

"Can't you see? Everything I've done, I've done for you. For us."

I scoffed.

"Is that supposed to make this better? Am I supposed to thank you?"

"No, just to understand."

I chuckled darkly.

"Forgive me. This is a lot to swallow."

He nodded.

"These last millennia have been like the twilight hours of

summer. I believed I achieved the impossible. That I won. Until the visions returned. Until that day you mentioned Sigyn."

The hairs on my neck raised. I didn't like her name rolling off his tongue.

"That's why you didn't want me near her."

"It alarmed me the Destroyer and the one who bears the sign of Ragnarok should form an attachment. There are no coincidences. It had to be ended."

He stared out, as if lost in thought.

"And what does that mean? 'Bear the sign?'"

"I don't know," he said. "Trust me, I've tried to figure it out. But somehow, despite my every effort, Ragnarok is coming."

My stomach twisted.

"Is Sigyn safe?" I asked. "Is she exempt from you believing she plays any further role in this tragedy? A sign is not a threat."

He met my gaze again. It darkened.

"As long as she doesn't give us cause."

I didn't like this at all.

"Leave her out of this," I snapped. "I swear to you I will never bring Ragnarok. I will never seek to destroy you. I don't want to."

His mouth twisted into a frown.

"What we want, and what will be are always at odds. No one can say for certain what the future holds."

My core quaked as it all dawned on me. How far Odin had always gone for what he wanted. How far he was willing to go to protect himself from Ragnarok. He imprisoned my own children. He sacrificed his own life.

And he killed.

"I must ask, now that we're being honest with each

other, why did you want the king's sons? Why couldn't you spare that boy?"

Confusion knit his brow.

"What?"

"You were consumed with creating an army for your precious Valhalla. Endlessly searching the Nine Worlds for the worthy, collecting their souls for your hall. I want you to tell me the reason."

I wanted to hear him admit it.

"As I've always told you. I needed an army of specialized troops to protect our borders. Those damn Jotnar are always causing trouble. I had to be prepared to face them."

I scoffed.

"Liar. The true reason."

He rubbed his thumbs against his fingertips and sat on the chaise, sinking into the silk pillows. I enjoyed the sweat beading at his temples.

"Why does this event continue to haunt you so much? You've killed nearly as many as me."

I put out my finger to him.

"Killing a child is an evil I cannot stomach. And now I finally see. You wanted his life to save your own."

He tightened his jaw.

"I gave the king a way to rid famine from his lands."

I laughed.

"A famine you caused," I said. "You are a devilish con, Odin. A first rate hustler. You wouldn't rest until you had what you wanted from that man. Until you had his sons."

He shifted in the pillows.

"I admit, his sons were excellent warriors, with braver souls than most gods in Asgard, but..."

"Unfortunately still alive," I finished. "An itsy, bitsy

problem when only the souls of the dead can pass into Valhalla. But you found a way to fix that little snag."

He narrowed his eye and ground his teeth.

"You make me out like I'm some monster. I didn't bring down the blade on them."

"Oh, of course not!" I mocked. "You never liked getting your hands dirty. That's why you sent me to tell their father the only way to make his lands fertile again was to sacrifice his own sons. All of his sons. To you."

"You know such spells carry a cost."

"A cost you made sure he would pay," I seethed. "I watched one after the next hang, their bodies cut down and ripped open so their blood could be sprinkled across the fields to cleanse the soil. It churned my stomach." I stopped. Emotion bit the back of my throat recalling it at all. "But when the last son remained, still only a boy...and you sent me again to his father to tell him...for the first time, I refused you."

He leaned forward, pressing his elbows into his legs and leaning his chin on his steepled fingers. He stared out into the distance. As if staring out into the past.

"You warned me if I went through with it, we were done," he whispered. "But there was no other way."

I sneered.

"Of course not. Not when you craved him for your great army to complete the collection," I said. "That boy's screams as they pulled him up the gallows still cling to my bones, along with the clean snap of his small, fragile neck."

"I gained the boy's soul and lost the heart of the only man I'd ever love."

"Because one soul was worth more to you than our love," I said. "Your protection worth more to you than what was right."

He snapped his gaze to mine. Standing, he walked to me and leaned in.

"I didn't rejoice in their deaths, but the future is always unsettled," he said. "I needed his sons. I was desperate."

"Again, I ask you, tell me the true reason."

He bared his teeth.

"I needed the best I could find, and those sons were the best. I had to prepare. I had to be ready for the destruction I saw, and you at the center of it all. My army in Valhalla isn't for our borders. It's for Ragnarok."

I smiled.

"And you said you weren't a monster."

He grasped me around my throat, sinking his nails into my skin. He never liked it when I was right.

His eye searched me.

"I've risked everything on a love for a man destined to destroy me. I've lied. I've tortured and cheated. I've murdered. I've done terrible things, but I've done them all for you. It's only ever been for you."

I hated how my heart thrashed against his stiff fingers. How his heat sank into me. How it all thrilled me.

"I never wanted any of this pain."

He loosened his grip and rested his hands on my shoulders. He squeezed me tenderly, letting his fingers slide across my skin as if wanting to memorize me.

I kept my eyes open though they wanted to close.

"What choice did I have?" His hot breath skimmed my chin and cheeks. "It was the only way we could be together."

He leaned his forehead against mine and all my defenses shattered.

I sank into him. Surrendered to the pain squeezing my heart at the horror of it all. We could have had it all. Odin could have held the entire universe in his palm, instead he chose to become this thing.

I cradled his face in my hands, wishing it all to be different. *Why couldn't it be different?*

"Trust me," I begged, tracing his cheeks with my thumbs. "Stop this torment infecting you."

He grasped my arms, desperate to hold on to me. As if I slipped away from him. As if he slipped away from deliverance.

"Don't forsake me," he breathed.

He clung to my waist. I dug my fingers into his hair, pressing my nails into his scalp.

The air thickened between us with what we once were.

Need crept in my bones. A desire for a moment of the past. A moment of what we could have been.

Our lips crushed against each other.

Unforgiving. Starving.

His ambition surged into me, filling my mouth, filling my lungs until he filled me to the brim. I sucked more of him into me. I pushed my chaos out into him. Searing his chambers, broiling his blood.

I tore at his clothes, clawing at his chest, hating his edges that kept more of him from me. He scratched across my back, the pain and the pleasure splintering me into oblivion.

His ambition pulled harder, colder through my veins, into my core, mixing into my marrow. Tearing me open and drowning me in him.

My drug.

My addiction.

No.

I paused, my hand clutching his belt. The roar of my heartbeat deafened my ears.

I put my hand against his mouth and pushed him back. His cheeks and lips were flushed as my own.

"We can't go back to how it was," I said through ragged breaths.

"Why not?"

He reached for me. I pulled away.

"Because we both need something the other doesn't have."

His mouth parted, as if lost in what to say.

There was nothing to say.

I walked to my wardrobe and put on a fresh pair of trousers and tunic. I grabbed my purse of coins, and a bottle of akvavit for the road.

Strong again.

Determined.

His shadow lengthened over my shoulder.

"What are you doing?" he asked.

"Leaving. I think that's the best for everyone now, given the circumstances," I said. "I hear the Southern Isles of Vanaheim are quite lovely. Perhaps I'll get a hut with a goat or two and call it a day."

I marched towards the door. He stepped in front of me, blocking my way.

"I don't think that's wise," he said.

I stiffened. I didn't like how he said it.

"Why? Do you have a problem with goats? They can be a bit feisty, but nothing I can't handle."

He glowered.

"It's not about the damn goats!" he spat. "You are not to leave."

"Oh, so you were just threatening me, then?" I asked.

"No, just cautioning you. As a friend."

I'm sure he was.

"Everyone keeps forgetting the most important aspect of this whole prophecy. That we all have a choice, and I will always choose to honor the oath I made to you. I will not destroy you, I will not bring Ragnarok," I said. "Just...let me go."

The lines of his face softened. He reached out and touched my shoulder.

"I believe you," he said. "I believe you when you say you won't cause Ragnarok, but..." he faltered. He didn't have to say the rest.

He always could cut me into pieces.

"But," I echoed. "You will never trust me."

"This isn't choice we are speaking of. It's destiny."

I shook him off of me.

"Am I a prisoner, then?"

His face got stern.

"No," he said. "Not yet. Not if you do what I say."

I laughed.

"When have I ever done what I was told?"

He gripped into my tunic and shoved me against the wall.

"If you wrinkle this new tunic, I will never forgive you," I said.

He twisted his fingers tighter into the silk.

"I can make your time here pleasant, or very unpleasant," he hissed. "If you haven't noticed, there's no one else left in your corner but me. I stand between you and those who want nothing more than to rip out your throat. Don't push me."

Frigid cold slipped down my spine. He made an excellent point, and I hated the flash of fear he triggered in my gut. And while his threats terrified me, I thought only of Sigyn.

He let me go and walked towards the door.

"If I stay," I called after him. He stopped, but didn't turn. "Can you promise me one thing?"

"What?"

"Promise me, no matter how this plays out, no harm will come to Sigyn," I said. I hated the desperation in my voice. "Promise me, and...I will obey you."

No word had ever been harder for me to say.

He turned to me slowly.

"If I were you, I'd not breathe her name again. For her sake, and yours."

He left, slamming the door shut behind him.

Anger flooded my veins. He'd leave her a sitting duck.

Terror replaced my anger.

That's what he wanted.

He wanted her right where she was. And if she ever stepped one foot out of line, if she ever gave them cause, it would take no effort to crush her beneath his heel.

Did he really expect me to accept that?

He should have known better.

21

THE BOOK IS MIGHTIER

Midgard

Basel, Switzerland

The winter air of Midgard bit my lungs until they burned as I raced through the sky towards Basel.

I didn't know how long I had until Odin discovered me gone. And he would know exactly where I'd go.

I pushed myself harder. Faster.

Flecks of white and blue moonlight shimmered beneath me as I soared over the Rhine's rushing current.

Frost crusted the city. The red spires of the Münster cathedral stood black against the night.

I never thought I'd see this city again.

I never thought I'd see her again.

My insides were a wreck of excitement and nerves. Even a flutter of hope she might be happy at us being reunited. I chuckled darkly at such a stupid thought.

After how I left her...How could she see me as anything other than a cad?

I couldn't worry about that now.

With no time for grace, I crashed against the cold cobblestones of a side alley and shook off my falcon aspect, shifting back into my usual self in three seconds flat. A personal best.

I took off running up the slick street of Heuberg, the scent of roasting chestnuts and chimney soot filling my every heaving breath.

I had to get to her.

Sigyn should be finished with her duties at the print shop and back home mashing ginger roots in her study. I really didn't want to race through the whole city looking for her. Not when every second counted.

Reaching her house, my heart tightened.

I didn't know what to expect from her with this reunion, but as long as she came with me, as long as she let me hide her away in some nook in the realms, I didn't care if she hated me for an eternity.

I pounded at her door, the painted oak smooth against my fist.

The latch clicked.

The door opened.

I took in a breath.

Silvia, Sigyn's maid, stood before me.

Damn.

Her pink mouth parted.

Delicate twirls of blonde hair fell beneath her linen cap, and apple peels stuck to her apron that she slowly clasped tight in a fist.

Her shock melted into the nastiest scowl I'd ever received.

It impressed me.

"You," she said, her voice deep and deadly.

"It's a bit nippy out here. Do you mind if we do this inside?"

I tried to squeeze past her, but she pushed me back.

"I think you're fine where you are," she replied.

So this was how it was going to be. Thought as much.

"I can tell you're brimming with hatred for me," I said. "Let me save you the trouble. I'm a cur, a scoundrel, a louse, and a bastard. Does that about cover it?"

I made to walk in again. She put out her arm, bracing it against the doorframe and blocking my way.

"It's a start."

"While I appreciate your loyalty to your mistress, I'm afraid I really have no time for this. I need to speak to her. Urgently."

"Oh, it's urgent?"

"Quite."

She smiled.

"Herr Lanter, my mistress told me if you ever dared return, I was to do this."

"And what's that?"

She slammed the door in my face.

I grumbled beneath my breath as I banged against the door harder.

"Silvia! Let me in! I need to see her! Silvia!"

I smacked the oak with my open palms, clattering the iron hinges and latches.

"Sigyn! You're in danger. You've got to listen to me."

"You will cease these dramatics," a voice called from inside. "Or I will call the Watch."

Sigyn's voice.

Hearing it again kicked me back eight months to when I first saw her. To when I fell in love with her.

And now an inch of oak kept us apart.

"Sigyn. Please. Let me in."

"I did that once before, it didn't turn out too well for me."

Still a cheeky spitfire.

"I know you're angry, but I must speak with you."

"Leave me alone."

The entire door shook in its frame as I continued my assault. Sweat started to bead on my brow as my desperation grew.

"If you want me to stop let me in, otherwise I will keep going until I break down the door. This is dire."

A clean click rang out. The door swung open.

Relief washed over me.

I stepped inside, narrowly missing striking my forehead against the low door frame. Just as the first time I ever entered her home.

A cozy warmth heated my skin, and the always present wood smoke and lavender perked my nose.

My gaze found Sigyn's and I was unable to look at anything else but her eyes.

A force grabbed hold of me, wanting me to rush to her and take her into my arms. To cover her cheeks in kisses and beg her forgiveness.

But her frigid face told me not to dare take a step closer. She looked older somehow. Disillusioned.

Done.

And I knew it had been my fault.

I heard myself swallow.

"Sigyn, I..."

My mind swirled with everything I wanted to say. Everything I needed to say.

Then I noticed something else that was different about her.

My eyes trailed down her dark green velvet gown to her waist. Any words I hoped to speak died in my mouth.

I only felt terror.

Cold, crushing, profound terror.

"You're with child," I breathed.

My gaze couldn't leave her large and round stomach. The child would soon be born.

"A lovely parting gift from you."

My throat dried. Panic tore into my guts.

"It's mine?"

She turned to Silvia, who remained standing next to us. The girl sighed, curtsied and headed back towards the kitchen. She muttered curses beneath her breath at me the entire way, each more graphic than the last.

"Let's go where it's more private," Sigyn said. "Voices carry too well down here."

She tightened her shawl around her shoulders and took off up the stairs. The wood groaned beneath her every slow step.

I followed her into the sitting room stuffed with wainscot chairs and heavy furniture. I couldn't help casting a glance at the Persian rug between the settle and the fireplace.

The spot where I had left her.

She went to the massive desk shoved against the back wall between the two leaded windows. Open books cluttered the surface. She picked up one at a time, snapping each shut, and stacked them on the edge of the desk.

I struggled to keep my memories from wandering to

when I set her on that edge and sank to my knees
before her.

"How is this possible?" I asked.

"It's a common side effect when you bed a woman," she
said. "Do you really not know how this works?"

I combed my fingers through my hair, trying to take it
all in.

Gods were not beholden to the same erratic rules of
reproduction mortals were. We could decide if and when we
wanted to produce children, and I swore to never have
another after Angrboda.

What went wrong?

Golda's voice rang clear and terrible in my mind.

*The children of Loki are who the gods fear above all others.
They are their undoing.*

If Odin discovered I'd fathered another child...If any of
them found this out.

I scrubbed my face with my hand.

It would only be a matter of time. They would come, and
they would take my child away from Sigyn.

I had to get her out.

She clapped another book shut and slammed it on the
growing stack, making the desk quake.

"Do you have any idea what I've endured?" she asked,
breaking me from my thoughts. "You hated the gossip my
brother left to eat at my reputation. That was nothing
compared to the scandal you gave me."

She rubbed her stomach. A flash of her fidelity ignited
in her chest for a heartbeat, then extinguished.

I dared a step towards her. The air condensed with her
anger.

She kept her back to me, her honeyed ginger hair bound

tight and secured with bone pins. I twisted my silver onyx ring around my middle finger.

"I know I owe you a million explanations," I said. "But can we delay all this for another time? We have to go."

She grasped a book, turned, and threw it at my head. I ducked. The book struck the wall behind me.

I deserved that.

"I've waited long enough to hear any reason from you!" she screamed. "I will not wait one second more."

She hurled another book at me, a thicker one. It whacked my shoulder with a stinging punch.

I deserved that, too.

I crouched and put up my hands in surrender. My rule was an angry woman always won.

"I didn't want to hurt you," I said.

Red inflamed her cheeks and spread across her chest.

"Too late."

She chucked a third book directly into my kneecap, sending a jolt of pain down my leg.

Ok, this was getting excessive now.

"You don't understand. I was trying to help you."

She clasped a fourth book in her hand, digging the tips of her nails into the leather.

"By abandoning me? Was this all some twisted game?" she seethed.

"No," I said. "This has never been a game."

"Did you love me at all?"

I started to rise slowly back to my feet, wincing as I straightened my still throbbing knee.

"If I didn't, I wouldn't be standing here before you now, risking everything. I came here at great peril to myself. For you."

She pushed out a hoarse laugh.

"You're full of shit."

"Excuse me?"

"You expect me to believe your false excuses? To fall back into your arms because of a few noble words?

"I'm telling you the truth."

"I'm sure you are, because when have you ever lied to me?"

I flattened my lips. Frustration twisted my insides. How much longer was this going to go on?

"What do you want from me?" I snapped. "Do you want to horse whip me? Kick me? Would that make you feel better?"

She flung the book to the floor splitting the spine on impact.

"Only I have the right to be angry!" she yelled. "I woke to find you gone." She paused. Red misted her eyes. "You promised you'd never leave me. And you just left."

She leaned against the desk and her hands shook as she wiped her eyes.

Pain tightened my chest. If she only knew the agony I suffered choosing to go. Choosing to do what was best for her.

Choosing her above myself.

"I never just left," I said.

She snapped her eyes up to mine.

"It doesn't matter anymore," she said. "I've struck you from my heart, and I am free of you."

She pushed herself off the desk and walked towards the door. The dagger I'd given her all those months past glinted at her hip in the firelight.

"Then why do you still have the dagger I gave you?" I asked.

She stopped and faced me. Pulling the dagger from its sheath, she gripped the hilt and stared at the blade.

"It's a reminder to never rely on anyone but myself again."

She might have well stabbed me in the chest with it and twisted.

Clear ticks rang in my ears coming from the firegilt brass turret clock on the wall. Time continued to run.

"Hate me," I said. "Despise me for what I did to you, but you must come with me and leave this house. If not for yourself, then for our child."

She scoffed.

"I will never go with you."

Damn this woman and her stubbornness! I knew I loved it about her, but right now it started to give me anxiety. And I didn't do anxiety.

I neared her. She stepped back.

"You are in grave danger. Please, listen to me."

"This is insanity. I think it's time you left."

"Not without you."

I grabbed her wrist and tugged her towards the door.

"No! Let me go!" she cried.

She dug her heels into the carpets and tugged, wrenching herself free from me. She swung out her dagger in front of her, pointing it at my throat.

I put out my hands.

"I cannot let you face them," I said. "I will not surrender you to them."

Confusion tightened her brow.

"Who is them?"

Here it came.

The awkward bit.

"The gods."

She raised her right eyebrow and lowered her blade.

"There is only one God. The rest are fiction. Myth."

"About that," I said. "You told me once you wanted to believe that the myths you loved were true. Remember what you told me about St. George killing the dragon to save the maiden? I'm telling you you can believe it."

Her expression hardened.

"You really must think me a fool," she hissed. "You are the grandest liar I've ever met."

If only she knew how right her words were.

"You are right. I am a liar," I said. "I am the god of lies, asking you to trust him."

Her shoulders tensed and she shut her eyes, pointing at the door.

"Lukas, get out. I'm done."

I stepped towards her.

"My name never was Lukas."

"There's always another layer of deception with you."

"I told you, that's who I am."

She narrowed her eyes.

"And who is that?"

I paused.

"Loki."

She let out a deep chuckle.

"Well, that's very fitting, I'll give you that," she said. "The god who is the most eloquent, charming, and always stabs you in the back. That's exactly who I'd put my faith in when he asked."

That hurt.

"The irony isn't lost on me, I assure you."

She ground her teeth.

"You mock me with this."

"I don't mock."

She walked to the fireplace and lifted a painted vase off the mantle. Turning to me, she let it slip from her fingers. Porcelain exploded into splinters at her feet.

"Fix it."

"What?"

"If you are a god, prove it. Fix the vase."

I rubbed behind my ear.

"I'm afraid that's not exactly in my repertoire."

Her lips curled into a victorious smile, as if she got me.

"Of course not. Because you are a fraud."

No one called me a fraud.

"I'm the god of chaos, not vases," I said.

She shrugged.

"I'm afraid I will need a little more than your word, especially if you claim to be the literal god of lies."

I sighed, pressing my head in my hands.

The ticking from the clock grew louder in my ears, reminding me of every second we wasted locked in this fight.

She left me no recourse.

I lowered my hands and met her eyes.

"If you won't take my word for it, I'll just have to show you."

I gave her my most charming smile and linked my fingers while I stretched my arms. Satisfying cracks played down my knuckles.

"Prepare yourself, my dear, things may get a bit heated."

She crossed her arms and tapped her foot.

"Oh, I can't wait," she said.

I shivered as I summoned my element, willing it to rise to the surface and consume me.

Fire exploded in my chest and ripped through my veins.

Down my neck it spread, searing throughout my torso, chasing the sinew into my fingertips.

My eyes erupted in flames. The blaze raced within me, and outside me, licking my arms and legs, wrapping me completely in an inferno of hissing and snapping fire.

Sigyn's arms fell at her sides. The anger creasing her forehead softened.

"Is this what you wanted to see?" I asked.

Her mouth parted as she stepped closer to me.

Sparks snapped in my hair, and embers spiraled around me in seconds of yellow and orange flecks.

"It is true," she whispered. "All of it."

The fire burning on my skin drenched her face in warm light.

"Even the god of lies can occasionally tell the truth."

She reached out her hand, letting it hover over me, as if wanting to feel the heat rise from my chest.

"That's why you didn't die in the fire when you ran in and saved my print shop," she said. "You couldn't, because you *are* fire."

"To my core," I said, my breath scalding.

Her fidelity burst within her chest, bright and pure, sending a rush of peace through me.

Before I could stop her, she laid her hand on my chest. But I didn't burn her. I didn't even sear her flesh though my fire licked over her hand and between her fingers.

I tilted my head.

No one had ever been able to touch me in my true form.

Except her.

She was like a cooling balm, her wholeness, her over-powering joy, calming the fire raging inside of me. Controlling the wildness of my nature.

She smiled, and her own element strengthened, light flowing out her pores and dousing her in bright gold.

"You're beautiful," she said.

If only she knew of her own beauty.

Steadfastness pulsed through her palm into my heart. Hope rocked through me. Cinders cracked between my fingers as I placed my hand on top of hers and gripped it tight.

Our elements did not repel, they entwined, complemented, in some esoteric way. We were two sides of a coin.

"This is what I am, Sigyn. I am chaos. I am lies. I am tricks," I said. "I thought by leaving you, I was protecting you from what I am. But I only placed you in greater danger than I could have ever imagined. Loving you was my greatest sin."

She traced her thumb across my burning cheek.

"Love is never a sin."

"It is if your love will only ever cause the other pain. I couldn't damn you to that fate. It wouldn't have been fair to you."

I sank my fingers into her hair, dislodging the bone pins securing her braid in place. I breathed in her rosemary, filled my lungs with the ginger floating beneath.

She skated her hands to my shoulders. I slid mine along the arch of her back.

"Fair would have been giving me the choice to decide," she said. "It should have been mine to make, and I would have chosen you."

Her lips met mine, and I fell away into her kiss.

Fire and fidelity mixed and twisted around us in blinding light, wind rushing through our hair and rippling our clothes.

For those seconds, the dangers outside our door didn't matter. There was only she and I.

We parted.

The light extinguished.

We returned to our normal selves.

She looked into my eyes with love, and I thought I'd go weak. Her gaze fell to my lips.

I made to kiss her again. She stopped me.

"What happened to your mouth?" She traced my lips that continued to burn from her kiss. "It's riddled with red marks."

I swallowed, forced back into the world.

Reality was a bitch.

"A little token of what happens when you cross the gods," I said. "Far worse is awaiting if they catch us. We need to go."

I pulled her towards the door.

"Why am I in danger from them?" she asked. "What crime have I committed?"

"You exist," I said. "They believe this stupid prophecy that claims you will bear the sign that instigates Ragnarok."

"Ragnarok?"

"The end of the worlds. The end of everything."

She stroked her stomach, as if trying to protect our child in her.

"This is ridiculous," she said. "I'm just Sigyn. I'm not any immortal."

I stopped and looked at her. She had to be told.

"No, but you have the element of one."

Her eyes widened.

"What?"

"You should have burned when you touched me, but you didn't," I said. "I can't explain why, just as I can't explain why in all my millennia I've never encountered the element you contain. Why it lives within you. It is the most precious, the most elusive. You are fidelity, Sigyn. You are hope."

She didn't answer, as if lost in the abyss of trying to understand what I said.

"And..." she stopped. "And is this element in me significant to the prophecy?"

I grimaced.

"I don't know, but there are no coincidences," I said. "And it's not good the one who bears the sign that instigates Ragnarok, should find the one that summons it."

Confusion twisted in her brow.

I put my hand on her stomach for the first time. Devotion and love swelled in my chest for the life we made growing inside her.

"I am the Destroyer, and you carry my child," I said. "They will hunt you. They will hunt our child. And they will take it. I gave them my family once before, I swear I will not again. This is why we must run."

I took her hand, and we rushed towards the stairs.

She tugged me back.

"Loki..."

Concern tightened the lines of her face as she looked down. She lifted her skirts.

My heart thundered in my ears.

A puddle of water spread at her feet.

22

WHEN IT RAINS

She cried out as a wave of pain clutched her insides. Her contractions came more rapidly and with more violence.

I almost wanted to scream with her as panic shredded my nerves. I had no idea what to do. Birth was a subject I always felt best avoided.

I despised this feeling of not knowing. Like I was free falling, and not in a fun way.

Her cheeks flushed red, and her chest heaved as she sucked in large breaths.

"What should I do?" I asked.

Sweat beaded across Sigyn's forehead as I helped her into her bedroom crammed with dark oak furniture. A fire raged in the hearth, and the scent of wood filled my lungs.

"You can get this baby out of me," she grunted.

Floorboards creaked. Silvia appeared in the doorway, eyes glaring with murder. She gripped a cast iron pan.

What the blazes?

"Get off of her, you fiend!" Silvia warned me.

She stepped towards me, raising her pan to strike me.

"Silvia," Sigyn said, forcing the name out between her clenched teeth. "Put that down. The baby is coming."

The scowl melted from Silvia's face, replaced by shock. The pan fell from her hand and struck the floor with a good bang.

"I'm sorry, I heard a scream, and..."

"Obviously thought me to blame," I said. "It's fine, it's not the first time I've been attacked today."

She narrowed her eyes and dropped her hands to her hips.

"You've done this to her! To me you still deserve a hard wallop across the head."

I forgot how much I enjoyed her.

Sigyn grasped hold of the sturdy bed post and bent forward, wincing as another crash of agony rolled through her.

"Enough!" she grunted. "This baby is actively trying to shred my insides. I cannot take your bickering."

She looked at Silvia. "Make yourself useful and get that clean linen off the dresser and bring it here."

She shot her gaze to me.

"And you, get this damn dress off of me. I'm stifling."

Now that was something in which I was quite adept.

I tore at her laces, pulling the cords through the eyelets. My fingers might have well become useless sticks. I could usually undress a woman in two shakes of a lamb's tail, but now I trembled and fumbled and tangled. Damn these nerves!

This was embarrassing.

I breathed out in relief, finally slipping her out of her gown and kirtle, leaving only the thin smock to cover her.

Silvia rushed across the Persian rug and laid the stack of linen on the bed thick with mattresses.

Sigyn dug her nails into the bed post, panting. Sweat glistened on her skin in the candlelight, and a twinkling drop rolled off her nose and splashed against the floor.

Silvia stared at Sigyn, clutching her arms tight across her chest.

"Let me fetch the midwife," she begged.

"Yes, I agree," I said.

Sigyn shook her head.

"Frau Horber has a bad back, and she's well into bed. The baby will be here by the time she hobbles to the front door."

"Then who will deliver this baby?" I asked.

She faced Silvia.

"You."

Sigyn took in a breath and shut her eyes. Another rush of pain and contractions seized her.

"Me?" she shrieked.

"I need you both to do exactly as I say..." She winced. "...and we should be done before the hour is through."

I didn't like this idea.

Neither did Silvia from the look of the green shading her skin. She wrung her hands.

"What if I get sick on you!" she said. "What if I get sick on the baby? You know I don't do well with blood and globby bits."

This girl would not have survived Jotunheim. Blood and globby bits were just a part of life where I came from. In fact, I could say ninety percent of my childhood consisted only of those two things.

"You won't get sick," Sigyn assured. "I've taught you the basics in tending. Just consider this a jump in your training. You can do this."

Silvia wavered and her shoulders slumped as if her body prepared to faint.

"What must we do?" I asked, having to do something before I crawled out of my skin.

"Get me to the birthing stool."

Silvia and I each took one of Sigyn's arms over our shoulders and sat her on a stool shaped like a crescent moon. We lifted her smock and slowly sat her down. The wood groaned as she helped us position herself until her back was straight, and legs spread open.

"You." She tapped my shoulder. "Get behind me."

Had the circumstances been different, I would have been excited by such a command.

As it was, I obeyed her immediately.

Taking a chair I sat behind her and straddled my legs on either side of her. I wrapped my arms around her, and she latched onto my hands, lacing her fingers between my own.

She took in three short breaths and squeezed my hands with rigid fingers.

She craned her neck back, pressing her head against my shoulder. I kept her upright, bracing myself and digging my heels into the floorboards as she thrashed. Her entire body fought against mine.

Sigyn gasped for air and leaned forward. Down she pushed our arms, forcefully pressing our hands into the tops of her legs. Her fingernails bit into my skin, cutting between my knuckles.

For being only a human, she damn near crushed my fingers.

She relaxed, and took in another breath, and let it slowly out between her lips.

"It's coming," she rasped. "Silvia, tell me what you see."

Silvia swallowed. Her green pallor deepened.

But she knelt between Sigyn's legs and squinted trying to make it all out. Wonder flooded her eyes.

"I can see a head!" she exclaimed. "Red hair. Bright red."

I inwardly somersaulted. My child was coming into the world, and it was ours.

My heart pounded with eagerness to meet the little tyke. Would they take after their stoic mother, or after their hellion of a father? I smiled as my mind raced imagining it all.

"Good...good," Sigyn said. "Now comes the tricky part. I need to let the body do the work. I shouldn't push too hard until the next pain, even if," she stiffened and yelped, "I want to."

I reinforced my embrace around her.

"Just breathe," I whispered in her ear.

Her hair was damp with sweat, and salt and coriander rose from her hot skin into my nose. She tightened her grip on my hands and she pressed her shoulders into my chest.

"Take your time. It's coming," Silvia encouraged.

Though she looked like death, she stayed the course.

Sigyn cried and strained again. I pressed my thumbs into her hands, wishing I could give her more, do more, for her. I hated her agony and hoped it to end.

"The head is out!"

Sigyn screamed, calling out to all manner of saints.

A cry. A clear, beautiful, loud cry filled the room.

Silvia lifted a wriggling, wrinkled pink thing to Sigyn's chest. Tears streamed down her flushed cheeks as she held our child in her arms.

"It's a boy," she said, as Silvia handed her a clean cloth to wrap him in.

I don't believe I ever smiled as wide as I did in that moment. Emotion swelled in me as I gently stroked my son's soft skin. Well, perhaps sticky was the more accurate word. But it didn't matter. Only he mattered.

A deep, unceasing love for this child, *my* child, filled every nook and cranny of my being.

Sigyn's smile vanished. Her face twisted, and she bent forward. Silvia rushed to her and took the baby and placed him in the prepared crib beside us.

"What is it?" I asked.

"I...I don't think this is over."

Silvia knelt again and looked. Her mouth parted.

"Another comes."

"Another?" Sigyn and I both asked in unison.

My heart exploded with pride. Twins! When I did something, I really did it a hundred and ten percent.

Sigyn braced herself against me and grunted. She seemed weaker than with the first child. I supposed she was exhausted. That's all.

I hoped that was all.

She huffed and strained as Silvia and I both coached her as the hour turned into two.

The child was stubborn. This one obviously took after its mother.

Sigyn tired. But childbearing was a tiring process.

Although, why did her skin become so cold?

"Another boy!"

A blaring wail spilled out of the child's fresh lungs as Silvia put him in Sigyn's arms. My love deepened even more.

My sons.

"He's perfect," Sigyn whispered, running her fingertips over his curled fists. Her voice faltered.

"Perfect," I echoed.

"You better take him, I'm feeling a bit light headed."

Silvia placed him beside his brother, who now slept. Two shocks of red hair in a crib.

Could life get any better?

Sigyn slackened in my arms. Her head flopped on my shoulder.

Alarm raced through me.

"Sigyn?" I said. "Can you hear me?"

Silvia walked in front of her to check. The color in her face faded into ash.

Blood pooled at Sigyn's feet.

She took a step back, the red chasing her across the floorboards and soaking the carpets as it continued to rush out of Sigyn.

My throat dried.

I knew what this meant.

It crushed me to know what this meant.

"I don't know what to do!" Silvia cried. "There's so much blood."

She ran to a chamber pot and retched.

Even in the most dire of circumstances I never once skipped a beat in forming a course of action. But now? I paced trying to force my mind out of the weeds tangling and choking me.

Silvia pulled her head out of the pot and wiped her mouth.

"Go," I told her. "Fetch a doctor. Anyone."

She nodded and ran out the door. Weeping.

She knew what this meant, too.

I lifted Sigyn and kicked the stool away and laid her on the floor. Kneeling over her, I patted her cheek.

"Sigyn...Sigyn!"

She remained silent. Blood continued to spill, spreading

out from between her legs. Her life drained into the cracks in the floorboards. Into the fibers of the rugs.

And there was nothing I could do to stop it.

She was dying.

My chest tightened as all my fears rose like monsters from the recesses of my mind.

I cradled her face between my hands. Our children cried. As if they knew they were losing their mother.

"Come back to me," I said.

Her heart struggled beneath my fingertips. She was lost to unconsciousness. To darkness.

And soon, darkness eternal.

I moved back. Away.

Her children wailed for her. They needed her.

I needed her.

Something in me shifted.

And I came to a decision.

A terrifying decision.

Odin had once told me what I wanted could kill her. That her mortal body might not be able to withstand such a transformation.

Circumstances had changed.

I scrambled back to her side. More blood rushed away from her. Emptied her.

Could.

Might.

Those words ricocheted between my ears. I clung to them as glittering diamonds. Dug my nails into the edges of their possibility. Their potential.

I didn't know if it would work. I didn't even know if it were something I could perform.

But all I had was the gamble.

The chance.

I tore my tunic to get to my bare flesh and pressed my fingers against my chest. As I remembered Odin had done an eon ago.

My skin and bone pushed back, but I continued to force my fingers in.

Pain swelled. Pressure built.

I closed my eyes imagining what I wanted. Needed.

I thrust them into me.

I buckled forward, agony twisting as I stretched my fingers, sinking deeper into my cavity.

I sensed heat. Burning, smoldering heat coming from my core.

My element.

I touched it, and my entire body quaked.

Taking a deep breath, I tore off a piece. A shock of pain rocked to the soles of my feet, and I believe I heard myself scream as everything around me darkened. Flickered.

It focused again.

I yanked and believed I wrenched my own self from my roots. As if I tugged on strings attached to my toes.

I had no choice.

I grunted and ripped it out.

A white flash.

A strike of an axe in my sternum.

An orb glowed between my thumb and forefinger. One tiny bite of chaos.

I looked down at my chest and breathed through the dulling pain. No wound. No sign at all that I'd just stuck my entire fist into me.

Sigyn's skin was a nasty shade of blue.

Not much time remained.

Exposing her naked skin between her breasts, I hovered the orb above her heart. Biting my lip, I pressed the piece of my chaos into her chest, sinking it into her depths.

And I thought. I thought of this piece giving her renewed life. Of my energy feeding her fidelity. Of my chaos transforming her element into what it was always meant to be.

Immortal.

A goddess.

Her eyes opened.

She gasped in a breath.

Sigyn pressed her palms against the floorboards and sat herself up. As if she'd woken from a refreshing nap.

She touched her head.

I stared at her in shock.

In disbelief.

I did it.

"I must have fainted," she said. "I got so woozy and then...I don't remember. Oh, the poor babies! Why are you letting them cry?"

She stood, swayed slightly, then walked to the crib and rocked it gently. Looking down at them she smiled.

"There, there," she cooed.

The babies quieted.

She shifted her attention to her smock. Her pupils dilated following the trail of crimson staining the fabric.

Her smile turned to horror.

She stepped back, gripping her smock drenched in blood from her waist to her feet.

"What happened?" she asked.

I stood, but I couldn't speak.

Her eyes continued down her smock to the smooth lake of blood coating the floor and saturating the rugs.

She looked at me. Pierced me.

"How am I standing?" she asked, her voice deep. Shaken. "How am I alive at all?"

I opened my mouth to explain.

Thunder rolled in the distance.

I turned from her and marched to the window. Throwing the leaded glass open I leaned out over the sill and looked out.

The clouds churned, lightning blazing within the boiling sky.

"Loki, what did you do to me?" she asked.

Terror twisted my stomach.

I turned back to her.

"They've found us. We must run."

23

IT POURS

W e fled along the slick cobblestones of Heuberg and out beneath the massive Spalentor gate, leaving Basel behind us.

Frigid air stung my eyes, and Sigyn's heaving breaths filled my ears as we ran into the winter's night. I held one child tight under my furs, while the other Sigyn swaddled within her thick cloak.

Lightning split the darkness, throwing the fields and gardens in and out of purples and blues.

We kept on racing South into the countryside, our feet pounding against the sheet of frost covering the dirt road.

The storm strengthened, Thor, and whoever else joined the hunt, gaining on us.

I would not suffer the embarrassment of that oaf catching me a second time.

I split off duplicates of Sigyn and myself, sending one pair of illusions scurrying North, another running East, and the last speeding West.

Thunder cracked the sky, and the earth trembled

beneath my boots. Probably a demonstration of Thor's brain exploding, not knowing which of us to follow.

I couldn't help smiling. Even in these circumstances I could still irritate him.

The churning clouds stilled for a second or two, then took off chasing the pair headed North towards the Rhine and Germany.

Relief calmed my hammering heart despite only buying us a little time. They were adept hunters, and we their prey.

If only we could make it out of Midgard...That was impossible. Sigyn did not yet possess the ability to realm jump as a fledgling goddess, and the children even less so.

We had to stay the course towards the Alps. Hiding away in some remote mountain valley was our only shot until Sigyn and the children were strong enough to flee to Alfheim. Queen Elénaril of Nilhanor owed me a favor.

Knowing her, she'd take us in just for the joy of refusing to hand us over to Odin. He had no jurisdiction in Alfheim, and the Elves loved rubbing it in his face.

Elénaril was our only hope of surviving this.

We kept sprinting along the Birs river, twisting with it between pastures and hills hour after agonizing hour.

Dawn broke. Deep reds and pinks slowly dissolved the inky black of the sky.

Cold ate further through my leather boots and numbed my toes.

We skimmed the edges of Dornach, a small village of no consequence nestled in nowhere.

"We need to stop," Sigyn huffed. Rolls of her breath faded into the air.

"We can't," I said. "They will soon realize they chase an illusion. They will return."

She slowed her pace.

"Our children are only hours old. They're hungry, and this air will chill their lungs."

I stared out at the empty road, knowing we had to keep going. Knowing we couldn't. My shoulders dropped.

Lifting my furs I checked my son. He stirred huddled against my chest, nuzzling for food. I could feel the coolness starting to spread across his skin. Though he and his brother shared half my immortal blood, it wasn't enough to protect them fully.

Not yet, anyway.

I closed my eyes for a heartbeat and took in a breath.

"Then we must find cover," I said. "But it has to be concealed, obscured. Tucked away in a forgotten pocket where their eyes cannot find us."

She turned and faced the forest. Bitter wind tore through her hair, sweeping red ringlets across her neck and cheeks. The morning sun coated her with pale light.

"A labyrinth of caves rests beneath the forest floor," she said. "I used to play in them as a child with my brother. One could be lost in their depths forever and never be found."

"Never to be found is exactly what we need."

She took off, and I followed her, leaving the straight road behind and entering a muddle of dense woods.

Ice glazed the tall pines, and hoarfrost crusted the fallen leaves of the surrounding walnut and larch trees. We trekked deeper, twigs and earth cracking, snapping, and popping, breaking the hard silence of winter.

Wild goats leapt over fallen logs. The ground grew rockier, slicker, and the din of a waterfall crashed in the distance. I could smell ice and wet stone.

"It's not much farther," she said, catching herself as her heel slipped on the slope we struggled down.

I hoped not. I'd rather had my fill of traveling these past days.

Pressing my son harder against me, I held onto tree trunks and branches, whatever I could to keep steady. The hill steepened more. The frozen soil split beneath my heels as I struck the edge of my boot into the cold earth that threatened to make me fall.

We descended past damp boulders and squeezed between pine trees. Walls of stone rose higher on either side of us until we reached the bottom of a gulch.

Water gushed over the lip of the cave entrance splattering the rock below, and my trousers, as we ventured into the cavern.

The bite of winter softened, along with the sunlight as twilight swallowed us.

Humid air condensed dew on my face and hair.

"Watch your step," she said.

We crept beside the rough cavern wall, avoiding the slick rivulets of water trickling along the ground to our left.

The first vault rose over our heads, and I had to crane my neck to even see the top. Our steps and the prattle of the miniature streams mixed into haunting echoes.

I hated how small I felt. The abyss surrounding us. The emptiness.

"How deep can you lead us?" I asked.

"I've never dared venture past where we stand," she said. "I wouldn't risk losing the light."

I peered out into the cavities and chambers of pitch black. It made me shiver.

One was so...alone.

I snapped my fingers, igniting a small ball of fire. It flickered within my palm. Light flooded the cavern, reflecting off sheets of white, glistening flowstone. Salamanders scurried off into crevices and chasms.

"Good thing you have me," I said.

Bats clung to the walls as we groped our way deeper into the cave. We clambered over rock, and pressed between narrow openings, and scooted beneath slabs of limestone. Grit and mud covered our knees and elbows.

The babies started to fuss more as their hunger grew. But we had to press on into the void.

The entire time I tried not to think how my fire was the only thing between us and being lost in darkness forever. If it ever went out...The thought gave me chills again.

Caves were nasty, sinister formations. I couldn't wait to leave.

We passed into a new chamber crowded with stalagmites and stalactites. Water purred into a pool alive with squirming white cavefish. Finally able to stand straight, I stretched my back and my vertebrae rejoiced.

I moved several small stones into a circle with my foot. Three centipedes scuttled away into the gloom. Caves were a treasure trove of all the lovely creepy crawlies.

I threw the fire burning in my hand down into the pit and swelled the flames to get some decent heat into the twins' bones.

That was the benefit of being me. My fire didn't require fuel to keep crackling, only my will.

Sigyn sat near the fire and leaned against the cave wall. She uncovered the child in her arms and rocked him gently.

I pressed my back to the rock and slid down, sitting beside her.

She fed one, and then the other.

With my free arm, I reached behind her shoulder and pulled her against me. We both stared at our sons as they finally drifted off to sleep, full and content. I marveled at their short and fast breaths. How their faces contorted and fingers stiffened and relaxed lost in their dreams.

Firelight washed them in gold. In warmth. In love.

My little family.

Happiness gripped me again, and I dared to hope...

"We haven't even named them yet," she said, her voice soft. "What shall it be? Gerhardt? No, how about Balthazar?"

How about neither?

"I think we have bigger problems than choosing names," I said.

"I just want them to have a name, in case..."

She bit her lip.

I could sense her fear. It mirrored my own. I despised fear. I had no use for it, and now it infected me. Because for the first time, I had something more significant than my own skin to lose.

"I've never run from literal gods before," she finished.

I held her tighter against me, rubbing her upper arm with my thumb.

"I swear nothing will happen to them," I said. "To you."

I forced a smile, though inside my confidence wavered.

"Even so," she said. "It will take my mind to better places. To the future."

The future.

Why did that word taste so bitter? Like it mocked me?

I handed her the baby sleeping in my arms, and she cradled both against her bosom. My heart somersaulted again.

"Then we will call them Narfi and Nari," I said.

She smiled.

I leaned in and kissed her forehead.

We sat in silence, huddled together, as a family. Us

against the world. A very angry world. But it didn't matter, because in that slice of time, we had each other.

"I will protect you, Sigyn," I said. "All I am is yours."

"How nauseatingly sentimental," a familiar voice said from the darkness.

My muscles tensed.

* * *

I PULLED Sigyn's cloak tight around her, hiding the children beneath, and stood in front of her. If they found the children...

Frigg stepped out of the black and into the flickering light. Mud streaked her simple linen gown, and her usually flowing hair was bound tight behind her head. A tidy row of daggers hung from her wide, leather belt.

She came prepared to fight.

"I love the warrior vibe you're sporting," I said. "Very menacing."

She strutted across the twisting rock towards us. Ghostly shapes moved behind her.

"And you've brought friends," I said. "How nice."

Thor, Balder, Tyr, and Odin slunk into the gold, their shadows stretching up the walls and reaching the ceiling. Weapons glinted at their sides, and dirt smeared across their straight and grim faces.

"Why so glum?" I asked. "It looks like you're about to attend a funeral."

Question was, theirs or mine?

Odin narrowed his eye, staring at Sigyn who remained crouched behind me. He lifted his gaze to my own and set his jaw.

"I knew you'd come back for her," he said, his voice a mix of emotions.

He took a step closer. I remained standing firm.

"Congratulations," I said, slow clapping. "You are a master sleuth. What gave you the first clue? The obvious, or the fact any numbskull with half a brain cell could figure it out?"

Odin let out an exasperated sigh, and rubbed his forehead, as if already done with me.

Balder seemed equally done.

He clenched his teeth and dropped his hand to the sword at his hip. Grit filled his usually manicured fingernails.

"For once in your life can you just shut up?" Balder asked. "It's always one quip after the next with you."

"Is that a problem?" I asked. "I think it helps liven up an otherwise dull conversation."

He unsheathed his weapon, and walked towards me, pointing the blade at my chest.

"You have no regard for what you are. For what you are destined to do to us. You stomp out virtue, you raze honesty, and you kill goodness. And you don't care. You take joy in it."

I laughed. His nonsensical outburst was incredibly endearing.

"Are you going to jab me with your little sword, then?" I asked. "I know you've been dying to sink it into me for two millennia at least."

He tightened his grip on his hilt.

"Try five."

I smiled, enjoying his spite. I was glad to know he had it in him.

Odin snapped his fingers and motioned for Balder to

back down. He glared at me, but obeyed his daddy. I waved at him as he crept away.

"Loki," Odin said. "You have one last chance. I suggest you don't waste it."

"How generous."

"Leave the girl, and return with us."

I crossed my arms over my chest.

"What for?" I asked. "So you can shackle me? Slaughter me as you once planned? Make me endure a stern lecture on responsibility?"

He dared a step closer. The lines of his face softened, as if trying to appeal to my reason and good sense.

"We can move forward from this," he said. Almost pleading.

"I appreciate the optimism, but I think that ship sailed long ago."

He flattened his lips. Tension stiffened the air between us.

Thor cracked his knuckles, breaking the silence.

"Then I can't wait to finally crush your bones," he snarled, tossing Mjolnir in the air and catching it. "First, for telling everyone I wore a dress, and second for bedding my wife."

He bared his teeth that gleamed white behind his thick, red beard.

Thor really was intent on making life difficult for me. Thank gods Sigyn couldn't understand Asgardian.

"What are they all saying?" Sigyn questioned.

Frigg shot her gaze to Sigyn behind me, and a wicked smile pulled at her lips.

"How you gave your heart to a wolf," she answered, switching to Sigyn's tongue. "He seduces his way through the Nine Worlds for the pleasure of adding to his list.

You're one of a thousand who he's claimed to love. Don't fool yourself thinking you're anything but a notch in a bedpost."

I crushed my nails into my palms, pretending they were Frigg's throat.

I braced myself for the coming storm from Sigyn. The questions, the demand for explanations. The inevitable hate.

I had done those things.

But never to her.

"The past doesn't define who we are in the present," she said. "I trust him, and I always will, no matter how hard you try to undermine our connection."

I turned and faced her, still amazed how she could continually surprise me with her constancy. She gave me a reassuring smile.

"Stupid girl!" Frigg said. "You stand before danger now because of him. Because he doesn't care who he harms, as long as he gets his thrill."

The muscles in Sigyn's neck flexed.

"I stand before danger because of you," she spat.

"You insolent human!" Frigg snapped. "Do you realize who you address?"

"Of course," she replied. "A bitch."

I loved this woman.

Frigg's right eye twitched, and she clutched her dagger for two seconds before letting her hand fall back to her side.

Odin stepped between us and Frigg.

"Enough," he said. "Loki, end this now, or I swear I will rip out your spine and beat you to death with it."

"You seem to think I'm just going to surrender at a few veiled threats," I said. "That's a bit anticlimactic, don't you think?"

A sharp cry echoed off the cave walls. A second joined in.

My blood went cold.

Narfi and Nari.

Odin's mouth parted. The others snapped their gazes on Sigyn, as if lions spotting their prey.

The twins continued to wail. Sigyn looked at me, terror in her features.

"Take off your cloak, girl," Odin said.

He marched towards us.

"It's just some bats fighting over a spider," I said, pushing the words through my tightening throat. "The echos in here play with your mind. Sound like all manner of ghosts and goblins."

"Don't insult me. You reproduced with her."

"They're not mine. I found her this way."

"Take off the cloak," Odin commanded again, ignoring me.

He slid out his small battle axe from the belt at his side. The sharp edge glinted with warning in the firelight.

"I haven't the time for this," Frigg said, rushing towards us.

She tried to get behind me and snatch Sigyn's cloak away. I blocked her.

"Don't," I warned.

Frigg tried to claw at her again.

"You're awfully protective of children you claim aren't yours."

She lunged her hand behind me and gripped Sigyn's arm and pulled her out of my shadow.

The cloak fell and pooled at her feet. Sigyn stood in her blood soaked smock before them, an infant in each arm, with red hair undeniably the same shade as my own.

My stomach lurched.

Horror stiffened Frigg's face.

"This can't stand," she said.

She tugged Sigyn towards the others, I raced to her side and wrapped my arms around my little family and pulled them back. Frigg wouldn't let go.

Sigyn stepped on Frigg's foot, which only made her tighten her fingers into Sigyn's arm. I feared her bruising her.

Sigyn's eyes turned vivid blue. Her element of fidelity awoke in her.

"Get away from our children, you witch!"

Blue light burst beneath Frigg's hold on Sigyn's arm, a rush of pure fidelity tossing her to the ground. She yelped, striking her back against the limestone.

Thor dropped Mjolnir, his eyes widening in shock. Tyr and Balder scratched their heads.

And Odin...Odin knew producing children wasn't all I had done...

"What just came out of me?" Sigyn asked.

Odin looked at me. Bewilderment and anger etching his face, tightening it until he almost didn't resemble himself anymore.

"How?" he asked.

There was no point in denying it.

"It really wasn't as hard as you claimed," I said. I didn't like how he kept looking at me. I couldn't read him, which unnerved me. "I did what I had to do."

"And what was that?" Sigyn asked me.

"He made you a goddess," Tyr answered.

"He made you a threat," Balder added.

I let out a breath and turned to Sigyn. If I owed anyone an explanation, it was her alone.

"Our children would have been without a mother," I said. "Watching you die...I couldn't let that happen if I had a chance to save you. Transforming your element and making you an immortal was the only way."

Her eyes searched me as if trying to take it all in.

"She will bear the sign that instigates Ragnarok," Odin whispered.

He stroked his russet beard as clarity descended his gaze, making alarm raise in my blood.

"I've always wondered what it meant. Was it a metaphor, a riddle, or literal? It's clear now." He pointed at Sigyn. "These children are the sign. They instigate Ragnarok. Their existence ensures the end of the worlds."

A cold sweat beaded along my back, and my nostrils flared. Heartache I thought long dead surfaced fresh and raw, reminding me of the last time Odin came between me and my children.

I shifted my family behind me.

"I won't let you take them like you did before," I said.

Frigg pushed herself off the damp limestone. A stream of blood trickled from a gash on her forehead.

"This won't be like before," she grunted, wiping away the crimson with her sleeve.

She dropped one hand to her dagger. I feared her pouch of runes more.

"You know what the prophecy says," Odin replied. "Your children are our undoing. And these children? They are the most dangerous of all. They are the tipping point. Billions will die, entire universes will die, because whatever they do causes the Destroyer to fulfill their destiny. You."

All five approached us.

Balder unsheathed his broadsword and clasped a battle

axe in his other hand. His eyes blazed white with his element of light as he drew strength from its well.

My every muscle tensed, and I planted my feet wide apart.

"Step no further," I warned.

They continued their advance.

Sparks ran the length of Thor's arms, and lit his eyes with lightning as he dug his nails into Mjolnir's handle.

"These children have too much prophecy in their blood," Frigg said, her gaze darkening. "You can't possibly think we can allow them to survive to fulfill their role in making you fulfill your own?"

My pulse pounded in my ears, and my breath heated.

"I will not step aside a second time and let you rip my family from me. I will fight to protect what's mine."

"Loki, think," Tyr cautioned. "This can only end badly for you. You are outnumbered."

I snapped my fingers and let a small orb of fire dance over my knuckles.

"I'm well aware, but you know what I'm capable of," I said. "And you're in my way."

"Take them," Odin commanded. "But take Loki alive."

I summoned all my heat, all my fire, all my rage. The flame grew in my hand, churning and roiling.

The blaze inside me burst within my eyes.

I hurled the fireball directly at him.

Tyr pulled out his massive sword and held it in front of his face, blocking my dose of heat. The flames dispersed off the cold steel, leaving behind a thin layer of soot.

Balder rushed me as I generated another fireball.

I shot the spinning flames towards his chest. He crossed his blade and axe, ricocheting the fire straight into a colony of bats clutching the high vault.

They swooped down and screeched around our faces, fluttering wildly.

I took out my daggers, sending my flames coursing through the steel. I ran towards Tyr, dodging bats left and right. He brought down his sword. I caught it between my blades.

His muscles flexed as he struggled to free himself. The flames blackened his sword further, eating into the metal. My boots slid across the wet rock as he pushed and pulled. I clenched my teeth, locking him in. Refusing to let him go.

Balder came up behind me.

Grunting, I burst a surge of fire out of me, blowing him ten feet away and into a swarm of angry bats.

Balder caught my arm with his axe and swung me around to face him. He dug the edge of his sword into the base of my throat.

"I've waited for this day," he grunted.

"To lose to me? I am honored."

I kicked him hard in the knee, and again in the chest forcing him back. Twisting, I rammed my elbow into Tyr's abdomen. He fell to his knees, trying to catch his breath.

Sweat rolled down Balder's face as he lunged at me, cutting his blade across my upper arm. Pain seared into my flesh and I cursed as blood soaked into my tunic.

I sent a charge of fire at Balder. His eyes widened, and he jumped to the right narrowly avoiding being singed. Losing his footing, he fell into a pool of water, scattering cave fish across the rock.

The floor shook. I turned.

Thor ran at me, lightning sparking over his body. He raised Mjolnir high over his head and jumped, preparing to bring it down on my head.

This wasn't good.

I forced more of my fire out of me, summoning every last spark, every last ember, to my palms and formed a blazing shield.

Lightning struck chaos.

Fire struck steel.

Thor flew backwards, his arms and legs flailing out in front of him. His back struck a stalactite. A crack rocked through the cave. Thor fell to the limestone, the stalactite following, breaking into chunks across Thor's arms and shoulders.

I didn't fare much better.

A wall of extremely hard and unforgiving flowstone broke my fall. The dribbling water skimming the surface snuffed out my heat where it wet my skin.

Frigg stood over me.

Her eyes were completely black.

She dug her hand into her bag of runes.

Shit.

I got up and stepped back. She pulled out Hagalaz, pain, which made grown men weep for their mothers.

She threw it at my feet. A stream of green, wicked magic burst from it.

I jumped behind a stalagmite. The curse hit the formation, leaving me luckily unscathed.

I wiped the sweat from my brow.

My heart stopped.

Odin cornered Sigyn. Her feet slid on the wet stone as she backed away, clutching our children tight against her.

I rushed to her, placing myself between them. I twisted a rope of fire into a ring.

Odin stopped. My fire shaded his face in deep yellows and oranges.

"I don't want to do this," I said.

His iris disappeared, overtaken by a flash of gray as he summoned his own powers.

"Nor I," he said.

Clenching my teeth, I pushed the ring of fire towards him, letting it lengthen and rouse into a vicious cyclone.

He held out his arms.

Silver light coated him.

And he called upon the rune Laguz.

Water.

I braced myself. He always did play dirty.

A spinning stream of water gushed from his palms and tore into my blaze.

I grunted as I demanded more of myself out into my conflagration. I needed it stronger, faster.

I ignored the ache deep in my muscles.

I ignored the fatigue starting to eat into my bones as I demanded more.

He took one step towards me. Another deluge forced me one step back.

My arms shook.

I kept on.

But I didn't know for how much longer.

I turned my head and looked at Sigyn.

"Hide," I said.

"No," she replied. "I won't leave you."

"I will follow," I said. "Head for that tunnel and wait."

I motioned with my head. She ran towards the black void, disappearing into shadow.

The whirring water inched closer and closer. He stepped one foot after the next. Our hands were but feet apart, fire and water mixing, boiling.

He cried out shoving a wave into my chest, drenching me. Extinguishing me.

Smoke rose from my sopping skin.

I tried to summon my flames back, but not even a spark would ignite. His spell smothered my fire completely.

Odin fared little better. He approached me, but he wavered. Odin's magic carried a price, and that was leaving him utterly drained for a good ten minutes.

Enough time for me to get away.

I turned. Tyr and Balder raced towards me. Frigg followed.

"Why are you always in my way?" I seethed.

I took in a quick breath, despite my growing tiredness. I had to keep fighting.

My daggers out, I lunged at them and locked blades with Frigg, knocking her dagger out of her hand, and kicked my boot into Tyr's solid chest.

He smiled.

He grabbed my ankle.

Shit.

My lungs burned as he slammed me on my back, knocking the breath out of me. His face glistened with sweat and dirt. He dug the tip of his sword into my side.

"What are you waiting for?" I rasped.

Excitement lifted his features out of exhaustion.

"Thor."

Lightning flashed in the corner of my eye.

Thor screamed, shaking the cavern as he charged me, lifting Mjolnir high over his head.

"You'll pay for that trick!" he bellowed at me.

I would not die having Thor smash my brains into mush.

I kicked Tyr in the groin with my other foot. He cried out, and dropped his sword.

I scrambled away just as Thor brought his hammer

down, splitting the rock, sending a fissure breaking through half the cavern.

The vault quaked, and stalactites cracked and crashed all around me as I caught up with Sigyn and we dove into the tunnel.

I couldn't see a thing as we stumbled and scrabbled our way deeper into the cave.

I kept trying to summon my fire, but Odin's damn spell stamped out anything I produced.

Come on! Just one spark!

Lightning scattered through the tunnel, bouncing off the walls, throwing our path in and out of vivid white and complete black.

Mjolnir zoomed past my ear, slamming into flowstone to our right, then flew back to Thor's hand. I didn't dare look back to see how far behind us he chased.

Another flare of light.

Sigyn took a sharp left, I followed, narrowly missing Mjolnir pummeling into my skull. Rock rumbled above our heads with thunder.

The tight cavern flickered in purples and frigid blues as Thor kept on our heels.

I ran into Sigyn's back.

The children started to cry.

"Why have you stopped?" I huffed, out of breath.

Seconds of violet lit Sigyn's face.

And lit the end of the tunnel.

We were trapped.

Thor's curses and threats echoed within the walls. We only had a heartbeat.

My pulse trashed.

Had I lost?

I didn't lose.

I just found another way.

It chilled my bones knowing what way that was.

Lightning cast Sigyn in garish white.

I clasped her face between my hands and leaned my forehead against hers. I breathed her in. I felt her skin, running my thumbs over her cheeks and hot tears. Wanting to memorize her...

Our children wriggled against my chest, their tiny heartbeats mixing with my own.

My throat burned.

Crackling flickers of purple jumped around us, lighting my little family for a glance, until snuffing them out back into the darkness.

"I'm afraid," she said, her breath curling along my neck.

I sank my fingers into her hair. I lowered my hands down her back and held her. Held my family.

I needed to hold on to them. I didn't know what awaited me, but I knew they could not follow.

"I know. I am too."

The ground quaked beneath my feet.

Just a little longer...

"But I promised I'd protect you."

I turned from her.

Thor stomped right beside us. Sheets of white doused him, and he no longer looked like an oaf, but my reckoning.

He raised his hammer.

I put out my hands.

Surrendering.

24

THE DEVILS ARE HERE

We returned to the firelight of the main chamber.

Beaten.

But not broken.

And with one last ace to play.

Thor shoved us into the center, the vault stretching high above our heads where the others waited. Their shadows loomed over us like five devils.

Frigg fingered her pouch of runes, readying to strike if I made one errant step. Tyr and Balder held their weapons out, their breaths hard and deep.

Odin stood tall and rigid. A warrior's stance. But when our eyes met, he wavered. As if straining to keep himself standing despite the weight of all this pressing down on his shoulders.

I sneered.

He ground his footing and returned his face to stone.

"You never can make anything easy," Odin said.

He wrung a stream of water out of his mud splattered tunic.

"Afraid not," I said. "But that's about to change. I want to do you a favor."

He chuckled.

"A favor? You seem to think you have leverage."

"I have all the leverage in the world."

"From where I stand, it doesn't appear that way."

He snapped his fingers.

"Take the children and the girl."

Balder and Tyr walked towards us, the edges of their blades flashing catching the light.

Sigyn stepped back.

I stepped forward.

It was time for the show.

Even though I wasn't ready for what it meant.

"I'm surprised you think this prophecy so cut and dry," I said. "You know prophecies are wibbly wobbly, bereft of details, and full of uncertainty. Never can exactly know what they really predict until the thing has happened."

"Which is why we are taking measures to fix the problem," Balder said. "We must protect the Nine Worlds at all cost."

Lifting my arm, I inspected my nails, running my thumb over the chipped edges. A travesty.

"Even if you kill my children, the *instigators*." I grimaced at the state of my cuticles. "You'd never be certain your fiery fates were avoided."

Frigg narrowed her eyes and chewed her lip.

Tyr and Balder stopped their approach.

"What do you mean?" Tyr asked.

I brushed the caked mud off my shoulder.

"You only know these children instigate Ragnarok, but you don't know how, or when. It could have already happened. And if that were the case..." I paused. "Their deaths would not help you escape your destinies. You're simply rolling dice."

Odin twisted his gold rings, the rubies and sapphires glinting in the firelight.

"Meaning Ragnarok would remain imminent," he said.

I smiled, gorging on his fear. His fear, his uncertainty, was what I needed.

"Exactly," I replied. "Which is why I want to offer you something better than a gamble."

He lowered his hands to his sides and took three steps towards me.

"And what's that?"

"Assurance," I said. "Assurance that Ragnarok will never take place."

He tilted his head.

"And how do you suggest we achieve such 'assurance'?"

I turned my gaze to Sigyn for a heartbeat, wanting to remember her standing next to me. The heat of her skin, the softness of her breath skating across my neck that slowly slicked with sweat.

There would be no returning to her side after this.

I slowly met Odin's eye again.

"Yggdrasil showed you how," I said. "There is only one way to stop the Destroyer. To stop all of this carnage from taking place. I offer you myself, so you can do what must be done."

Odin's face tightened flattening his lips into thin lines.

"You dare ask this of me?" His voice was deeper than I'd ever heard it. Dangerous. "You know what I gave, what I sacrificed, to avoid the fate it showed for you."

I lowered my eyes to his neck where his beard met his skin.

A thick, red scar wrapped around his throat where the

rope had cut into his flesh when he hung from Yggdrasil for nine days. When he sacrificed himself to himself.

He always told me it was from a fight with a frost giant. But it had really been because of me.

For me.

And now I shat on it.

"I know," I whispered. "But I must do what I have to, to protect my family, as you must do to protect the Nine Worlds from the Destroyer. From me."

His shoulders stiffened, and he stared at me as silence colder than the limestone set in.

"What are you asking him to do, Loki?" Sigyn asked, worry saturating her every word.

Each was an arrow in my gut.

I refused to look at her. I couldn't have my resolve shaken.

"What's been put off far too long." Frigg replied. "Odin, listen to him. We never would even be at this point had you finished the job in the beginning."

Odin's nostrils flared. Sweat beaded across his forehead.

"No. It's not possible." He scrubbed his face. "We struck a blood oath with one another. Our fealty remains binding and no harm can be done to the other unless it's broken."

I stepped right in front of him until I could smell the salt and sweat of his skin.

"Then I break it."

I knew the gravity of what I said. What it meant to break an oath. Especially an oath as ours had been...

But it was the only way to give us both what we wanted.

Anger tugged at the lines of his face. Grief deepened them.

"You can't break it," he said. Begged. "I will lose you forever."

I forced a pitying smile for him, for his callow reluctance to mourn with me the bitter truth.

"You already have."

He trembled. Hard denial set his jaw.

"I still won't do what you ask. What Yggdrasil showed must happen..."

Something in me shifted. My vision clouded red. Heat flooded my body, and my fire sped through my veins despite the dampening residue of his spell.

"Damn you!" I yelled. "It's me you fear, not them! They don't deserve this fate. Only I do."

I seized his forearm and snapped him against me. Sparks crackled between my fingers and knuckles as I curled my fingers around him.

"Let me go!" he shouted, tugging back, trying to pull free.

I ground my nails deeper into his muscle, feeling his bones flex beneath my grip.

"It's me alone who summons Ragnarok. Only I bring it to your door."

Cinders fell at our feet as I started to burn through his leather bracers. Then his tunic.

"You know not what horrors you ask of me."

Couldn't he see? None of that mattered now.

"The only way to ensure your life, to ensure the safety of the Nine Worlds, is doing what must be done to me," I said. "If you don't..."

I seared into his flesh. Inside my heart was breaking, but I tightened my grasp on him harder. Charring his chambers to ash. Incinerating the final links of the oath we had made to each other eons ago on that riverbank. He had to understand there was no other choice.

His eyes searched mine, for some mercy. For some saving grace.

I had none to give.

Because none existed.

"Is this a risk you're truly willing to take?" I asked, grinding deeper into him. Burning deeper into him. "Spare my family, take my deal, and for the first time in your life, you will have escaped your fate, wholly and utterly. I'm giving you what you've always truly hungered for. Deliverance from the Destroyer. Deliverance from me."

I released him and he hissed clapping his hand over his arm. Wincing, he peeled back his hand revealing a map of red blisters bubbling across his skin.

And he finally understood.

He locked eyes with me. A breath of shock, and then it all came crumbling down. Every wish he ever wanted. Every hope I ever had. A million shattered pieces at our feet.

"Must this really be how it ends?" he asked, though he already knew the answer.

I forced out my hand to him. I hoped he didn't notice it tremble.

He stared at it. Long. Hard.

"It must."

A deep sorrow darkened with anger rolled behind his gaze.

"Then our oath is broken. We are no longer brothers."

He took my hand, breaking one promise and cinching us to another. Sealing both our fates.

"What's happened?" Sigyn asked.

I dared glancing at her. Red misted her eyes as she held our boys.

"I've given my family its best chance," I said, hoping she

saw my love for her, for Narfi and Nari, bleeding through my eyes.

"Let the girl and the children go," Odin pushed through a tight throat. "Only Loki remains."

"You can't take him from me," Sigyn yelled, panic overtaking her. She tried to race towards me, but Tyr caught her and wrapped his arms around her waist, holding her back. I was grateful. I didn't want her to see what came next...whatever that would be.

"You can't go to him anymore," Tyr whispered to her, pulling her away, taking them all towards the cave entrance and to freedom. Leaving me behind...Sigyn looked at me, tears streaming down her flushed cheeks.

"No," Frigg shouted. The word curdled my blood. "I'm done making exceptions for this man. Taking risks. This beast is a traitor, and his spawn our undoing. As long as they breathe they are a danger to us all."

Tyr kept pulling Sigyn away despite her protestations and begging for my freedom. For mercy.

"The deal is struck," Odin snapped at Frigg. "We made a bargain. They live. He stays."

Her face reddened.

"I won't allow this," she spat. "I've endured millennia of you risking us all for this man. Not anymore. Today it ends."

Frigg rushed Tyr and Sigyn. A heartbeat. A slice of a second. She ripped Narfi and Nari away from Sigyn's arms.

"No!" I shouted.

I raced towards Frigg. Towards my sons screaming in her clawed hands.

I was inches away.

I could just graze their soft skin...

And I did not notice.

Frigg hurled a rune at my feet.

Hard magic laced around my torso and tugged, ensnaring me tight. Another rune followed.

I was thrown, hurtled through the air. I struck three large stones. The back of my skull cracked against the rock and invisible bonds flew out of the rune and trapped me to the stone.

Sigyn cursed and flailed in Tyr's hold. Narfi and Nari screamed in Frigg's arms, crying out for their mother. For me...

Helpless and fragile.

Frigg looked at them as if worms.

I wrestled against her binding spell, ignoring the pain splinting down my muscles and sinew. I knew it was no use until the spell weakened, not even my fire could do anything against the curse, but I couldn't stop trying...I wouldn't.

Tyr tightened his hold on Sigyn trying to force her still from her squirming and biting.

"Return those infants to the mother," Tyr growled. "I will ensure they are taken away."

Sigyn kicked and clawed at him.

I strained against my bonds.

"It's not enough," Frigg said. "I'm ensuring our salvation. I'm saving our lives, and the lives of the entire Nine Worlds. It's for the greater good. Can't you see?"

"No," Odin said, his voice hard. "The deal was his life for theirs."

Realization overtook her eyes. Disappointment. And beneath, wild desperation.

"You can't see, can you? You never could...That's why I must do this."

She pulled out a blade.

My stomach lurched.

"No!" Odin shouted. "I won't allow another oath broken tonight!"

He scrambled over the uneven rock towards Frigg.

Sigyn broke free of Tyr and followed on Odin's heels, her face flushed and filled with rage.

I strained against the bonds holding me back. Forcing all my strength and summoning all my magic to break through...

Narfi and Nari's cries ricocheted in my ears. Pulling at all of me to help them...

A flash of a blade.

Silence followed.

A grisly hush that ripped out my insides.

Looking at the aftermath I shook, cold, splintered. I swallowed down hot sick.

Sigyn turned white. She staggered towards their broken bodies. She let out a wail of sorrow from the roots of her heart.

She looked at Frigg. Death glared in her eyes. Arms stretched out and fingers rigid like claws, she tackled Frigg and slammed her against the rock. Her head whacked the stone so forcefully a clear split rang out. Lifting back her hand, Sigyn prepared to bring it down on Frigg, as if to tear out her beating heart from her chest in recompense for crushing her own.

Sigyn's eyes glowed blue again with her element.

Blood trickled down Frigg's forehead.

Sigyn's element dissolved.

She looked down at a slender blade of Dwarven steel sticking out of her stomach. The only thing capable of killing a god.

Frigg released her hold on the handle. A victorious smile pulling at her lips.

"Sigyn!" I rasped.

She faltered and stepped back.

She looked at me, fear and despair in her gaze. Crimson trickled out between her lips. Odin went behind her and caught her as she collapsed in his arms.

And I knew...

She went with our sons where I could not follow.

She was gone.

My little family was gone.

And I was alone.

With only my grief.

My rage.

A deep rage.

I cried out through hot tears. Breaking.

Broken.

Odin lowered Sigyn's limp body to the ground.

Frigg wiped the blood from her brow and knelt beside my sons. Only gore and death and flesh. She set to work on something I could not watch.

"What are you doing, Mother?" Balder asked Frigg, his voice shaken and strained.

"Ensuring we have what we need to keep him where he is."

Odin combed Sigyn's hair away from her face. She looked asleep. He felt for a pulse. Inspected her. Whispered over her as if trying to preserve something that wasn't there. Couldn't he see? She was gone.

They all were gone.

Because of him.

"Stop touching them!" I cried.

Odin backed away from her. Frigg stood, a pair of dark cords in her hands. They shined gruesomely in the light.

I scratched my nails against the stone, my fingers stiff and hungering for their lives.

They broke their promise to me.

They took what I loved because they rather trust the idiotic words of a prophecy than me, who they knew.

Something woke in me. In those horrifying seconds. A madness. A clarity. A beautiful thing that swept through me, incinerating any remnant of who I was and left me with only the coldness of a steel knife. Righteousness descended like a crown atop my head, and in that righteousness...A just promise. A just purpose.

For judgement.

For wrath.

With this act they fulfilled the very prophecy they tried to prevent. They made me the very thing they feared. The thing I feared.

All I never wanted.

I who was and I who am.

Loki the Breaker of Worlds.

The Destroyer.

I hated them for it.

And I loved them for it more because now I could drink their souls.

"I will burn you all for what you've done this day," I roared. "I will strip you to the bone and turn you into ash."

The cavern shook. Bits of stone fell like hail around us.

My fire blazed through my eyes as I fought against the hex still keeping me against that damned rock.

"Oh shut up," Frigg snapped.

She shoved the cords into Thor's hands. His pallor turned green. I'd never seen him so sickened.

"Tie him down to the rock with these before the hex

weakens. These will keep him bound for the next five millennia."

He shook his head.

He shoved them back to her.

"No. I want no further part in this...this...cruelty," Thor said.

"This is wrong..." Tyr added.

Balder looked ill.

Frigg's lips flattened.

"You are all disgusting man children," she said. "If you won't do it..."

She stomped towards me and coiled the ropes around my wrists and ankles.

I twisted, trying to break free, hurling dark curses at them one after the next.

I stopped.

The cords were wet. *Warm.*

And I knew what they were. I knew what she had done hunched over my sons' lifeless bodies.

"You sick fuck!" I shouted at Frigg. Horror doused me as I struggled to free myself from them. To stop their entrails from touching me. "You broke your promise to me, and so I break mine. I swear to you I will bring Ragnarok for this, and you can all know it was your doing."

She smiled and pulled them tighter, burying the cords deep into my flesh until they stung, until I could not move.

The flames in my eyes went out. My chaos shriveled. My element, my fire, extinguished as the cords drained my powers.

"We've caused our own deaths with this," Thor said, anxiety dripping off him. "We've caused them trying to stop them."

"Don't let him get into your head," Frigg said. "Why do

you think I had to use the guts of his sons? Only blood magic can arrest his element of chaos and keep him bound to this rock for eternity. We are safe."

Odin's fingers curled into fists.

"Safe?" Odin barked at her. "Safe would have been not breaking our bargain. What you've done is..." he trailed off. "This will cost you dearly."

"What I've done is protect entire worlds. Universes! You heard his threats of Ragnarok. You see how easily he would snap our necks. Now end it."

"No...this is too much bloodshed."

Her face sharpened.

"When has that stopped you before? Yggdrasil set you this task. It is your duty as protector of the Nine Worlds..."

His eye flashed, her words running off him.

"You dare tell me my duties?" he roared.

He raced her, his hands aiming for her throat.

Balder stepped between them.

I kept hurling my curses. My promises of death and ash and smoke.

"Father..." he warned. "This is horror, but it must be finished."

Odin gripped into Balder's tunic, curling his fingers and pulling him against him. I thought he would eat Balder whole.

"Step out of my way, boy," he spat.

"What's done is done," he said. "There is only upholding what Yggdrasil commanded now. You know it's the only way to stop the Destroyer. You know it must be you." He paused. "It's all our lives, or his."

Odin's eye lit and magic sparked around him as if his mind raced with finding another loophole, another way.

But there was only one.

He wailed, the sound like a lost creature left to die.

He shoved Balder back and stepped away.

Odin locked eyes with me and everything dissolved. There was only he and I. Friend against friend lost to undoing, and reunited in hatred.

He walked towards me, dragging his feet as if each step were agony. And with each step he got closer, the more I wanted to attack. To bite and snarl. To rip his eye from his socket and crush it between the palms of my hands.

"I never wanted this for you," he whispered. "And I will never forgive you for taking my choice from me."

"As you've taken mine," I growled, squirming beneath my bonds, trying to lunge at him. To shred him to pieces.

He turned away.

He moved his hands and recited some spell.

I heard a hiss above my head.

I looked up, seeing a serpent longer than Thor was tall. A Vanir Viper. Its eyes glowed yellow, and its pink tongue flicked between its gray scaled jowls. It was somehow fixed to the stone, trapped the same as I was.

I understood now. I was to be tortured for eternity. My body made a tomb and my mind fogged with pain. Left to darkness. Left to be forgotten.

I laughed.

"You think this enough to stop me?" I asked. "I will be free, Odin. And I will end you. All of you. Ragnarok is inevitable. As am I."

He spoke his spell harder. Forcing all his power into each binding word.

Did he really believe it would work? Please. I had a prophecy to uphold.

I set my eyes firmly on those of the snake and faced my destiny head on.

"Ragnarok is inevitable."

The cavern rumbled as my voice filled the space with my promise.

Odin's words stilled.

And there was only hot agony.

Venom rushed down over me. I arched my back, roaring as it burned through my clothes and into my flesh, sending a million cuts screaming through my body.

"Ragnarok is inevitable."

I choked on venom. On scalding death. But I continued to swear my wrath on them.

The cave quaked. Rock collapsed and fell, locking me in. Snuffing out the light.

In that blinding pain, in that darkness, I was not alone.

I heard a whisper.

The voice. The spirit from Vigridr where we would all meet again.

"Ragnarok is inevitable."

I smiled, despite the venom charring my throat.

I smiled, despite my skin blistering and splitting.

I smiled, despite a thousand scorching needles impaling my eyes over, and over, and over...

I had the gift of purpose and the promise of freedom.

Kill them.

Burn them.

Destroy them.

Ragnarok is inevitable.

Ragnarok is inevitable.

25

FOR A RAINY DAY

Asgard

Three Weeks Later

The Asgardian Sea crashed in the distance muffled by the strike of horse hooves. Odin took in a breath spotting a light in a window. Moonlight coated the thatch of a small cabin tucked deep in the Black Woods.

Dismounting his horse, he walked down the gravel path and stopped at a closed door. He shot a glance behind his shoulder for two seconds.

A wolf howled.

He took out a brass key from his pocket and shoved it into the worn lock. Odin pushed the oak door open and stepped inside, the floorboards groaning beneath each step.

Idunn stood from a comfortable chair by a fire. Her usually calm face was pinched and worried. He walked towards her, passing a table topped with a bowl filled with golden apples.

"Has anyone been here?" He shot his gaze from point to point, making sure there were no other ears or eyes.

"Not today," she said. "Not ever since you hid her here."

Good....good.

He couldn't afford any more mistakes. Not now. Not when he could already feel the sear of Loki's warning on the back of his neck. Of the scorching flames of Ragnarok he promised...

He rubbed the sweat away.

"Does the prisoner improve?" Odin asked.

Idunn went to the table and picked out a large apple, and cut into the crisp flesh with a knife.

"I've never brought one back so close to death. But the apples are working."

"Then she will survive?"

"Yes, though she wishes she wouldn't." Idunn cut thick slices onto a plate. "She mourns for her family. She mourns for *him*."

Odin's lips thinned at that.

"I've made arrangements to send her to Alfheim."

Idunn grimaced

"She hasn't her strength back for such a journey."

"We haven't the time. I need her out of Asgard before anyone besides you or me finds out."

Almost losing her once before had been too close for Odin's comfort. She was valuable. The most valuable being in all the Nine Worlds. No risks could be taken.

If Loki ever escaped...

That thought sent a chill down his spine.

He walked past Idunn and opened the door behind her.

The woman sat on a clean bed dressed in a clean shift. Her arms were wrapped around her knees. She pressed them against her chest. Her red hair draped down her cheeks, obscuring most of her face.

He smiled, seeing his salvation in her. All their salvation.

The woman's eyes met his.

"Sigyn, it's time we leave."

26

LET CHAOS REIGN

Present Day

Basel, Switzerland

He kept staring at the burning candle beside the open Bible, as if he remained lost in that cave.

In the torment.

The chatter and warble of birds filled the cathedral, waking me from the savagery of his tale. I rubbed my eyes, surprised by the pale morning light streaming through the stained glass windows.

My God. We've been here all night.

He cleared his throat, reaching towards the candle and snuffed out the wick. Curls of gray smoke rose gently into the buttresses.

"Now you understand what they've done," he said, his voice husky. "Sigyn died because of them. And Narfi and Nari...They killed my family. Left me in the dark, submitting me to unimaginable torture for five hundred years."

My stomach pitted.

"They broke their promise," I said.

He shot his gaze to mine, his green eyes cutting into me.

"Broke their promise?" he asked. "They annihilated it!"

The stone arches shook from the timbre of his voice. His silken, lethal voice.

He flickered, the same as he had before he started telling me why he wanted to destroy the world. All worlds.

His strikingly beautiful image melted into a man disfigured with mangled patches of red scars.

Only tufts remained of his thick hair. His eyes were clouded and bloodshot.

And his face...

Distorted skin peeled and split on his cheeks and chin, while tracks of blisters raced down his neck. A lacework of knotted and mutilated skin pulled tight between his fingers and over the bones of his hands. His nails were burnt away, leaving only the raw, delicate flesh beneath.

He looked at his hands, and stared at the gnarled mess.

His lips stretched into a ghoulish smile, the fine red points from Frigg's needle dotting his mouth.

An utterly amused chuckle erupted from his lungs.

"And to think, I was worried about a few pricks of a needle," he said. "This will be a bitch to clear up."

In a second his divine form returned as he coated himself in an illusion of his past self, the ghoulish smile replaced by one brazenly charming.

He straightened his collar around his perfect neck, and ran his elegant fingers through his copper hair, taming the waves that moved like flames.

He walked past me towards the nave, the scent of salt and cedar rising from him, along with a rush of fierce and seductive energy.

"How...How did you escape," I called after him. "Odin

said it was impossible. I don't see how it was ever anything but impossible."

He stopped and faced me. He sighed and crossed his arms as if deeply disappointed.

"Impossible is such an unimaginative word," he said. "There's no fun in that."

I dared a step towards him.

"But how are you standing here?" I pressed. "They chained you with unbreakable magic."

His lips pulled into a wry smile. His eyes flashed with mirth, as if he held onto a delicious bite of gossip.

"It would seem I've become a sort of legend," he said. "A clan of adventurers stumbled upon me in my little crack in the earth, brandishing odd, compact cube telescopes with enchanted glowing mirrors. They kept jabbering about questing for something called 'content.' Apparently it's highly desirable in their realm of 'yootoob'."

I tilted my head and rubbed the back of my neck. Should I correct him?

"Do you mean *YouTube*?" I asked.

He shrugged.

"Possibly," he said. "I'll be honest, it was hard to understand a damn word they said with all their incessant screaming and begging for mercy. Like sniveling children. You'd think they'd never seen a little fire before."

His smile widened. Irreverence in his eyes again.

He started again down the aisle of red limestone towards the heavy doors, his every step powerful and sinuous.

If he reached them, it would be too late. For me, for the world.

I didn't want to die.

I didn't want the world to end.

"You don't have to do this," I said.

"I'm afraid I do," he replied. "I promised Odin I'd bring Ragnarok, and it would be rude of me to not come through."

"But you'll die, too," I said.

He stopped again and stared into me.

"Yes, but I'll be with her."

He looked back at the candle. His face stilled and the wry smile softened as ghosts danced across his face. Of Sigyn lighting the candle. Of them talking hours into the night over anatomy books. Of them holding their children in the darkness of that cave...

"We will be a family again." He didn't speak to me anymore. He spoke to Sigyn. "And then, I will have the peace you prayed for me to find."

It was an odd thing, the anger his soft spoken words lit in me.

Anger because he thought he had the right to make us all his sacrificial lamb. Anger because he thought he could get away with it. That his peace came at our expense.

He was the thief in the night.

With no thought but survival, I grasped the tall cast iron candlestick beside the Bible, and held it out as if a sword. I pointed it at his chest and widened my stance.

"I know you feel slighted."

"Slighted? That's the understatement of the millennium."

"But I won't let you cut us down in recompense. I won't let you decimate all life because you are incapable of forgiveness."

Laughter quaked out from deep in his gut. Tears rolled out the corners of his eyes.

Faster than I could see, he grasped the rod, his skin pulling taut over his knuckles. Cinders snapped wild within his hair. The iron started to glow orange beneath his fingers.

My pulse thundered in my ears.

"You are a dear to try to save the worlds. I appreciate the nobility, but you're forgetting the moral of my little story," he said. "I'm the Destroyer, and Ragnarok is inevitable."

Fire erupted within his eyes, making my blood run cold.

The iron rod crackled beneath his grip, smoldering yellows and reds running down the length. Heat broiled my cheeks as he kicked me back square in the chest.

I fell to my knees before him, my shins striking the hard stone. This is what he wanted. For us all to fall.

He admired the rod liquifying in ropes of molten metal, flowing between his fingers and dripping to the limestone at his feet.

Fear as I'd never known froze my core, shattering me and all I knew. There was only dread. Defeat.

Reckoning.

Him.

He glanced down at me, a pitying smile twisting his perfect mouth.

"I know..." he cooed. "It's terrifying facing your fate. But I've found it's best to accept these things instead of fighting them."

Squaring his shoulders, he adjusted his lapels, and smoothed the creases of his black suit.

He stepped around me and opened the massive oak doors to the expansive cobblestones of Münsterplatz.

My mouth opened.

Snow.

Snow fell in great, heavy sheets over Basel even though it was still July.

He breathed in a breath, as if taking it all in, the thrill of the end, the excitement of the awaiting destruction.

"I love a good omen first thing in the morning, don't you?" he asked.

He marched out across Münsterplatz, steam rising around him as snow melted beneath his every step.

Chaos was freed and walked among us.

EXCERPT FROM "THE ORDER OF CHAOS"

(THE NINE WORLDS RISING BOOK 2)

Present Day

Basel, Switzerland

I was back.

As if the gods could keep me down.

Bitch, please. It would take more than a little scalding snake venom to stop me.

The gods only achieved making me angrier with their pathetic attempt to trap me. To torture me. Every drop of liquid fire that slipped from that snake's fangs branded my purpose deeper into my chest. Every second I endured lost in that darkness hardened my resolve to take their lives as they took the lives of my family.

A pure and exquisite wrath filled me. I starved for blood. For judgement.

For Ragnarok. The end of everything.

And I loved it.

I was going to burn them all to the ground for what they did.

This would be such fun.

As eager for the show as I was, I unfortunately had a to-do list a mile long. It didn't help the world was nothing how I left it in 1526.

After narrowly avoiding getting struck by a growling block of metal on wheels, and then by something I later learned was a bus, and an old woman riding a bee-cycle, I realized it was far more interesting.

Car engines roared and trams rattled along metal tracks. Music blared from white buds in people's ears, and voices spoke into enchanted rectangles while other larger rectangles yelled back from shop windows and inside people's apartments.

Lives were no longer simple. They were much more complicated. Faster. Louder. Chaotic.

Perfect.

I even ate something marvelous called an ice cream cone.

I found it a shame to destroy this new world, really. But what can one do?

I took another bite of my pistachio ice cream and looked down at my plain black suit and grimaced.

The man in the Münster Cathedral, my first stop on my grand tour of the cosmos, did his best giving me some clothes after I'd shown up naked at the altar. But I couldn't destroy the worlds in a poly-blend suit.

That would be the true tragedy.

I needed something new. Something fabulous.

I would make Ragnarok look good.

I caught humans chattering about a place called a "department store," which seemed the very thing I required. And the best apparently was on Marktplatz, the main square in Basel's city center. I headed there at once.

Doors of glass slid open and I walked across polished, white tiles that reflected the glaring lights from the ceiling. An odd place stuffed with clothes on metal racks, bins filled with merino wool scarves, and perfume bottles lining back-lit shelves.

I felt eyes on me. I turned. A woman stared at me from behind a glass counter. Perfect painted red lips. Legs for days. She twirled her brunette hair around a manicured finger. I understood. I had a certain effect on women. And men. And everyone.

I flashed her my most devastating smile. After a few words back and forth brimming with euphemisms, Elena offered to help me navigate these new Midgardian fashions.

She picked out a pair of black, tight-fitting trousers and insisted helping me put on a black t-shirt. She said it really showed off the chiseled definition of my chest. I enjoyed her perfume of jasmine as she clasped silver chains around my neck that matched the silver rings she stacked on my fingers.

To complete the look, an extravagant jacquard tuxedo jacket with red stitched floral embroidery caught my eye. Elena tried to talk me out of it for something more subdued. I never was one for anything subdued. Besides, the jacket reminded me of the heavy patterned fabrics I had adored in the 16th century. I was a sucker for embroidery.

Total damage amounted to 2,340.09 francs.

Oh.

Now, this was embarrassing.

I had no money. Elena bit her lip. What to do? Her eyes darkened and roved down my chest. Then lower.

I brushed the side of her hand with my fingertips. I could feel her quiver beneath my touch.

Perhaps an arrangement could be made?

The dressing room walls shook and clothes fell off hangers. We got quite carried away. Unspeakable acts.

She muffled her cries into a wool coat.

Can I be blamed? Five hundred years was a lengthy time to go without sex. Without food. Light.

Hope.

I pushed the dark and damp of the cave from my mind, forcing myself to focus only on the heat and sweat and pleasure of the dressing room.

Once finished, she stuffed a hundred franc note in my back pocket and whispered a "thank you" in my ear. A pink flush of complete satisfaction brightened her cheeks.

I still had it.

Leaving the store, I straightened my aviator sunglasses and walked out into the wind that howled through Marktplatz. Heavy flakes of snow fell from a gray sky, catching in the waves of my copper hair.

Winter in July.

The first sign of Ragnarok.

My fault, I'm afraid.

I breathed in the rush of the cold and what I as the Destroyer promised. I held the fates of all living creatures in my hand like a small bird.

Such a thought sickened me when I learned what Odin had kept from me. The truth of what I was. What my destiny meant.

But certain events changed all that.

I took off across the cobblestones, dodging the green trams that slithered through the city like snakes. The massive Rathaus spread the length of the square, looking the same as the last time I walked here.

Looking the same as the first time I caught sight of her.

Sigyn.

Memories rose around me as I started up the steep alley of Totengässlein. I stretched out my arm and ran my fingers along the lime plaster homes as I climbed the steps. I could almost feel her beside me again. Her warmth. Her fidelity...

The noise of Marktplatz dissolved into stillness as I kept on, as if I stepped into the past. Into a hush where I could pretend I'd see her running to me after her day working at her father's printing press.

I sauntered on, out of one memory and into another.

Into Herr Burgi's apothecary, where she bought all her ingredients for the salves and medicines she made. To help others. To share her passion for medicine and science.

Gods I missed her.

I missed them.

I chased the ghosts I conjured through the streets that remained untouched by modernity. And in those seconds, the ghosts were real.

I had them back.

I had my family back.

I stopped. Clouds of hot breath rolled out from my lungs.

Sigyn's house stood before me.

Nothing was straight about the house anymore, as if the entire structure had sighed and relaxed into the city.

I pulled out a votive candle I'd bought (*bought*, because Sigyn didn't approve of petty theft) at a grocery store and placed it in front of the green door. Snapping my fingers, I ignited the wick. It burst into a beautiful flame. She loved prayer candles, and now I lit one for her as she had once done for me in the Münster Cathedral. When I knew I loved her.

I closed my eyes, thinking of Sigyn. Thinking of Narfi and Narvi, our twin boys.

They had been born in this house. I thought my life whole.

And then everything changed.

The gods believed our children the instigators of Ragnarok. All because some stupid prophecy said so. And Odin believed it. They all believed it. They would kill my family to stop my destiny. I couldn't allow that.

I gave my life for theirs. What better deal could the gods hope for than the Destroyer himself? But they betrayed me. They murdered Sigyn. They killed my sons and ripped out their guts and used them to tie me to that rock.

Then there was only darkness. Suffocating pain.

That's when I became what I never wanted to become. And it was their fault.

I made a fist and leaned my forehead against the chilled door.

"They promised you'd all be safe," I whispered, as if this inch of oak was all that separated her from hearing me. "It should have only been me."

I tightened my fist and cinders cracked between my fingers. Heavy snow melted against my cheeks and steam rose off my shoulders and arms.

"I will make them pay for their betrayal. And then, I can be with you. We will be a family again."

I took in a shivery breath and stepped backward and into something solid.

No.

Someone.

"Watch it, asshole."

Asshole? No one called me an asshole.

I swung and stared down at a sniveling thirteen-year-old boy. He wore a slouchy knit cap that unfortunately didn't hide enough of his scrunched, mean face. I would fix that problem.

I reached for his scrawny neck, but stopped.

He held a thin booklet jam-packed with colors and figures wearing winged helmets and red capes. At the top, written in bright, big, bold letters was the word *THOR*.

What the f—

I ripped it out of the boy's grubby hands, ignoring his rampage of threats and curses. I flipped through glossed pages covered in images of Thor and Odin, of all the gods, fighting enemies and vanquishing foes with one mighty strike of Thor's hammer, Mjolnir.

Of course, their likenesses weren't exactly accurate, but where was...

...oh gods.

A snarly looking figure clad in tights and wearing an impractical horned helmet stared back at me.

The villain.

Me.

While Thor and Odin and the rest were hailed as heroes, they made me the monster of the story? After what they did?

A voice whispered in my mind.

Burn them. Kill them. Destroy them.

The boy and the street dissolved into a field of dead grass that stretched for miles around me. Hot wind blew through my hair, and that familiar stench of ash and death filled my lungs. I was no longer in Basel. I was on Vigridr. The battlefield of Ragnarok.

Twirling sparks snapped within the red haze, smothering this place. And there it stood. As always.

A figure covered in a shroud of white linen. The spirit of this place. At least, that's what I assumed it was. I honestly didn't know, and I didn't care. Our tête-à-têtes offered me momentary escapes from the horror the gods had trapped me within.

"This is shameful fodder." I pointed at the comic book. "I refuse to wait a second more for their blood."

"Patience. You shall have your war." Brimstone saturated its voice.

"Patience?" I snapped. "I've done five hundred years of patience."

"Have I failed you yet?" it asked. "During your bondage, your suffering, I gave you purpose. I made you what you are. Ragnarok is here and you walk free because of me."

This spirit never failed at being cocky.

I walked towards it, a fan of heat exploding beneath my every step.

"You? You seem to forget I'm the Destroyer. I've ignited Ragnarok, and it's mine to command."

It laughed. I wasn't sure with me, or at me.

"Your position is quite precarious," it said. "The gods will discover you've escaped. They will hunt you down and throw you back into that darkness and pain. Until you secure an army, you remain exposed."

That thought sliced through my guts. I wouldn't return there.

I couldn't.

But only one army was formidable enough against Odin's precious warriors of Valhalla.

Odin collected their souls like a miser collected gold coins. He cut down healthy men. Let the better side lose. Did worse to get what he wanted. All for a gambit to stop little ol' me.

"I guess acquiring an unbeatable army just made my to-do list."

I sensed it grin.

"Once the army is yours, once you are untouchable, you will complete your most important task."

Now this part I liked.

My fire spiraled hot and wicked in my veins. It wanted out, and I would let it out in the most cataclysmic way. It was going to be amazing.

"I will wake Surtr." Embers crackled within my words. "And the final battle will begin."

Surtr. Fire giant. Pure darkness spat out of the bowels of Muspelheim itself. Paired with my chaos...my heart somersaulted imagining the carnage we would unleash together.

The spirit took a step closer to me. Molten points of orange and yellow light swept around us.

"And when Surtr drives its flaming sword into the heart of Vigridr, it will finish Ragnarok," it said. "All will end and your destiny as the Destroyer will be fulfilled."

Fire erupted behind my eyes. They were only fire. And soon would be all the Nine Worlds.

"Now go burn them. Kill them. Destroy them."

Each word swelled in my bones with the beautiful carnage I was about to unleash.

The figure vanished.

Vigridr shifted beneath my feet. The dried grass blurred within the crimson fog.

A jerk and a shove.

Another shove.

Something was shoving me.

No.

Someone.

"Give it back asshole, or I'm going to break your nose."

I was back in front of Sigyn's house and the teenager obviously wasn't finished with me yet.

As I wasn't with him.

I twisted my lips slowly into a smile as I met the boy's gaze. His nostrils flared and his glare was pure menace. I loved it when humans challenged me. As if they stood a chance.

"Some kindly advice from me to you," I said. "I'd start preparing that nasty, greasy soul of yours, because in a matter of days, you won't be worrying over such trivial possessions as this drivel anymore."

I fluttered his book just out of his reach.

He jumped for it, only an inch short of grazing the smooth pages. Pity.

I laughed and sent a rush of flames down the cover. Thor and Odin's images blistered and peeled. The colors blackened into ash. It was all extremely poetic.

The menace in the boy's eyes iced into fear.

A shrill scream burst out of his lungs and he took off running, his heels sliding across the slick cobblestone and arms waving to keep his balance. He resembled a very flabbergasted penguin.

Humans never could keep their wits when faced with divinity.

And I never could keep to a schedule.

With one final glance back at the house, I turned and left into the blowing snow. I had an army to obtain, after all.

But why did it have to be hers?

* * *

I SHOVED the last bite of a strawberry ice cream cone in my mouth and stepped off the tram onto the cement platform of Dreispitz. Drab didn't even begin to describe this South-East scab of Basel languishing in smoke and industry.

Crisscrossing wires jostled over my head as the tram left the platform. Cars snarled along the roads lined with aluminum street lamps and ugly homes. My nostrils burned from the diesel and other acrid chemicals.

I already regretted this visit.

I crossed the street and strode towards a gateway made of limestone and arches and wrought iron bars.

Wolfgottesacker Cemetery. One of the few remaining cemeteries in the city. The Swiss were too pragmatic to cherish a bunch of slacking skeletons eternally. The dead took up an awful lot of space, contributing nothing. Cold? True. But it was better than when they buried them beneath cathedrals. Summers were quite ripe.

Entering the cemetery, the pavement split into several paths that cut through grass coated in gray frost. Robins huddled against the cold in tree branches above me as I kept to a trail that edged a wall lined with massive headstones. Bushes and wilting wild flowers crammed around the stones, each more ornate than the last.

I almost felt back in the eras I remembered. When marble and heavy architecture were favored to glass and steel.

Drinking songs from raucous feasts pulsed inside my ears, while mead bursting with honey and orange tingled my tongue. The scratch of wool pricked my fingertips and wood smoke filled my breaths from a spitting fire.

It was all so warm. Inviting...

The screech of a train from the train yard behind the cemetery plunged me into a frigid truth. The world moved on leaving the old world behind.

Leaving me behind.

Pain bit into my palms. I forced my fingers out of fists I

hadn't realized I'd made and glanced down. Eight red, crescent moons marked my skin from my own nails.

This is why I hated cemeteries. It always brought out the glummest of sentiments in me.

Glum was so boring.

And it would only get worse where I headed.

Helheim.

The realm of the dishonorable dead. A catch-all for those who died cowards, or behaved a touch too naughty.

It also happened to be ruled by my daughter, Hel. Because if you're given your own realm to rule, you might as well name it after yourself. Narcissistic? Perhaps. But a little self confidence never hurt anyone.

I stood in front of the doors of an immense mausoleum and gripped the doorknob. The grit of the tarnished brass scratched my palm as I forced the door open. The rusted hinges squealed.

I walked inside the crypt and into swirling dust and dirt. Ten alcoves lined the walls in neat rows, each stuffed with a wooden coffin in varying stages of decay.

I guess one was as good as any.

I pulled out a coffin from the bottom row, splintering the wood against the stone as I slid it into the center of the room.

I flung open the lid. A leathered corpse looked back at me with empty eye sockets and a yawning mouth. Kneeling, I lowered my hands into the coffin and clasped its upper arms. I tried not to think how my fingers plunged through its brittle, silk tuxedo.

"My apologies," I said to the corpse. "But I need this more than you."

I tossed the shriveled thing out of the coffin and brushed away the wood shavings from the bottom.

I was not looking forward to this reunion.

Taking in a breath, I tapped my knuckles against the bottom.

Knock. Knock. Knock.

The stone floor shook beneath my knees. I shot up and skipped back as the entire mausoleum quaked. Coffins rattled out of their alcoves and cracked open, striking the ground. Corpses and skeletons burst out in gray clouds of dust that covered my shoulders and shoes.

Of course.

The bottom of the coffin shifted and gave way, revealing a narrow staircase inside.

All graves were the gateway to Helheim, you see.

I snapped my fingers and ignited a small flame in my palm and descended the steps. Cobwebs clung to my clothes and silverfish skittered away from the light, retreating into the gloom.

The air cooled.

Damp and rot filled my every breath.

A light suction and a pop.

A bit of a tickle.

And I stepped out of one realm and into another.

My heels sank into black sand as I plodded along a beach littered with swords and human skulls. The Shore of Corpses. As lovely a place as it sounded.

The Veiled Sea thundered against sharp rocks and mounds of rusted armor, coating me in a fine mist that cut a shiver down to my bones.

Gods I hated this realm. I just prayed my brand new Louboutin Chelsea boots survived. If they got scuffed...

I shook the mummy dust out of my clothes and trudged up a hill and onto a path strewn with rocks and pebbles that led directly to Hel's palace, Eljudnir.

I could already make out its pointed spires rising above a layer of fog. A hundred windows of halls and wings reflected the blood reds and bruised purples of the darkening sky. The entire palace looked simultaneously cruel and melancholy, much like its mistress.

I stepped onto a bridge that spanned the Gjoll River, which separated the living from the dead. The planks bowed and cracked beneath my feet, the wood as rotten as the woman standing at the far end waiting for me.

Modgur. The guardian of this bridge who possessed all the charm of a pissed off wasp.

"Hello Modgur," I said. "My, are you using a new stitching pattern to keep your head sewn on your neck? It's done wonders for your whole, uhhh, *thing*, you have going on here. Very fetching."

She eyed me, which was a problem. I never knew which eye actually looked at me. I decided it was the blue one.

"She's not pleased with you being here," Modgur growled.

"That makes two of us."

Hel could always sense when a new soul crossed into her realm. And the fact I was still alive was like a foghorn. She always said the living gave her a headache.

I made to pass Modgur, but she put out a withered arm and stopped me.

"You cannot pass until I know your business," she said.

I rolled my eyes. The dead were always sticklers for rules. I guess rules were all they had left to worry about.

"As lovely as this little interrogation is, I'm in a bit of a rush."

"No business, no entrance."

It took everything in me not to tear off her leg and shove it up her—

"Let him in." A voice with all the sweetness of a razor called from a window. Hel's voice. "The quicker we let him in, the quicker we get him out."

A warm welcome, as always.

* * *

The Order of Chaos
(The Nine Worlds Rising Book 2)
is available on Amazon

THANK YOU!

I sincerely hope you enjoyed reading this book as much as I enjoyed writing it. If you did, I would greatly appreciate a short review on Amazon or your favorite book website, such as Goodreads or Bookbub! Reviews are crucial for any author, and even just a line or two can make a huge difference.

ALSO BY LYRA WOLF

The Nine Worlds Rising

Novellas

Thunder, Blood, and Goats

Novels

Truth and Other Lies (Book 1)

The Order of Chaos (Book 2)

That Good Mischief (Book 3)

The Fire in the Frost (Book 4)

Untitled (Book 5)

Untitled (Book 6)

ACKNOWLEDGMENTS

I don't even know where to start. I've been blessed to be surrounded by truly wonderful and supportive friends and family.

To my dear, dear husband, who has all the patience of a saint, thank you for always being there and listening to me yammer on about fictitious people in fictitious, and highly improbable, situations.

To my friend Hannah, thank you for not being afraid to tell me the truth when I needed to hear it. Thank you for all those long talks working through plot holes. Thank you for believing in Loki and his journey...And for stopping me that one time I threatened to throw this entire book into a bonfire and roast marshmallows over its burning pages...(I swear I'm not a dramatic person. Really.)

To my parents, thank you for cheering me on and always being there, even if I don't always write about nice people doing nice things. Sorry Mom.

I also want to thank Dr. Jackson Crawford, whose videos on the Norse myths and language have been an indispensable resource for me. I highly encourage anyone who has an interest in Viking lore, language, and culture, to check out his Youtube channel.

Finally, I want to thank you, the reader. You make all the work and effort and trials worth it. I really do hope you enjoy your adventures with Loki and friends.

And before I close, I want to take this time to formally apologize to my characters for all I put them through. Especially Loki. Don't worry buddy, it will get better.

*A special shoutout to my Keurig. You provided me with all the coffee I needed to get me through. Thank you.

ABOUT THE AUTHOR

Lyra Wolf is a Swiss-American author of fantasy and mythic fiction.

Raised in Indiana, home to a billion corn mazes, she now lives in Central Florida, home to a billion mosquitoes. She enjoys drinking espresso, wandering through old city streets, and being tragically drawn to 18th century rogues.

When Lyra isn't fulfilling the wishes of her overly demanding Chihuahua, you can find her writing about other worlds and the complicated people who live there.

Lyra has earned a B.A. in History and M.A. in English.

Sign up for the **Lyra Wolf Pack VIP Newsletter** for exclusive content, updates, and other delicious goodies.
Sign up Here

You can connect with Lyra on her website, or by following her on social media!

lyrawolf.com

Milton Keynes UK
Ingram Content Group UK Ltd.
UKHW031458240724
1019UKWH00017B/128

9 781944 912369